Robert Rankin used to inhabit Brentford but now lives in deepest Sussex. *Bizarre* ̶̶̶*pelling, dangerous, challenging, subversive* and *sexy* are ̶̶̶̶̶̶̶̶̶̶̶̶ ̶ave been used to describe his unique and ̶̶̶̶̶̶̶̶̶̶̶̶̶̶̶̶̶̶*d* and *in serious need of therapy* ̶̶ ̶̶̶̶̶̶̶̶̶̶̶̶̶̶̶̶̶̶̶ man himself.

Robert Rankin is the ̶̶̶̶̶̶̶̶̶̶̶̶̶̶̶̶̶̶̶̶̶̶̶̶̶̶̶̶̶̶̶*r*, *Web Site Story, Waiti̶̶̶̶̶̶̶̶̶̶̶̶̶̶̶̶̶̶̶̶̶̶̶̶̶̶̶̶nd Sausage Rolls, Snuff Fi̶̶̶̶̶̶̶̶̶̶̶̶̶̶̶̶̶̶̶̶̶̶oo Handbag, Sprout Mask ̶̶̶̶̶̶̶̶, ̶̶̶̶̶̶̶̶̶̶̶̶̶̶̶̶̶̶̶̶̶̶̶̶*r*, A Dog Called Demolition, The Garden of Unearthly Delights, The Most Amazing Man Who Ever Lived, The Greatest Show Off Earth, Raiders of the Lost Car Park, The Book of Ultimate Truths*, the *Armageddon* quartet (three books), and the *Brentford* trilogy (five books) which are all published by Corgi Books.

For more information on Robert Rankin and his books, see his website at:
www.lostcarpark.com/sproutlore

What they say about Robert Rankin:

'One of the rare guys who can always make me laugh'
Terry Pratchett

'To the top-selling ranks of humorists such as Douglas Adams and Terry Pratchett, let us welcome Mr Rankin'
Tom Hutchinson, *The Times*

'A born writer with a taste for the occult. Robert Rankin is to Brentford what William Faulkner was to Yoknap-tawpha County'
Time Out

'One of the finest living comic writers . . . a sort of drinking man's H.G. Wells'
Midweek

Also by Robert Rankin

ARMAGEDDON THE MUSICAL

THEY CAME AND ATE US,
ARMAGEDDON II: THE B-MOVIE

THE SUBURBAN BOOK OF THE DEAD,
ARMAGEDDON III: THE REMAKE

THE ANTIPOPE

THE BRENTFORD TRIANGLE

EAST OF EALING

THE SPROUTS OF WRATH

THE BOOK OF ULTIMATE TRUTHS

RAIDERS OF THE LAST CAR PARK

THE GREATEST SHOW OFF EARTH

THE MOST AMAZING MAN WHO EVER LIVED

THE GARDEN OF UNEARTHLY DELIGHTS

A DOG CALLED DEMOLITION

NOSTRADAMUS ATE MY HAMSTER

SPROUT MASK REPLICA

THE DANCE OF THE VOODOO HANDBAG

APOCALYPSO

SNUFF FICTION

SEX AND DRUGS AND SAUSAGE ROLLS

WAITING FOR GODALMING

WEB SITE STORY

THE FANDOM OF THE OPERATOR

and published by Corgi Books

THE BRENTFORD CHAINSTORE MASSACRE

Robert Rankin

CORGI BOOKS

THE BRENTFORD CHAINSTORE MASSACRE
A CORGI BOOK : 0 552 14357 X

Originally published in Great Britain by Doubleday,
a division of Transworld Publishers

PRINTING HISTORY
Doubleday edition published 1997
Corgi edition published 1998

7 9 10 8 6

Set in 11/13pt Bembo by
Kestrel Data, Exeter, Devon.

Corgi Books are published by Transworld Publishers,
61–63 Uxbridge Road, London W5 5SA,
a division of The Random House Group Ltd,
in Australia by Random House Australia (Pty) Ltd,
20 Alfred Street, Milsons Point, Sydney, NSW 2061, Australia,
in New Zealand by Random House New Zealand Ltd,
18 Poland Road, Glenfield, Auckland 10, New Zealand
and in South Africa by Random House (Pty) Ltd,
Endulini, 5a Jubilee Road, Parktown 2193, South Africa.

Printed and bound in Great Britain by
Cox & Wyman Ltd, Reading, Berkshire.

This book is dedicated to
VERITY
Beautiful daughter of
James and Evette

THE BRENTFORD
CHAINSTORE
MASSACRE

SHAGGY DOG STORY

What a wonderful lurcher you have there, Mrs Bryant,
I haven't seen as fine a one since long before the war.
Can you make it roll about, play dead, or beg a biscuit?
Nod its head or shake your hand by sticking out its paw?

'Actually,' said the lovely Mrs Bryant, whose
dresses tended to terminate a mere six inches below
her waist, 'it's a Dane, not a lurcher.'

'Come off it,' I said. 'That's a lurcher. My dad
used to keep them back in the nineteen fifties.'

'It's a Dane,' said Mrs Bryant. 'A Dane, that's what
it is.'

I shook my head and hailed a passer-by. 'Is this
dog a lurcher or a Dane?' I asked him.

The passer-by stroked his bearded chin. 'Looks
more like an Irish wolfhound to me,' he said. 'This
woman is wearing a very short dress,' he continued.

I dismissed the hirsute passer-by and addressed
the dog directly. 'Are you Dane or lurcher?' I asked
it.

'Dane,' said one of the dog's heads.

'Lurcher,' said the other.

GHOST STORY

The gambler was old and frail. The shoulders of his tired tuxedo hung like wounded wings, the cuffs were frayed and lacked their gilded buttons. Once he had worn a silk cravat, secured by a diamond pin, but now about his neck hung an old school tie.

With a trembling hand he laid his final chip upon the gaming board. 'Twelve black,' he said. 'It's all or nothing.'

The croupier called out something which sounded like 'Noo-rem-va-ma-ploo', and spun the roulette wheel. The silver ball danced round and round and finally came to rest.

'Thirteen red,' said the croupier.

'Ruination,' said the gambler.

With dragging feet he left the casino, stepped onto the terrace, drew his ancient service revolver from his pocket, put it to his temple and took 'the gentleman's way out'.

The casino too now lies in ruins. Fifty years have passed. But they do say that should you dare to visit here upon this very night, upon the anniversary of

11

the tragedy, you can watch the whole sad scene re-enacted by its ghostly players.

The three ghost-hunters watched the needles on their sensitive equipment dip and flutter. Professor Rawl made torch-lit notes on his clipboard, then studied the faces of his two companions, lit eerily by the moonlight. 'Did anybody see anything?' he asked.

Indigo Tombs shook his head. 'Not a thing,' he whispered. 'But I thought I heard—'

'What did you hear?'

'A whirling sound.'

'A roulette wheel,' said Dr Norman. 'I heard it too.'

'And then—'

'A gunshot,' said Professor Rawl. 'We all heard that, I'm sure.'

'We did,' the two agreed.

Professor Rawl tucked his pen into his pocket. 'The readings are inconclusive. We may have heard something, or nothing. It can't be proved either way.'

The three ghost-hunters dismantled their equipment and carried it back to the Land Rover. Professor Rawl keyed the ignition and they drove away into the night.

A tramp called Tony watched the tail-lights dim into the darkness. 'There you go, Tom,' he said to his chum. 'I told you it was true, and now you've seen them for yourself. Three scientists they were, or so

12

the old story goes, died of fright or something, they did, many years ago.'

His chum Tom coughed and spat into the night. 'You're drunk,' said he. 'I never saw a thing. Now come inside, it's turning cold.'

FAIRY STORY

Once upon a time there were two men. An Irishman called John Omally, who was young and tall and dark and handsome, and an elder called Old Pete, who was none of these things.

And it being lunchtime, these two stood at the bar counter of an alehouse discussing the ways of the world. The ways of the world have long been a subject for discussion. Ever since there have been any ways of the world, in fact. And an alehouse has always been a good place to discuss them.

'The ways of the world leave me oft-times perplexed,' said Old Pete, sipping rum.

John Omally nodded. 'Which ones in particular?' he asked.

'Well, you know that Mrs Bryant, who lives next door to me?'

'The one with the two-headed dog?'

'That's her.'

'And the very short dresses?'

'That's her as well.'

'I know *of* her,' said Omally.

'Well, last night her husband came home early

from his shift at the windscreen wiper works to find an alien in bed with her.'

'An illegal alien?'

'No, a space alien, although I suppose they must be illegal also.'

'Sounds a bit of a tall one,' said Omally.

'Yes, he described him as tall, and young and dark and handsome.'

'Ahem,' said Omally. 'Doesn't sound that much like a space alien to me.'

'That's what I thought,' said Old Pete. 'Sounded more like an incubus in my opinion.'

'A *what*?'

'An incubus. It's a sort of demon that takes on human form, creeps into the bedrooms of sleeping women and does the old business.'

'The old business?'

'The old jigger-jig. My wife, God rest her soul, suffered from them something terrible while I was away at the war. They used to appear in the shape of American servicemen back in those days.'

'Really?' said Omally. 'So you think Mrs Bryant was had by one of those?'

'I think it's more likely than a space alien. Don't you?'

Omally nodded. He could think of an even more likely explanation, one he could personally vouch for. 'So she told her husband that this bedroom intruder was a space alien, did she?'

'As soon as he regained consciousness. The bedroom intruder, as you put it, walloped him with a bedpan, and then took flight.'

'In a spaceship?'

'According to Mrs Bryant, yes.'

'Makes you think,' said John Omally.

'Makes you think what?'

'No, just makes you think. It's a figure of speech.'

'Well, I think there should be a law against it,' said Old Pete. 'If a woman can't lie safely in her bed without some incubus claiming to be a space alien taking advantage of her. Where's it all going to end?'

'Search me,' said Omally.

'Why?' asked Old Pete.

'No, it's another figure of speech.'

'But you do think there should be a law against it?'

'Absolutely,' said John Omally. 'There should be an Act of Parliament.'

'Then you actually believe all that old rubbish, do you, Omally?'

'Pardon me?'

'About space aliens and incubi. You actually believe all that's true and there should be an Act of Parliament?'

'I do, as it happens, yes.'

'I see.' Old Pete finished his rum and placed the empty glass upon the bar counter. 'Then what if I were to tell you that I personally witnessed the "incubus" making his getaway down the drainpipe? In fact I even recognized him.'

Omally's self-composure was a marvel to behold. 'I wouldn't be at all surprised,' said he.

'You wouldn't?'

'Not at all, and if you were to tell me that this shape-shifting incubus had taken on the appearance

17

of, well . . .' Omally glanced about the alehouse, as if in search of a suitable candidate. 'Well, let's say myself, for example. It wouldn't surprise me one little bit.'

Old Pete ground his dentures. This was not the way he had planned things at all. The wind-up, followed by the sting, was the way he'd planned things. Good for at least a bottle of rum.

'Would you care for another drink?' asked Omally. 'Perhaps a double this time? You look a bit shaky. Encounters with the supernatural can have that effect on people.'

Omally ordered the drinks.

Old Pete accepted his with a surly grunt. Omally pressed a five-pound note into his hand. 'Why not get yourself a half-bottle for later on?' said he. 'For medicinal purposes.'

'You're a gentleman,' said Old Pete.

'I'm a scoundrel,' said Omally, 'and so are you.'

The two men raised glasses and drank each other's health.

'But I'll tell you this,' said Omally. 'Back in the old country we don't make light of incubi and faerie folk and things of that nature.'

'Don't you, though?' said Old Pete.

'We do not. There's a strong belief in such things in Holy Ireland.'

'Is there?' said Old Pete.

'There is, and shall I tell you for why?'

'Please do,' said Old Pete.

'Souls,' said Omally. 'The souls of the dead.'

'Go on.'

'It is popularly believed', said Omally, 'that the faerie folk are the souls of the dead, the soul being an exact facsimile of the human form, though far smaller and subject to an entirely different set of laws and principles. Now, fairies are notoriously mischievous, are they not?'

'So I've heard it said.' Old Pete swallowed rum.

'And this is because they are the earthbound souls of folk who were neither good enough to go to heaven nor bad enough to go to the other place.' Omally crossed himself. 'The mirthmakers, the folk who could never take life seriously.'

'Folk such as yourself,' Old Pete suggested.

Omally ignored him. 'Why do you think it is', he asked, 'that only certain folk are able to see the fairies?'

'Several answers spring immediately to mind,' said Old Pete. 'It might be that there aren't too many fairies about. Or that they employ an advanced form of camouflage. Or that they are for the most part invisible. Or, most likely, that those who claim to see them are in fact mentally disturbed.'

Omally shook his head. 'It's down to susceptibility,' he said. 'Psychically speaking, of course.'

'Oh, of course.' Old Pete rolled his eyes.

'To perceive the faerie folk requires a certain type of mentality.'

'I think I gave that as one of my answers.'

'Hence the Irish.'

'Hence the Irish *what*? Or was that another figure of speech?'

'The greatest proliferation of faerie lore and belief

19

in the entire world, Ireland. And you will admit that the Irish mentality differs somewhat from the accepted norm.'

'Willingly,' said Old Pete. 'Of course, your theory might gain greater credibility were you able to offer me some convincing account of an encounter you yourself have personally had with the faerie folk.'

Omally grinned. 'Well, I couldn't do that now, could I?'

'Could you not? Well, that is a surprise.'

'Because', said John, 'the kind of mentality required to understand the whys and wherefores of the faerie folk is not the kind suited to their actual observation. I am too sophisticated, more's the pity. A simple mind is required. A child-like mind.'

'Hm,' said Old Pete, regarding his now empty glass.

'So tell me, Pete,' said Omally, 'have *you* ever seen a fairy?'

Old Pete peered over his glass at Omally's tweedy form. Throughout the conversation he had watched the ring of hobgoblins that encircled the Irishman's head, the bogles and boggarts that skipped to and fro around his feet singing songs about shoemending, the fat elf that sat upon his shoulder and the unruly pixie that nestled in his turn-up.

'Leave it out,' said Old Pete. 'There ain't no such things as fairies.'

And they all lived happily ever after.

1

If you ever had to describe Dr Steven Malone to someone who'd never met him, all you'd have to say was, 'He's the bloke who looks like Sherlock Holmes in the Sidney Paget drawings.' Of course, there will always be some people who will immediately say Sidney who? And there may even be a few who will say Sherlock who? And you can bet your life that there's a whole lot of others who will say Doctor Who. But to them you need only say *Doctor* Steven Malone. (Eh?)

It wasn't a curse to look like a Sidney Paget drawing of Sherlock Holmes, even if it did mean you were only in black and white and spent most of your life in profile, pointing at something off the page. It had never proved to be a big bird-puller, but it had served Dr Steven well at school for plays and suchlike, and it did mean that he looked dignified. Which very few people ever do, when you come to think about it.

He looked dignified now, as he stood upon the rostrum in the lecture theatre of the Royal College of Physicians at Henley-upon-Thames. And he *was* dignified. He had carriage, he had deportment, and he had a really splendid grey with white check Boleskine tweed three-piece suit. It had the double-breasted flat-bottomed waistcoat with the flap on the watch pocket and everything. Tinker used to wear one in *Lovejoy*, but his had been in the traditional green with the yellow check.

Dr Steven looked the business. And he *was* the business. Top of the tree in the field of bio-chemistry. The icing on the cake of DNA transfer symbiotics. And the ivory mouthpiece on the chromium-plated megaphone of destiny when it came to genetic engineering. He was also very good to his dear little white-haired old mother, a 33° Grand Master in the Hermetic Order of the Golden Sprout and a piercing enthusiast who boasted not only a *Prince Albert* but a double *ampallang* and *apadravya*.

Dr Steven sipped from a glass of liquid ether and gazed at the ranks of students with his cool grey eyes.

'And so,' he said. 'What do we learn from these three short stories?'

The students gazed back at him, none, it seemed, inclined to offer comment.

'Come on, someone.' Dr Steven made an encouraging face in profile. By the law of averages, some of the students must have been listening. Some might even have been interested. One might even have got the point.

'Someone? Anyone?' Dr Steven eyed his audience once more. His gaze fell upon a young man with a beard. His name was Paul Mason and he was a first-year student of genetics. Dr Steven pointed. 'Mason, what of you?'

The lad's eyes focused upon his tutor. 'Me, sir? Pardon?'

'What do we learn from these three short stories?'

'Not to believe the evidence of our own eyes?'

Dr Steven raised his grey eyebrows and lowered his off-white ears (a trick he had learned in Tibet). Mason's eyes went blink, blink, blink. 'I'm very impressed,' said the doctor. 'Would you care to enlarge?'

Mason shook his hirsute head. 'I think I'll get out when I'm winning. If you don't mind.'

'All right. But just before you do, tell me this: were they *true* stories?'

'Well, certainly the first one. Because I was the bearded passer-by in that.'

'And the other two?'

'I really couldn't say.'

Dr Steven lowered his eyebrows and raised his ears once more. 'Anybody else? Pushkin, what of you?'

Larry Pushkin, back for yet another year at the taxpayer's expense and a chap who had as much chance of becoming the next Doctor Who as he had of becoming a medical doctor, was rooting about in his left nostril with a biro. 'I'd rather not comment at this time, sir,' he said, in a Dalekian tone. 'I think a cockroach has laid its eggs in my nose.'

'Anybody? Anybody at all?'

Those who could be bothered shook their heads. Most just stared on blankly. But then, somewhere near the back of the auditorium, a little hand went up.

'Who's that back there?' asked Dr Steven.

'It's me, sir. Molekemp, Harry Molekemp.'

'Why, Molekemp, this is an honour. You are out of your cosy bed somewhat early.'

'Wednesday, sir. The landlady always vacuums my room on a Wednesday.'

'Rotten luck. And so, do you have some erudite comment to make?'

'Yes I do, sir. I don't believe Mason. You told the shaggy dog story in the first person. If Mason had been the bearded passer-by, you would have known.'

'Very good. Well, at least you were listening.'

'Yeah, but I wasn't very interested.'

'But you were listening.'

'Oh yeah, I was listening. But only in the hope that there might be some mention of genetic engineering. As that is what this course of lectures is supposed to be about.'

A rumble of mumbles signified that Molekemp was not all alone in this hope.

'Touché,' said the monochrome doctor. 'But the stories did have a purpose. What do we really know about our own genetic makeup?'

'*We* don't really know much at all, sir. We were hoping that *you* might enlighten us.'

'And that I was endeavouring to do. Let me briefly summarize. Firstly, the shaggy dog story. Here we have a mythic archetype. Cerberus, several-headed canine guardian of the Underworld. Ancient belief, brought fleetingly into a modern day setting. Of course, Mason was lying. The story was not true. It was a shaggy dog story with a twist in its tail. But think *archetype*, if you will. Think of old gods and old belief systems. Think of THE BIG IDEA, which existed in the beginning and from which all ideas come. I will return to this.

'Secondly we have the ghost story. The present-day scientists are studying the ghosts of the past. They can't actually *see* them, but they think perhaps they might be able to *hear* them, to *sense* them. But then we discover that the scientists themselves are not of the present day. That they too are ghosts, mere shades and shadows. And the story could continue endlessly. The tramps turn out to be ghosts, witnessed by others who turn out to be ghosts and so on and so forth.

'So think here, *the march of science*, half-truth superseding half-truth superseding half-truth, on and on and on, towards what? Ultimate discovery? Ultimate revelation? Are you following any of this, Molekemp?'

'I suppose so, sir.'

'Jolly good. Third story. The fairy tale. The Old Pete character knows of the existence of fairies, he can see them with his own two eyes. But he cannot admit this to his friend who has just told him that only people with child-like minds can see fairies. Tricky dichotomy there, and one that cannot be resolved. The Old Pete character's observation of the fairies is purely subjective. He may be a dullard, or he may be a visionary. And we all know how the scientific fraternity loves to mock the visionary. Science demands a provable hypothesis, repeatable experiments, double-blind testing and the seal of approval by those in authority. How well would fairies fare?'

Molekemp's hand was once more in the air. 'Surely this is all somewhat circuitous, sir,' he said. 'Fascinating though it is, or, as far as I'm concerned, is not.'

Dr Steven shook his head. 'I felt that the stories had a certain elegance,' he said, 'and this too I wished to touch upon. Science holds elegance to be something worthy of veneration. The poetry of mathematics, always in stanzas rather than blank verse. The beauty of the models science creates to convey what can never truly be understood. The pigeon-holing of reason. The belief that one thing should actually balance another.'

'I'm lost again,' said Molekemp.

'Then you are a twat,' said Dr Steven, 'and I shall waste no more time upon philosophical concepts.' He turned to the blackboard and chalked up the letters DNA. 'So,' said he, 'DNA. Deoxyribonucleic acid, the main constituent of the chromosomes from which we are composed. The DNA molecule consists of two polynucleotide chains, in the form of a double helix, which contain—'

Somewhere in the distance a bell rang, and as if in silent tribute to Pavlov (whose lectures were apparently a howl a minute) the students gathered together their belongings and left the auditorium.

Dr Steven Malone stood alone before his blackboard. Top of the tree, icing on the cake and ivory mouthpiece he might have been, but communicator of wisdom to the young and impressionable he was not. He was a visionary and he had glimpsed THE BIG IDEA, but getting this across to his students was proving tricky.

He had been leading up to his conviction that present-day scientists in the field of genetics (that field with the big tree in the middle on which perched Dr Steven Malone) went about things in all the wrong ways. They were obsessed with the study of present-day man's DNA, in order to discover its secrets.

But the secrets did not lie in the DNA of present-day man. Present-day man was a genetic mutation, an evolutionary development. In order to learn the secrets of DNA you had to study it in its original form – the form that had existed in the very beginning. You would have to study the DNA of Adam and Eve. Or even go one better than that. God created man in his own image, so the DNA prototype was to be found in God himself.

But how could anyone study the DNA of God?

And what might you find if you did?

These were the thoughts that obsessed Dr Steven Malone, that had driven him into the field of genetics in the first place, and would drive him to his inevitable and devastating downfall.

But his downfall was still some months away.

Some years away, in fact, or even centuries, depending on just where you happened to be in time. So be it only said that Dr Steven had a plan. It was a brave plan and a bold one. It was daring; it was dire. And had it not already been given away on the cover of this book, it would have come as one hell of a surprise to the reader.

But such is the way of it, and so we must leave Dr Steven Malone for the present. A noble figure, all in black and white, still bearing an uncanny resemblance to Mr Sidney Paget's renderings of Sherlock Holmes.

Dr Steven stands in profile and points to something off the page.

2

And a great wind came out of the East,
as it were a burning cloud consuming all
before it. And the sons of Man did
weep and wail and rend their garments,
crying surely this is the breath of Pooley.

'*Surely this is the breath of Pooley?*' Jim Pooley re-read the computer print-out. 'How can this be?'

The obese genealogist leaned back in his creaking leather chair and clasped his plump fingers over an expanse of tweedy waistcoat. 'How it can, I do not know,' said he. 'But there you have it, for what it's worth.'

Jim, now breathing into his cupped hands and sniffing mightily, said, 'I might well have the twang of the brewer's craft about the gums myself. But as to *a burning cloud consuming all before it*, that's a little strong.'

'Hence all the weeping and wailing, I suppose.' The genealogist grinned.

'Are you sure it isn't a misinterpretation or something? These ancient scribes were subject to the occasional slip-up, you know. A transposed P here, a wayward ey round the corner.'

Mr Compton-Cummings shook his bulbous head. 'I'm sorry, Jim,' he said. 'But it looks as though your forebears were notable only for their extreme halitosis. They put the poo in Pooley, as it were.'

Pooley groaned. 'And this vile smear upon my ancestors you propose to publish in your book, *Brentford: A Study of its People and History*?'

'It would be folly to leave it out.'

Jim rose from his chair, leaned across the paper-crowded desk, knotted a fist and displayed it beneath the snubby nose of Mr Compton-Cummings. 'It would be a far greater folly to leave it in,' he suggested.

Mr Compton-Cummings put a thin smile upon his fat face. He was a Kent Compton-Cummings and could trace his own ancestry back to the Battle of Agincourt. 'I would strongly advise against a course of violence, Mr Pooley,' he said softly. 'For it is my duty to warn you that I am an exponent of Dimac, the deadliest form of martial art known to mankind. With a single finger I could disfigure and disable you.'

Jim's fist hovered in the air. A shaft of sunlight angling down through the Georgian casement of the genealogist's elegant office made it momentarily a thing of fragile beauty. Almost porcelain, it seemed. Hardly a weapon of terror.

Jim chewed upon his bottom lip. 'Sir, you wind me up,' said he.

'I never do,' the other replied. 'Schooled by no

less a man than the now legendary Count Danté himself, inventor of the Poison Hand technique. Perhaps you know of it.'

Jim did. 'I don't,' he said.

'To maim and mutilate with little more than a fingertip's pressure. It is banned now under the Geneva Convention, I believe.'

Jim's fist unfurled.

'Good man.' The fat one winked. 'Reseat yourself. I'll call for tea and crumpets.'

Jim sat down. 'It's just not fair,' he said.

'We cannot choose our parents, nor they theirs. Such is the way of the world.' Mr Compton-Cummings strained to rise from his chair and made good upon the third attempt. To the sound of considerable wheezing and the creak of floorboards, he manoeuvred his ponderous bulk to the door and coughed out a request for tea to a secretary who sat beyond, painting her toenails with Tipp-Ex.

Pooley's unfurled hand strayed towards a heavy onyx ashbowl. A single blow to the back of the head and a sworn testimony on his own part that the fat man had merely tripped and fallen were all that would be required. But the obscene thought passed on at the moment of its birth. Jim was not a man of violence, and certainly not a murderer. He was just plain old Jim Pooley, bachelor of the parish of Brentford, man of the turf and lounger at the bar counter of the Flying Swan.

He had hoped so much that he might have been more. That perhaps somewhere, way back down the ancestral trail, there might have been one noble

Pooley, who had achieved great ends, performed mighty deeds, written the poetry of passion . . .

Or left an unclaimed legacy!

But no.

Jim had been shafted again.

Not, as was usually the case, by the quirks of cruel fate, or the calumny of strangers, but by one of his own tribe, and a long-dead one to boot. It really wasn't fair.

Mr Compton-Cummings ladled himself back into his reinforced chair and smiled once more upon Jim, who leaned forward.

'Listen,' he said. 'What if, for a small remuneration, you were to change the name in the manuscript?'

'Change the name?' The genealogist puffed out his cheeks.

Jim nodded enthusiastically. 'To, say . . .' He plucked, as if from the air, the name of his closest friend. 'John Omally,' he said.

'John Omally?'

'Certainly. I've often heard John complain about how dull his forebears were. This kind of notoriety would be right up his street.'

Mr Compton-Cummings raised an eyebrow. 'But that would be to hoodwink and deceive the common man.'

'It is the lot of the common man to be hoodwinked and deceived,' said Jim. 'Believe me, I speak from long experience.'

'Out of the question. I have my reputation to think of.'

'And I mine, such as it is. Listen, if this gets out I will be the laughing stock of the borough.'

'I sympathize, of course. But it is my bounden duty as scholar, researcher, writer and gentleman to do all within my power to ensure absolute accuracy in the book I am compiling. Such is the standard I have set for myself – a standard which, were you to view it from a more objective viewpoint, you would find admirable and worthy of emulation.'

'I doubt that,' said Jim, making a grumpy face.

Mr Compton-Cummings turned up his pink palms.

'What more can I say? After all, it was you who answered my advertisement in the *Brentford Mercury* for local people, who felt that they might have had ancestors who played a part in the making of this fine town, to come forward and have their ancestry traced, for free. You who plied me with talk of blue blood coursing through your veins. You who swore upon your mother's life that it was a Pooley who had won the land upon which Brentford now stands in an I-spy-with-my-little-eye competition with Richard the Lionheart. You—'

'Enough,' cried Jim, waving his hands. 'My motives were entirely altruistic.'

'Then we are kindred spirits.'

Jim once more took up the computer print-out and perused its dismal details. Back they went, an unbroken chain of Pooleys, marching through time. Well, hardly marching, slouching was more like it, with their heads down, probably to mask their evil breath. Peons and peasants, sanitary engineers and shovellers of sh—

'Ah, here's the tea,' said Mr Compton-Cummings.

The secretary held Jim's towards him at arm's length. Her face was turned away.

'Thanks very much,' said Jim.

'Look on the bright side,' smiled the genealogist, sipping at his Earl Grey. 'My book will be a very expensive affair, pandering to an elite minority. The scholastic fraternity, Fellows of the Royal Society, the intelligentsia. Hardly the class of folk to be found flinging darts in the saloon bar of the Flying Swan. The chances are that your rowdy drinking chums will never even see a copy, let alone purchase and read it. The secret of your malodorous predecessor will most likely remain just that.'

Jim sipped at his own tea. The cup smelled strongly of Dettol. Mr Compton-Cummings was probably right. John Omally rarely read anything heavier than the *Morris Minor Handbook*. Archroy was a *Zane Grey* man and Neville the part-time barman subscribed to *SFX Magazine*; Old Pete stuck to the *People's Friend* and Norman of the corner shop to the *Meccano Modeller*. Though wise words were often spoken within the Flying Swan, those words derived not from books but rather from personal insight gained through the observation and intuitive understanding of natural lore. He was safe. Of course he was.

'Well, thus and so,' said Jim. 'You are no doubt right, I'm sure.'

The genealogist offered Pooley one fat smile for luck, the two shook hands and Jim took his leave.

As he trudged up Moby Dick Terrace towards the Ealing Road and the Flying Swan, Jim sighed a great deal inwardly, but put his best foot forward. So what if he hadn't sprung from noble stock? So what if he came from a long line of nobodies? So what if the only Pooley who had merited more than a statutory birth, occupation and death mention in the parish records had been some kind of brimstone-breathing ogre? So what indeed! Jim, though often daunted and done down, was an optimist ever. He rarely opened his eyes upon a new day without a sense of wonder and excitement. Certainly, on more than a few occasions, those eyes were somewhat bleary and bloodshot and the brain behind them still blurred from drink, but life was life and life was now. And Jim lived his life to the fullest he could manage.

Jim breathed in the healthy Brentford air, scented with honeysuckle, jasmine blossom and sweet pea. The sky was blue as a blue could do and the sun beamed down its blessings. Alive was a wonderful thing to be on such a day as this. Jim pulled back his shoulders, thrust out his chest, put a pace into his stride and found a tune to whistle. God was in his heaven and all was right with the world of Brentford.

Pooley had a fair old skip on by the time he reached the Flying Swan. He put his hand to the saloon bar door and pushed it open, to find himself confronted by a most bizarre spectacle.

Old Pete's half-terrier, Chips, lay upon its back in

the centre of the floor, a paw drawn across its canine snout. It appeared to be shaking with mirth. At the bar counter, several customers had handkerchiefs tied cowboy-bandit fashion about their faces. Two old fellas from the estate sat at their domino table holding their noses and fanning their beer, while John Omally stood with his arms folded and a Vick inhaler stuffed up each of his nostrils.

Neville the part-time barman stuck his head up from beneath the counter. He was wearing a gas mask. 'Wotcha, stinker,' he said in a muffled tone. 'Just breezed in from the East?'

And then the Swan's patrons collapsed in helpless laughter.

Pooley stood, slack-jawed and shaking, slowly clenching and unclenching his fists. 'Compton-Cummings,' he said in a cold and deadly voice.

'Got him in one,' declared Neville, removing his gas mask and mopping tears of laughter from his eyes. 'He phoned here five minutes ago, plugging his latest book. Thought we'd all be keen to buy a copy.'

Jim Pooley left the Flying Swan and went home to find his old school cricket bat.

3

The judge, in his final summing up of the case,
described the attack as vicious and cold-blooded.
He said that for all his long years at the bar, he
could not recall an incident of similar barbarity. He
drew the jury's attention once more to the horrific
photographs taken by the police scene-of-crime
photographer, which showed in gory detail the full
extent of the victim's injuries. He displayed the
broken blood-stained cricket bat and spoke of
the long drop from the second-floor window to the
pavement below.

He spoke of escalating violence, the influence of
television, the need to be firm (but fair), the need to
see justice well and truly done and the need to clear
the streets of inhuman monsters and make them safe
for dear little white-haired old ladies to walk upon.

And then he added that in his personal opinion
the attack was totally justified and dismissed the case
out of hand. He also dismissed Mr Pooley's claim
for one million pounds' compensation. Mr Pooley,
he said, had got the hiding he deserved.

'As a practitioner of Dimac myself,' the judge said,

'and a fellow Freemason in the same lodge as Mr Compton-Cummings, I would have dealt with you far more severely.'

Bang went the gavel onto the block, the court cleared and Jim was left alone in his wheelchair.

At a little after lunchtime closing John Omally arrived to push him home. 'Look on the bright side, Jim,' he said. 'At least you were on legal aid.'

Months passed, bruises healed and bones knitted themselves back together. Out of respect for the punishment Jim had taken, the patrons of the Flying Swan made no further reference to winds from the East. And after the brief excitement of the court case, the borough of Brentford settled itself down to do what it did best. Nothing. With style.

It was almost a year to the day of Jim's beating that a large brown envelope tumbled through his letter box and came to rest upon a welcome mat that had long worn out its welcome. Jim plucked the item up and perused it with interest. He hadn't ordered anything and it wasn't his birthday. A present from a well-wisher? An admirer? Ever the optimist, Jim took his treasure into the kitchenette, placed it upon the stained Formica worktop and worried it with the carving knife. Away came the wrappings and out came the book.

The book!

Brentford: A Study of its People and History.

Jim stared at it in disbelief. Compton-Cummings had actually had the bare-faced brutality to send him a copy. It beggared all belief.

'You *bastard*!' Jim snatched up the book and stared it in the glossy cover. 'I just don't believe this.' He put a foot to the pedal-bin pedal and raised the lid. A noxious stench rose from within, possibly even as noxious as the infamous, and now publicly chronicled, 'breath of Pooley'. Jim released the pedal and fanned his nose with the book. 'I've been meaning to empty you,' he told the bin. He carried the book over to the cooker. 'But you're gonna burn!'

It had been a slow month financially for Jim. The gas had been disconnected.

Jim carried the book to the sink. 'Drown, then,' he said, then shook his head. Drown a book? He sat down at the kitchen table and thumbed the pages. They fell one upon another with the silky flow of an old school Bible. Jim sighed once more and with weary resignation flicked through the index for P.

His finger travelled down the page.

Plague Origin of Black Death traced to Brentford.

Planetary Alignments Astrology invented here.

Plasma Vortex Engine Invented here.

Plastic Ditto.

Platform Tickets World's largest collection housed in museum.

Pooley's finger travelled further down.

Plot Guy Fawkes's confession fingers Brentonian.

Pocahontas Born here.

'Eh?' said Pooley.

Pomegranate Farming Doomed attempt by local man.

Poor House Location of.

Pooley's finger went up, then down again. 'I'm

39

not here,' he said with some elation. 'He's left me out. He's a decent fellow after all. Well, what about that? He sent me a free copy just to show there were no hard feelings about taking him to court for beating the life out of me. What a gent! I wonder if he signed it.' Jim flicked forward. 'No, he didn't. But I think he should. I'll go round there now, I've nothing else on.'

And so saying, he did.

For the reader who, now thoroughly won over by Jim's personality, is eager for a description of the man, let it be said that Jim Pooley looked the way he always has looked. Except when he was younger, of course.

A man of average height and average weight, or just a tad above the one and underneath the other. A well-constructed face, a trifle gaunt at times; a shock of hair. Well, not a shock. A kindly countenance. His most distinctive feature, the one that singled him out from all the rest, was of course his—

'Golly,' said Jim. 'Whatever is going on here?'

He had reached Golden Square, a byway leading from the historic Butts Estate. A Georgian triumph of mellow rosy brick, once home to the wealthy burghers of the borough, now offices for solicitors and other folk in 'the professions'.

Jim stopped short and stared. There was an ambulance drawn up in front of the offices of Mr Compton-Cummings. His door was open and out of it a number of men in paramedic uniforms were struggling beneath the weight of something spread across two stretchers. Something covered by a sheet.

Jim hastened forward. The genealogist's secretary, the one who had handed Pooley the teacup, stood on the pavement sobbing into a handkerchief. A crowd was beginning to gather. Jim pushed his way into it.

'What happened?' he asked.

'Robbery,' said somebody. 'Bloke shot dead.'

'He was never shot,' said somebody else. 'Axed, he was.'

'Garrotted,' said yet another somebody. 'Head right off.'

'Talk sense,' said Jim.

'Some big fat fellow's died,' said a lady in a straw hat. 'Myocardial collapse, probably. It's always your heart that gives out if you're overweight. I used to be eighteen stone, me, but I went on a diet, nothing but roughage. I—'

'Excuse me,' said Jim, pushing past. He caught the arm of the weeping secretary. 'Is it Mr Compton-Cummings?' he asked.

The secretary turned her red-rimmed eyes up to Jim. 'Oh, it's you,' she said, between sobs. 'I remember you.'

'Is it him?'

The secretary's head bobbed up and down. 'He had a heart attack, just like the lady said.'

'Told you,' said the straw-hatter.

'And he's dead?'

'I tried to, you know, the kiss of life, but he . . .' The secretary sank once more into tears. Jim put a kind arm about her shoulder. It was a pretty shoulder. Well formed. Actually, all of her was well

41

formed. The secretary was a fine-looking young woman, a fact that had not gone unnoticed by Jim. 'Come inside and sit down,' he told her.

The paramedics, now aided by several members of the crowd who were eager to get in on the action, were forcing the lifeless sheet-shrouded corpse of Mr Compton-Cummings into the back of the ambulance.

Jim led the secretary up the steps and through the front door. In the outer office Jim sat the secretary down in her chair. 'I'm terribly sorry,' he said. 'I came here to thank him for sending me a copy of his book, and for leaving the bit about me out of it.' Jim placed the book upon the secretary's desk. Unsigned it would always remain.

'He felt bad about that,' sniffed the secretary. 'And about beating you up. It played on his mind. He was a good man, I liked him a lot.'

'I'm sorry. Can I get you a cup of tea, or something?'

'Thanks.' The secretary blew her nose. 'The machine's over there.'

Pooley applied himself to the task of dispensing tea. He'd never been very good with machines. There was a knack to technology which Jim did not possess. He held a paper cup beneath a little spout and pressed a button. Boiling water struck him at trouser-fly-level.

'It does that sometimes,' sniffed the secretary.

Eyes starting from his head and mouth wide in a silent scream, Jim hobbled about the office, fanning at himself with one hand while holding his steaming

42

trousers away from his seared groin region with the other.

'I'll make my own then,' said the secretary. 'How do you like yours? Two lumps?'

Jim hobbled, flapped and held out his trousers.

'It was horrible,' said the secretary, handing Jim a paper cup.

'It still is,' croaked Jim.

'No, Mr Compton-Cummings, dropping down dead like that.'

'Oh yes. It must have been.'

'One moment, big jolly bear of a man with his trousers round his ankles, the next—'

'Hang about,' said Jim. 'You don't mean that you and he were—'

'Well, of course we were. It's Tuesday, isn't it?'

'Yes, but—'

'We always do it on Tuesdays.'

'What? You and him? I mean, well, you're so . . . and he was . . . well, I mean.'

'A Mason,' said the secretary.

'Eh?'

'A Freemason. I always helped him dress for the lodge meeting on Tuesdays. Here, you weren't suggesting . . .'

'Perish the thought,' said Jim, crossing his heart with his cup-holding hand and sending tea all over his shirt. 'Oh, damn.'

'You're very clumsy, aren't you?'

'I try not to be.' Jim plucked at his shirt and shook his head. 'So he died while he was putting on his Masonic regalia.'

'It was the way he would have wanted to go.'

'Was it?'

'Well, no, I suppose not really. But you can't choose how you die, can you? It's like you can't choose your parents. No offence meant.'

'None taken,' said Jim. 'So he just dropped down dead while you were helping him on with his apron and whatnots.'

'I never touched his whatnots.'

Jim looked the secretary up and down. She was a beautiful young woman, but she was clearly not for him. Jim had never harboured a love for the toilet gag or the double entendre. The entire *Carry On* canon left him cold. Imagine having a relationship with a woman who could turn anything you said into a willy reference. Nightmare.

'So,' said Jim, once more and slowly. 'You think that the exertion of putting on his Masonic vestments caused him to have a heart attack?'

'Well, it was either that or the blow job.'

4

'She said *that*?' Omally spluttered into his pint of Large. 'You're jesting.'

'I am not.' Jim crossed his heart once more, careful to use the hand that was not holding the drink. 'Of course, she then went on to explain that she meant the job of blowing into the spout of the tea dispenser to clear a blockage. I'd had enough by then, so I made my excuses and left.'

'And quite right too,' agreed Omally. 'That's not the way we do business in Brentford. A woman like that is quite out of place.'

Jim Pooley raised an eyebrow to this remark, coming as it did from John Omally, whose reputation as a womanizer was legend hereabouts. But he knew what his best friend meant. There was something very special about the little town of Brentford, something that singled it out from the surrounding territories, that could not be quantified and catalogued and tamed by definition. It was subtle and elusive; it was precious. It was magic. And the folk who lived there felt it and were glad.

Jim sighed and drained his glass and placed it on the counter.

The two stood in the saloon bar of the Flying Swan, that Victorian jewel in the battered crown of Brentford pubbery. Raking shores of sunlight venturing through the etched glass windows sparkled in the ashtrays and the optics, on the polished mahogany counter top and from the burnished brass. There was magic here all right.

'One of similar, Neville, please,' said Jim as he pushed his glass across the bar.

'And one for me,' said John.

Neville the part-time barman pulled the pints and smiled upon his patrons. 'You know, Jim,' said he, when the pints were drawn and paid for, 'that book you have there might prove to be worth a few bob.'

'This book?' asked Jim, turning the item which lay before him on the counter. 'How so?'

Neville took up Mr Compton-Cummings's posthumous publication and idly turned the pages. 'Well, I was talking just yesterday with that chap Gary. You know the fellow, tall, good-looking, posh suit, always carries the—' Neville paused and made a face.

'Mobile phone,' said Omally, crossing himself.

'The very same, and those abominations remain as ever barred from this establishment. Well, Gary works for Transglobe, the outfit responsible for the publication of this book. It came up in conversation.'

'Oh, did it?' said Jim. 'Just came up in conversation. You weren't perhaps hoping to get a free copy?'

Neville made the innocent face of the guilty man. 'As I was saying, it came up in conversation and Gary told me that it was scheduled for publication this very week, this very day in fact. But at the eleventh hour all copies were withdrawn and pulped.'

'Blow me!' said Jim.

'Language,' said Omally.

'All pulped,' said Neville. 'Even the original manuscript had to be destroyed.'

'But why?'

'Gary wasn't altogether sure. But he was mightily peeved. The book was destined for the world market. It was expected to sell millions.'

Jim glowered into his ale. 'So much for the "elite minority".'

'Gary was cursing because he hadn't actually got round to reading a copy himself. But he said the talk was that the book contained certain "sensational disclosures" and that the order to pulp it had come down "from above".'

Jim's eyes rolled towards the Swan's nicotined ceiling and stared unfocused, as if viewing through it the infinity that lay beyond. 'From God?' he whispered.

'From the board of directors,' said Neville.

Omally plucked the book from the part-time barman's fingers. 'You pair of buffoons,' said he. 'That Gary was winding you up, Neville. It would all be a publicity stunt.'

'You really think so?'

'I do. And to prove I'm right I will take this lad home with me now and read it from cover to cover.

47

If there's anything in it worth talking about, I'll let you know.'

'I think not.' Pooley availed himself of his book. It was a struggle, but he managed it in the end. 'It was I who suffered at the fingertips of the martial genealogist, and if this book contains anything of a sensational nature, which might be turned to a financial profit, then I should be the one to benefit.'

'The thought of turning a financial profit never entered my head,' said Omally, in a tone which might well have convinced those who didn't know him. 'But as it seems to have entered yours, then please do so with my blessing.'

'Thank you, John. I shall.'

Omally raised his glass in toast. 'There, Neville,' he said, 'you see a man of steely nerve and fearless disposition. An example to us all. Let us salute Jim Pooley, "he who dares".' Omally swallowed ale.

'He who *what*?' Jim asked.

'Dares,' said John. 'As in takes risks. Big risks.'

'What big risks?'

'The modesty of the man,' said John. 'As if he doesn't know.'

'What are you talking about?'

'Only this. Supposing that the book really does contain "sensational disclosures". They must be pretty damn sensational if they've caused a publishing house the size of Transglobe to call in and pulp millions of copies rather than risk the consequences of publication.'

'Hm,' said Jim. 'Perhaps.'

'And call me a conspiracy theorist, but isn't there

something highly suspicious in the fact that on the very day the book was due to be published, its author drops down dead from a so-called heart attack?'

'Coincidence,' said Jim.

'Oh, right,' said John. 'So if I find you lying dead in your kitchen, with your trousers round your ankles and the teapot stuck in your gob, I'll put that down to coincidence too.'

'I . . . er . . .'

'Stop it, John,' said Neville. 'You're frightening him.'

'I'm not scared,' said Pooley.

'I would be,' said Neville.

'Me too,' said Old Pete, shuffling up to the bar. 'What are we talking about?'

'Jim's book,' said John.

'Jim's written a book?'

'No, he's been given one.'

'Well, let me have a look at it when he's finished colouring it in.'

'Most amusing,' said Jim. 'You are as ever the wit.'

'Large dark rum please, Neville,' said Old Pete. 'And give Jim whatever he wants.'

'He wants a bodyguard,' said Omally, 'or possibly a change of identity.'

'Stop it, John.' Pooley held out the book. 'Go on, you take it then. I've quite lost interest in the thing.'

'Not me,' said Omally.

'You, Neville?' Jim asked.

'No thank you.' Neville shook his head.

'Cor blimey,' said Old Pete, 'reminds me of that

49

joke about the ten commandments.'

'What joke's that?' Jim asked.

'Well, you see, this is back in biblical times, right, and God goes to the Arabs and he says, "Would you like a commandment?" and the head Arab says, "What is it?" and God says, "Thou shalt not commit adultery," and the head Arab says, "No thanks, we do that all the time, we enjoy it."

'So God goes to the Egyptians and he says to the Pharaoh, "Would you like a commandment?" and the Pharaoh says, "What is it?" and God says, "Thou shalt not covet thy neighbour's wife, or his ass or whatever," and the Pharaoh says, "No thanks, coveting's what we do best, we thrive on it."

'So finally God goes to the Jews and he says to Moses, "Would you like a commandment?" and Moses says, "How much do they cost?" and God says, "They're free." So Moses says . . . "I'll take ten." ' Old Pete collapsed in laughter.

'Surely that is anti-Semitic,' said Jim.

'Not when it's told by a Jew. Especially one who's just bought you a drink. But I'll take that free book if it's still going.'

'That's all right,' said Omally. '*I'll* take it.'

When Neville called time for the lunchtime session, Pooley and Omally parted company. John returned to his rooms in Mafeking Avenue and Jim took himself to his favourite bench before the Memorial Library. It was here, on this almost sacred spot, that Jim did most of his really heavyweight thinking. Here where he dreamed his dreams and made his plans. Here too where he sat and smoked and soaked up sunshine.

Jim placed his bum upon the bench and stretched his legs before him. He'd been shafted again. Omally would root out whatever sensational disclosures the book held and profit therefrom and Jim would wind up empty-handed. But surely John wouldn't grab the lot? He was Jim's best friend, after all. There'd be something in it for Jim. But probably not a very substantial something.

Jim sighed and stretched and wriggled himself into comfort. Stuff the silly book. What did he care about that? He was destined for far higher things, financially speaking.

Jim rooted about in his jacket pockets and pulled out a crumpled pamphlet. This was his passport to fortune. He uncrumpled the pamphlet and smoothed out its edges.

Time Travel for Fun and Profit
by Hugo Rune

This was the kiddie. Jim had come across it quite by chance – if there really was such a thing as chance, which Mr Rune seemed to doubt. Jim had purchased a large cod and chips and Archie Karachi of the Star of Bombay Curry Garden (and Tasty-chip Patio) had wrapped them up in this very pamphlet.

Jim had studied the pamphlet with interest. It wasn't one of those build-your-own-time-machine science fiction jobbies, more one of your esoteric-new-age-power-of-the-mind sort of bodies. Astral bodies, probably.

Mr Rune explained, in words which the layman

could understand, that time really didn't exist at all. His premise was that the universe had always been here. It had never begun and would never end. So there was an infinite amount of 'time' in the past and an equally infinite amount of 'time' to come in the future. He drew the famous analogy of the infinitely long piece of string. If you had a piece of string that stretched endlessly from infinity to infinity, then any point you chose on that string must be its middle. You couldn't have more infinity on one side of it than on the other. And so it was with time. Wherever you were in it, you were right at its centre. No more time behind you than in front. It made perfect sense. Time, said Mr Rune, was a purely human concept. There was no past and no future, just an infinite number of presents.

So how could a human being travel into either the past or the future? The answer was, of course, that he couldn't. Not physically, anyway. For physical travel he'd have to travel faster than light and nothing can travel faster than light. Well, nothing except THOUGHT. It got capital letters in the pamphlet, which meant that it was important.

You can think about the sun instantly, but its light takes eight minutes to reach you. So, mentally, you can outrun light.

Rune argued (convincingly) that many people had already mastered the technique of mental time travel. These folk were, of course, the prophets. Those lucky few blessed with the powers of precognition. The Nostradamus types who could see into the future. And there had been loads of them.

Mother Shipton, Edgar Cayce. Rune offered a list. These folk had travelled into the future by the power of their minds. But the trouble was that the future, which consisted of an infinite number of presents yet to come, was simply too big for the average prophet to get his head round. There was too much of it. So he got overloaded and confused and made a lot of inaccurate predictions. Rune claimed to have formulated a set of mental exercises which concentrated the mind on one tiny little bit of the future – maybe the bit that was only half an hour away.

And this was the bit that had Jim hooked. Just *half an hour away*. What, if you knew it half an hour before it happened, would benefit you very much indeed?

It hadn't taken Jim half an hour to figure it out.

The result of the National Lottery.

And so Jim sat in the sun, his eyes closed and his face contorted by the anguish of his concentration.

It was a pity that the last page of the pamphlet, the page with the actual instructions for the mental exercises, had been torn off. Somebody else had got that round their cod and chips, but Jim had been unable to find out who. Still, he gritted his teeth none the less and *thought forward*.

Had Jim been able to foresee the eventual outcome of these mental exercises, he would have abandoned them there and then. In fact, he would probably have abandoned gambling there and then, along with drinking and all other things that he held dear, and retired at once to a monastery.

Because Jim's time travelling, added to John's imminent discovery of a certain sensational disclosure and multiplied by the abominable doings of Dr Steven Malone, would equal an apocalyptic total. And it would all begin with *A Most Exciting Tale*.

5

Prelude to the Most Eventful Day

Jack was scraping at his face with a razor, which, like his wit, had lost its edge a good many years before.

'It was a close shave getting out of that little scrape,' said Jack, as he all but finished the messy chore. 'As smooth as a baby's bum-tiddly-um-bum-bum,' he continued, as he applied shreds of Kleenex to the profusion of nicks and cuts that now speckled the shaven area beneath his nose. 'Pretty sharp,' he went on, as he examined his sagging features in the bathroom mirror. And 'You'll knock'm dead,' he concluded, straightening his tie.

Jack's wife, a beauty in her late forties, sliced bread in the kitchenette and worried quietly to herself. Worrying was good for her; it kept her mind off her problems.

Jack came down the stairs two at a time. 'Good morning, wife,' he said, limping painfully into the breakfast area.

'Good morning, Jack,' said Jack's wife. 'And how would you like your eggs this morning?'

'I would like them many, speckled and various,' said Jack. 'Ranging – *free* ranging, in fact – from those of the mythical Roc to those of the pygmy heron of Upper Sumatra.'

'They are on your plate,' said Jack's wife. 'Make of them what you will.'

It was going to be the most eventful day in Jack's long and uneventful life, but he did not as yet know this.

The Excitement Hots Up

'How would you like your tea, dear?' asked Jack's wife.

Jack worried a lot about her. Almost as much, in his own special way, as she did about him. Why does she say these things? he worried. Does she do it simply to annoy me? Or does she, perchance, believe that I am a different person every morning? Or possibly she is being unfaithful. Jack worried a lot about this.

'Sugar, dear?' asked Jack's wife.

'Twelve lumps please,' said Jack.

Jack's wife popped the usual two into his cup and stirred them with the usual spoon. And then she returned to her slicing and worrying.

Jack buttered up a slice of toast. 'You're a lovely bit of toast,' he told it. 'Would you like to come to the pictures on Friday night?'

In Jack's front garden a postman clung to the roof of Jack's porch. 'Treed by a bleeding lurcher,' he complained. 'Or was it a Dane?'

'I must be off to work now,' said Jack.

'Don't forget your sandwiches, dear.'

Jack thrust the brown paper packet into his brief-case. 'The price of butter is scandalous,' he told his wife. 'But not to worry, eh?' And he kissed her lightly on the cheek, hoisted his trilby hat onto his head, shrugged on his camelhair coat, tucked his case beneath his arm, picked up his umbrella and de-parted.

'Morning, postie,' said Jack to the figure cowering on the roof of his porch. 'I didn't know it was raining.'

'Raining?'

'Well, as they say, any porch in a storm.'

'Most amusing,' said the postman, who con-sidered it anything but. 'I thought you told me your dog didn't bite.'

'It doesn't,' said Jack.

'But it nearly had my leg off.'

'This isn't my dog,' said Jack. 'It belongs to the wife.'

Tension Mounts on the Bus

The 8.15 bus was crowded with 8.15 passengers.

'Morning, conductor,' said Jack.

'Morning, Jack,' said the conductor. 'Your mate Bill's up the front.'

Jack craned his neck and bulldozered his eyebrows. 'Morning, my mate Bill,' he cried.

'Morning, Jack,' Bill shouted back. 'And how are you today?'

'Fair to middling,' called Jack. 'Fair to middle-diddle-diddling.'

'I'm very pleased to hear it.' Bill returned to his study of the *Daily Sketch*. GIANT SPIDER CARRIES OFF WIDOW, ran the banner headline. She was probably asking for it anyway, thought Bill as his gaze left the tabloid and moved slowly up the legs of a particularly well-designed teenage schoolgirl. Shouldn't be allowed, his thought continued.

And meanwhile at Jack's house the postman was giving it to Jack's wife doggy style upon the kitchen floor. This lino needs a dose of *Flash*, worried the wife of Jack.

Two stops on Jack got a seat. 'We're running thirty-five seconds late this morning,' he informed a fellow traveller.

'Thirty-five seconds late for what?' asked the traveller, whose name was John Omally.

'For work.'

'But I'm not going to work.'

'Where then?'

'I'm going home.'

'But this is the 8.15 bus.'

'It was the 7.30 bus when I got onto it.'

'Ah, I see.' The conversation was interrupted by the sound of a thirteen-year-old fist striking Bill in the face.

'I never touched her,' cried Bill as the bus conductor fought his way through the standing passengers

58

to grasp him by the collar. 'A man is innocent until proved guilty,' he complained as the conductor flung him off at the next set of traffic lights.

'It's the same thing every day,' said Jack to his fellow traveller.

'Not for me it isn't,' said John. 'For I live the kind of life that most men only dream about. A riotous succession of society get-togethers, country week-ends, operatic first nights and charity functions.'

'Get away,' said Jack.

'True as true,' said Omally. 'Then there's the skateboarding, the sky diving and the riding of the big surf. Not to mention the North Sea oil drilling.'

'North Sea oil drilling?'

'I told you not to mention that.'

'Sorry.' Jack scratched at his hat. 'Do you do any crop spraying at all?'

'Heaps, and Formula One motor racing too.' Omally pulled off his cycle clips and adjusted his socks. 'And I'm judging the Miss World competition this afternoon.'

'That must be interesting.'

'Extremely,' said Omally. 'As long as you don't have to sit next to Tony Blackburn or Michael Aspel.'

The bus shuddered to a halt, regrouping its stand-ing cargo at the front end in an untidy scrum. As the struggling passengers regained their feet and began to dust themselves down, the driver put his foot down and they all bundled towards the rear.

A lady in a straw hat fell upon Omally.

'Is this a regular occurrence?' he asked.

'Sometimes we lose one or two at the round-about,' said Jack. 'Although I don't recall there ever being any fatalities.'

'What about that dwarf the fat butcher fell on last month?' said the lady in the straw hat.

'Oh yes, there was him.'

'And that Zulu who went up in a puff of smoke.'

'That was spontaneous human combustion. That could have happened anywhere.'

'This is my stop,' said Omally.

'It's very nice,' said the lady in the straw hat. 'How much did you have to pay for it?'

'Give my regards to Tony and Michael,' called Jack as Omally slipped off without paying.

The 65 bus swung over the Great West Road and headed south towards Brentford. In its path there might well have been a giant spider of outlandish proportions, its mutated mind set upon world domination. But upon this day, as upon others past, there wasn't.

But this *was* to be the most eventful day in Jack's long and uneventful life, although he still didn't know it as yet.

The Tension Almost Reaches Breaking Point

'Good morning, Jack,' said Jack's boss, Leslie. 'And how is your lovely wife?'

Jack looked at his watch. 'She'll be making the postman's breakfast about now,' he said. 'And how is your handsome husband?'

'Still delivering the Queen's mail.'

A thought entered Jack's head, but finding itself all alone in there it left by the emergency exit.

'Now, Jack,' said Leslie, boss of Jack. 'We have a very important despatch to make today and it must be handled with great care. We wouldn't want there to be any more unfortunate mistakes, now would we?'

'No we wouldn't,' said Jack. 'No-skiddly-oh-po-po.'

Leslie, Jack's boss, smiled upon her subordinate. She was a tall woman, slim, sleek, svelte. Brown-eyed and black-haired and carrying about with her that aura of a woman who knows exactly where she's going.

'I'm going to the toilet now,' said Leslie, boss of Jack. 'And when I get back I want to see you with your shoulder to the wheel and your nose to the grindstone. Do I make myself clear?'

'Well . . .' said Jack.

Nail-Biting Stuff

The company Jack worked for was called SURFIN' UFO.★ As far as Jack had been able to ascertain during his ten years of service, it had something to do with despatching fragile and precious cargoes from one place to another. The UFO part meant

---

★For company, he also worked on the night shift at the windscreen wiper works.

United Freight Operations, but the significance of the SURFIN' bit was lost on Jack.

Jack was the manager of the actual despatching department. He was, in fact, the only employee in this department. There had been some cutbacks. Once there had been lads with hair and tattoos, cavorting about on fork-lift trucks. Lads who read the *Sun* and smelled of cigarettes and the morning after. But now there was only Jack. And Jack didn't smoke or read the *Sun*. His office was a little glass partitioned-off corner of a vast warehouse. A vast and empty warehouse.

Jack hung up his hat and coat and rolled up the sleeves of his shirt. And then he sat down at his desk. It was an all-but-empty desk. Empty but for a telephone, a single package and a single piece of paper.

Jack perused this.

DESPATCH NOTE

SURFIN' UFO   1462

UNIT 4 + 2

OLD DOCK BUSINESS PARK   DATE: 23.5.97

HORSEFERRY LANE, BRENTFORD   VAT REG: 435 9424 666

TO:	NAME:	DR STEVEN MALONE	FROM:	NAME:	PROF. GUSTAV BOLNEY
	ADDRESS:	KETHER HOUSE		ADDRESS:	INC TECH
		BUTTS ESTATE			LOS ALAMOS
		BRENTFORD			NEVADA, USA

CONTENTS: ISOTOPES. HERMETICALLY SEALED.

<u>DO NOT OPEN FRAGILE FRAGILE FRAGILE</u>

Jack picked up the package and rattled it against his ear. Dr Steven Malone was SURFIN' UFO's only client nowadays. Stuff came to him from all over the world. From Turin, from Vienna, from Los Alamos and Latvia. Always by the most unlikely route and always under the tightest security.

Jack's job today would be to call up the local road haulage firm, impress upon them the highly important nature of the package and the need for its speedy and secure delivery, and then await the arrival of the van, sign numerous documents, hand over the package and return to his desk.

Jack picked up the telephone and tapped out numbers. Somewhere not too far away a phone began to ring.

And then a voice said, 'Yo, Leo Felix, who's dis?'

'Hello-skiddly-bo,' said Jack.

'Yo, Jack, my man. How's it 'anging?'

'The bus was late today,' said Jack.

'What? De ol' 8.15? That is truly dredd.' A Rasta-farian chuckle gurgled in Jack's ear.

A Veritable Cliff-hanger

'Can you pick up a package for immediate delivery to Dr Steven Malone?' asked Jack.

'Not 'ceptin' yo' pay yo' damn bill, Babylon.'

'Oh,' said Jack, replacing the receiver.

63

'Mr Felix says he won't pick up the package unless his bill is paid,' said Jack to his boss Leslie, who had just returned from the toilet.

'Leo Felix is a thieving nigger,' said Leslie.

'Surely that is a racist remark,' said Jack.

'Not when it's said by a black woman. Which I am, in case you hadn't noticed.'

'I thought you said you were Jewish.'

'I did.'

And Now Things Really Start to Happen

'You will just have to deliver the package yourself,' said the boss of Jack. 'Do you think you can manage that?'

'On foot?' asked Jack. 'And without an armed guard?'

'It's only two streets away.'

'But Mr Felix led me to believe it was in another Brentford, somewhere in Ethiopia.'

Leslie arched her eyebrows and bridged her nose.

'The thieving nigger,' said Jack.

'Enough of your racist jive, white boy.'

A Roller-coaster Ride to Hell

Jack trudged along Horseferry Lane, past the Shrunken Head and up to the High Street. He looked both ways before crossing and reached the other side in safety. There he sat down upon the bench outside Budgens and studied his *A-Z*. A lady in a straw hat sat down beside him. 'Are you lost?' she asked Jack.

Jack clutched his package to his chest. 'Certainly not,' he told her.

'Only I get lost sometimes. I have who'ja vu.'

'What's that?'

'It's the opposite of déjà vu. I can be in the middle of the supermarket and suddenly I get this feeling, I've never been *here* before.'

'I have to go,' said Jack. 'I have a very important package to deliver.'

'The doctor's put me on a course of placebos,' said the lady in the straw hat. 'But I don't take them. I'm saving them all up for a mock suicide attempt.'

'Goodbye,' said Jack.

'Goodbye,' said the lady in the straw hat.

How Much More Can We Take?

Jack tugged upon a brass bell pull. Somewhere within a brass bell rang and presently the front door opened.

Jack found himself gazing up at a gaunt black and white figure who bore an uncanny resemblance to the Sidney Paget drawings of Sherlock Holmes.

'Dr Steven Malone?' asked Jack.

'No,' said the figure, 'he lives next door.'

Jack went next door and tugged upon another bell

pull. A gentleman of identical appearance to the first opened the door.

'Dr Steven . . .'

'Malone,' said Dr Steven Malone. 'And you would be?'

'Jack,' said Jack. 'From SURFIN' UFO.'

'Please come in.'

'Thank you.'

Dr Steven Malone led Jack along a sparsely furnished hall and into a room of ample proportions. Here, upon boards of golden oak, spread faded kilims and upon these ponderous furniture of the Victorian persuasion. A gloomy room it was.

'You have my package. Do you want me to sign something?'

'I do, indeedy-do.' Jack pulled papers from his pocket. Dr Steven unscrewed the top of his fountain pen.

'Just there,' said Jack and Dr Steven signed.

'And there.'

'Here?'

'Just there. And there if you don't mind.'

'Here?'

'No, there.'

'Sorry.' Dr Steven signed again.

'And if you'd just put your initials here.'

'Certainly.'

'And tick this box.'

'Of course.'

'And put today's date.'

'My pleasure.'

'Then if you'll be so kind as to fill in the details here and sign this.'

Dr Steven raised his eyebrows and lowered his ears.

'Did you learn that in Tibet?' Jack asked.

'There's an awful lot of paperwork,' said Dr Steven.

'There is,' Jack agreed. 'And all of it unnecessary. I only insist upon it to be officious. Would you mind repeating all that you've just done on the carbon copy, please?'

'Actually I would.'

'How very trying for you. But you can't have the package if you don't.'

'What blood type are you?' asked Dr Steven Malone.

Hang on to your Hats

'AB negative,' said Jack. 'I used to bleed a lot as a child.'

'Nosebleeds?' Dr Steven asked.

'No, the top of my head.'

'How unusual.'

'Not really. My brother wanted to be a musician.'

'I don't think I quite follow you.'

'He wanted to play the xylophone, but my dad couldn't afford one, so my brother, my older brother, used to line up all us younger brothers in descending order of height, then go round behind us and strike each of us on the top of the head with a tent peg mallet. A sort of human xylophone, you see. He could do almost the entire Lennon and McCartney song book. I was Middle C. I used to suffer a lot from concussion.'

'Does your brother play the xylophone now?'

'In Broadmoor, yes.'

'I wonder if I might take a sample of your blood.'

'I don't see why not. What do you want it for?'

'It's a top secret experiment.'

'How interesting. What's it all about then?'

'It's top secret.'

'I can keep a secret,' said Jack. 'Listen to this one.' He whispered words into the still lowered ear of Dr Steven.

'She never does,' said the doctor.

'She does too, but don't tell anyone.'

'I certainly won't.'

'So what's the top secret then?'

Dr Steven Malone waved Jack into a fireside chair and seated himself upon another. 'For the last two years,' said he, 'I have been engaged upon a ground-breaking project. From all over the world I have gathered dried blood samples. From the Shroud of Turin, the Spear of Longinus, the purported crown of thorns in Troyes, nails from the true cross scattered in cathedrals across Europe, even an item claimed to be the holy prepuce. I have cross-matched two and I am certain that they come from the same being.'

'Jesus Christ!' said Jack.

'The very same. It is now my intention, using a reagent of my own formulation, to liquefy this blood

68

and extract the DNA. With this I intend to clone—'

'Jesus Christ!'

'Exactly. And not just the one. I am going to clone at least six.'

'Like in that film,' said Jack. '*The Boys from Brazil*. Where they cloned Hitler.'

'Exactly. Mine will be *The Boys from Bethlehem*.'

'But surely,' said Jack, 'you are tampering with forces that no man should dare to tamper with.'

'Oh, absolutely, yes. But then – do you mind if I stand up while I do this bit?'

'Not at all.'

Dr Steven Malone stood up, flung his pale arms in the air and began to stalk about the room. 'They thought me mad, you see!' he cried out in a ranting sort of a tone. 'Mad? I who have discovered the very secrets of Life itself?' He sat down again. 'What do you think?'

'Very impressive. But you could also add, "One day the whole world will know my name." '

'Thanks very much. I'll remember that in future. Now, about your blood.'

'How much do you want?'

'About eight pints.'

Close Your Eyes and Cover Your Ears

'Well, I'd like to,' said Jack. 'But I really should be getting back to work.'

'Another time, then. I'll show you out.'

'Thanks very much. Goodbye.'

'Well, I'd like to,' said Jack. 'But I really should be getting back to work.'

Dr Steven Malone produced a small automatic pistol from a trouser pocket and pointed it at Jack. 'Regrettably no,' said he. 'I cannot allow you to leave. I require your blood and I require it now. It's nothing personal, you understand. I would have used the blood of whoever had delivered the package. The isotopes are all I require to complete my procedures.'

Jack began to worry. 'Aw, come on,' he whined. 'You don't want my blood. My blood's just ordinary stuff. I could telephone my wife, she's got terrific blood.'

'Is your surname Bryant, by any chance?'

'That's right. Perhaps you know my wife. Wears a very short dress. Has this lurcher that's also a Dane, and—'

'Likes to make love with her head in the fridge?'

'She hasn't mentioned that to me,' said Jack.

'Move,' said Dr Steven. 'Along the corridor and down the steps.'

'Oh no-diddly-oh-no-no.'

This had undoubtedly been the most eventful day in Jack's long and uneventful life. Sadly it would also be the last.

Dr Steven stood in profile, pointing with his pistol to the basement off the page.

6

The dreaming mind of Pooley went on its walkabout, wading through a stream of semi-consciousness.

A cracked mug of darkened foliage by swollen ashtrays on limp carpets of faded heraldry where smells of stale cinemas and locked cars and fridges and magnets and bottom drawers in old boarding houses giving up their dying breaths and period paper ads for tennis shoes and foundation garments and Cadbury's twopenny bars of Bournville that give an athlete energy to run while underneath and undisturbed the rough drawer bottoms offer scents of camphor and sassafras and amber and Empire and then across the polished lino turning tiny rubber wheels *The Speed of the Wind* his favourite Dinky push and flip with the thumb to send it flying forwards past the potty deep into the dark beneath the bed where lying and looking up the silver shining spirals of springs ranked one beyond the next in crazy perspective out of focus from the fluff and fuzz of folk who pay by the day and the day you leave you must clear the room by ten and wipe the sink before you go downstairs to put your luggage in the sitting room we call the lounge and take a last walk along the promenade to watch the sea make fractious moves along the beach and suck the sand and lick the piles those cracked white piles beneath the pier all shuttered look there even the Palm Restaurant is closed and will not offer tea on trays to place upon its green glass table tops because the Lloyd Loom chairs are placed there now the arcades have their blinds pulled down by photo men and donkey men and those who bowl the penny maybe you can win the goldfish in the bag or simply watch and walk across the iron-trellised railway bridge as fast as you can to keep up with dad who has left it late to haul those cases up the asphalt stairs towards the empty platform where the train blows steam and shouts and sighs and streets of terraced houses with their grey slate roofs above the London stocks and strokes the orange cat upon the window sill that's glad to see you home and homework rushed upon that last weekend it's good to be back in the playground where the conkers rise and fall and fag cards flick and girls skip and show their knickers and the marbles and the whistle blows like a train—

'Jim Pooley, headmaster's room at the double.'

'But it wasn't me. Omally did it, not me, sir.'

But John did not own up.

And Pooley got the cane.

Jim stirred in his altered state. 'Move forward, you sod,' he told his brain. 'We keep going back to school, and I'm fed up with getting the cane again and again and again.'

There was a bit of a mental lap dissolve and what's this?

Fast music. Pete Townshend windmills. Marshall speakers. Mod dancing. Blue Triangle Club. Scooters. Parkas. Here's Jim here. Nice whistle. Burton's special. Fifteen pounds ten shillings over ten weeks. Slim Jim tie. Nice touch that. He's waiting for someone. Foolish haircut, Jim. Great loafers though. Ivy Shop, Richmond? Cost a packet, those, lads. Who are you waiting for, Jim, all alone outside with the music coming through the bog window and the bouncer on the door smoking a reefer?

'Sandra,' whispered Jim in his cosmic sleep. 'Oh, Sandra.'

Stand and wait and shuffle and look at your watch. Nice watch. Where d'you get that? Bought it off a bloke in a pub. You don't go into pubs, do you, not at your age? Bloke *outside* a pub. Outside a club. Just now! The bouncer sold it to me. Where is Sandra? Where *is* Sandra?

But Sandra is not coming. Sandra has gone off with John Omally, on the back of his Vespa.

Jim mumbled and grumbled. 'Bloody John. Forward, brain, forward. Into the future.'

Whir and click and *fast forward*.

And *freeze frame*.

And *play*.

What year is this? Get up, have breakfast. The bookies, then the pub. The pub and then the bench, then home for tea and then the pub again. Then ouch, get up and groan have breakfast, then the bookies, then the pub, the bench, then tea and then

73

the pub. What's this? The years becoming years, yet all the same? A small job here, a little fiddle there, a laugh, a sadness and another beer. Then sleep it off, then up, then breakfast, then the bookies and the pub, then—

'Forward,' moaned Pooley. 'Fast forward, please.'

Fast forward. Freeze frame. And *play*.

—the bench, then home for tea, then to the pub, then—

'Forward! Forward!'

Bubbling, turning, little spheres of red and white.

'Stop here and *play*!'

Bouncing, tumbling over, little numbers too.

'This is it,' sighed Jim, 'this is it. What week? *What week?*'

'It's the National Lottery draw for tonight, the *mmmph mmmph mmmph* 1997.'

'I didn't catch that date,' said Pooley.

'And the machine chosen for tonight . . .' The presenter's that bloke who used to be on *Blue Peter*, isn't it? 'Chosen by our beautiful guest star, is . . . *Leviathan.*'

'Ooooooooooh!' went the crowd. As if it really mattered at all.

'Ooooooooooh!' went Jim. Because here he is, sitting in a front-row seat, a lottery ticket in his hand. But he looks a bit odd. Somewhat battered. His left foot is all bandaged up. Has he been in a fight, or a war, or what?

'And to press the magic button,' says the *Blue Peter* bloke, or is he off that children's art programme where they do things with rubber bands and cling

74

film and tubes of adhesive, or was that a video with German subtitles? 'To press the magic button we have that American actress with the improbable breasts, who was in that film with Sylvester Stallone. You can't put a name to her face but you'd recognize her if she got her kit off.'

Jim made odd sounds under his breath. 'Just get on with it,' he muttered.

'Press that button, bimbo,' cried the *Blue Peter* bloke, or is he the fellow who does the chocolate bar commercial, where all that creamy stuff spurts everywhere? Or was *that* on the video with the German subtitles?

'That was on the video,' mumbled Jim. 'Roll them old balls.'

The American actress with the Woolworths frontage pushed the button. Down and plunge and round and round went the balls.

Jim studied the ticket in his lap. 'Come on,' he whispered.

And then the balls slide one after another into the tube, the tension mounting all the while. The *Blue Peter* bloke, who does mostly voice-overs nowadays, but is trying to rebuild his career with the help of Max Clifford, points to the first ball and shouts, '*Seventeen.*'

'Oooooooooooooh!' go the crowd. Do any of them actually have seventeen marked on their cards?

'I do,' whispers Jim.

'*Twenty-five.*'

Another 'Oooooooh'. Not quite so loud this time and lacking several Os.

Jim gives his card the old thumbs up.

Then '*Forty-two*' and '*Nineteen*' and '*Number five*'. And fewer 'Ooooohs' every time, except for Jim.

'Then thirty-one,' says Jim, all smiles.

'And *thirty-one*.'

'Oh yes! And then the bonus ball, which is—'

'*One hundred and eighty.*'

'*What?*'

'*One hundred and eighty.*'

'That's not right. The balls only go up to forty-nine. Hang about, you're not the *Blue Peter* bloke, you're—'

'One hundred and eighty and the Flying Swan scoops the darts tournament for the nineteenth year running.' And John Omally went 'Prrrrrrrt!' into Pooley's earhole.

Jim leapt from his studio seat to find himself leaping from the bench before the Memorial Library. Omally's grinning face filled all the world.

'Counting sheep?' grinned John. 'Hey—'

Jim caught him with an uppercut that swung the Irishman over the bench and into the bushes behind.

Omally rose in a flustering of foliage, clutching at his jaw. 'Mother Mary's handbag, Jim. You hit me.'

'And there's more to come, you robber of my millions.'

Jim took another mighty swing, but this time John ducked nimbly aside. Carried by the force of his own momentum, Jim too plunged over the bench. Omally helped him to his feet. 'Calm yourself, Jim, be at peace there.'

'*Be at peace?*I was there, right there, I had the

76

numbers, I . . . God, the numbers, what were the numbers?'

'One hundred and eighty was one of them.'

'You bloody fool, Omally.' Jim took yet another swing but this too missed its mark and Pooley went sprawling.

'Stop this nonsense, Jim. I've come to make you rich.'

'I was rich. I *was*. I had it. Help me up for God's sake, I'm stuck in brambles here.'

Omally helped him up once more and dusted him down. 'You didn't have it, Jim,' he said softly. 'And I heard the numbers you were mumbling. That was last week's lottery draw.'

'It was? But I was there and I was all bandaged up and—'

'Leave it, Jim. I've come to make you rich. I really have.'

Jim shook his head, dragged himself back over the bench and sat down hard upon it. Omally joined him.

'Go on, then,' said Jim. 'Let's hear it.'

John yanked Jim's book from his jacket pocket. It had about it now a somewhat dog-eared appearance.

'You've creased it all up,' said Jim sulkily.

'Never mind about that.' Omally leafed through the pages, then thrust the open book beneath Jim's nose. 'Cast your Sandra's over this,' he said.

'My *Sandra's*?'

'Sandra's thighs, eyes. I'm working on a new generation of rhyming slang, based upon the most memorable features of ladies I've known in the past.'

A young man on a Vespa rode by and Jim made a low groaning sound deep in his throat.

'Go on,' said Omally. 'Take a look.'

Jim took a look, although not with a great deal of interest. His eyes however had not travelled far down the page before an amazed expression appeared on his face and the words 'Sandra's crotch' came out of his mouth.

'Sandra's *what*?'

'Sandra's crotch. It's all too much!'

'Well, that isn't quite how it works, but it has a certain brutish charm.'

'This is barking mad,' said Jim.

'Yes, there is a small brown dog involved.'

'But it's a member of the . . . I never knew they were born in Brentford.'

'I don't think anyone did. And I don't think they know about *that* either.'

'*Chezolagnia?* What does that mean?'

'You really don't want to know, Jim. Have a look at the photo on the next page.'

'There's photos too?' Jim turned the page. 'Sylvia's—'

Omally put his hand across Jim's mouth. 'Crotch was distasteful enough,' said he.

'—mother,' said Pooley. 'John, this is dynamite. We'd end up in the Tower of London. Stuff like this could bring down the entire establishment.'

'Couldn't it too,' said Omally.

'Imagine if this fell into the hands of someone who had it in for the English.'

'Imagine that,' said John Omally, son of Eire.

'Oh no, John, you wouldn't? You couldn't?'

'No,' said John. 'I wouldn't and I couldn't. What a man gets up to in the privacy of his own love menagerie is his own business.'

Jim turned another page, then went 'Waaah!' and thrust the book back at John. 'Take it away. Burn it. I wish I'd never looked.'

John closed the book and tucked it back into his pocket.

'Then we're not rich at all,' said Pooley with a long and heartfelt sigh.

'Oh yes we are.'

'But you said you wouldn't and you couldn't.'

'I was only warming you up. That isn't the bit of the book that's going to make us rich.'

'You mean there's worse in there?'

'Not worse, Jim. And nothing like that at all. That was just a little footnote, but it set me thinking. What do you know about the Days of God and the Brentford Scrolls?'

'We did them at school. Something to do with Pope Gregory changing the calendar from the Julian to the Gregorian which meant cutting eleven days out of the year and this batty monk from Brentford going on a pilgrimage to Rome to demand God's Days back.'

'And?'

'Well, didn't the Pope get so fed up with him going on and on about it that he said the people of Brentford could have two extra days a year if they wanted them?'

'That was it, and gave him a special decree authorizing it.'

'The Brentford Scrolls.'

'Those very lads.'

'But the monk was murdered when he got back home so Brentford never got the extra days that it didn't want anyway and everyone lived happily ever after.'

'Well done, Jim. In a few short sentences you have reduced the most significant event in Brentford's history to a load of old cabbage.'

'I'm sorry, but I fail to see the significance of this significant event. Especially how it will make us rich.'

'Then allow me to explain. The Pope told the monk that Brentford could have two extra days a year, the Days of God, in perpetuity. But the option was never taken up. Now all this happened in 1582 and it's now 1997, four hundred and fifteen years later, which means . . . ?'

'I haven't the foggiest,' said Jim. 'What does it mean?'

'It means that by the end of this year Brentford has eight hundred and thirty days owing to it. That's over *two years*, Jim.'

'Do pardon me for missing the point here, John. But so what?'

'Jim, what is going to happen on December the thirty-first 1999?'

'A very big party.'

'Correct. The millennial celebrations. The biggest, most expensive, most heavily funded bash in history.'

'So?'

Omally threw up his hands. 'So the people of Brentford are actually entitled to celebrate the millennium two years earlier than the rest of the world, by special decree of Pope Gregory. He re-orientated the calendar and what he decreed goes.'

Jim opened his mouth to say 'So?' once more, but he said 'Come again?' instead.

'You're catching on, aren't you, Jim? The Millennium Fund. Millions and millions of pounds, set aside for all kinds of projects and schemes. And the people of Brentford are actually entitled to grab it two years before anybody else.'

'You have got to be jesting.'

'All the details are in this book of yours. All we have to do is to quietly check whether the Pope's decree was ever revoked, which I'm certain it never was. And then we put in our absolutely genuine and pukka claim for millions.'

'The Millennium Fund blokes will never swallow it.'

'They'll have no choice, Jim.' Omally pulled a crumpled piece of foolscap from his pocket. 'Now I've drawn up a bit of an itinerary here. Obviously as co-directors of the Brentford Millennium Committee we will require salaries suitable to our status. How does this figure seem to you?'

Pooley perused the figure. 'Stingy,' said he. 'Stick another nought on the end.'

'I'll stick on two, to be on the safe side. So, we'll want a big parade and a beauty contest—'

'Belles of Brentford,' said Jim.

81

'Belles of Brentford. I like that.' Omally made a note.

'And a beer festival,' said Jim.

'Let's have two,' said John, 'again to be on the safe side.'

'Let's have two beauty contests. Three, in fact. We'd be on the panel of judges, naturally.'

'Naturally. And I thought we should build something. How about a new library?'

'What's wrong with the old one?'

'The heating's pretty poor in the winter.'

'Right. Tear down the library, build a new one.'

'OK,' said Omally, making a tick. 'That's the John Omally Millennial Library taken care of.'

'The *what*?'

'Well, it will have to have a new name, won't it?'

'I suppose so, but if you're having a library named after you I want something too.'

'Have whatever you like, my friend.'

Pooley thought. 'I'll have the Jim Pooley,' said he.

'The Jim Pooley what?'

'No, just the Jim Pooley. It's a public house.'

'Nice one. I'll join you there for a pint. Do you think we should tear all the flatblocks down and build some nice mock-Georgian terraces, or should we—'

'John?' asked Jim.

'Jim?' asked John.

'John, about these Brentford Scrolls. The papal decree that papally decrees all this. Where exactly are the scrolls now?'

'Ah,' said John.

'And what exactly does "Ah" mean?'

' "Ah" means that when the monk got murdered, the scrolls disappeared. No one has actually seen them in over four hundred years.'

Jim Pooley swung his fist once more at John Omally.

And this time he didn't miss.

7

'Twenty of us in a ditch with just a bit of torn tarpaulin to keep the weather out.' Old Pete slumped back in his chair, then, gaining strength from the reaction of his audience, after-office types who had popped into the Swan for a swift half, he gestured meaningfully with the spittle end of his pipe. 'That's what I call hard times. None of this namby-pamby stuff about pyjamas and nightlights.'

Old Pete had certainly known hard times. For after all, hadn't he grubbed in the fields for roots to feed his four younger brothers? And didn't he once live for three months inside a barrel, until his beard was long enough to hide the shame that he could afford no shirt to be married in? And when his uncle died in a freak indecent exposure/hedge strimmer accident, hadn't it been Old Pete who gathered up the pieces and dug the grave himself?

Old Pete had seen real poverty. His tales of one jam sandwich between six and four to a cup never failed to bring a tear to the eye of the listener and a free drink or two to himself.

'How come', asked Omally, who had heard it all

before, 'that out of the twenty of you down the ditch, not one had the nous to earn the price of a dosshouse bed for the night?'

'There is always some cynical bugger', said Old Pete, 'prepared to spoil a good tale well told.'

Omally led Jim up to the bar.

'Good evening, Neville,' he said. 'Two pints of Large, please, and an unshared jam sandwich for Jim, who has missed his tea.'

Jim made a scowling face as Neville went about his business.

'So,' said the part-time barman, presenting his patrons with pints. 'Allow me to hazard a guess. My first thought was *Caught in a cattle stampede*, but this I feel is unlikely. So I am going to plump for *Taking a course of training with the SAS*.'

'Whatever are you on about?' Jim asked.

'You two,' said Neville, 'standing here utterly dishevelled, hair all over the place, cuts and bruises, bits of bramble hanging off your suits and a black eye apiece.'

'I'd rather we didn't discuss it,' said Jim.

'Quite so. Then tell me, John, have you come up with any sensational disclosures in Jim's book yet?'

Omally opened his mouth to speak.

Jim said, 'No he hasn't.'

'Shame,' said Neville. 'I had hoped that it might bring a few pennies more across the bar. The goddess knows, times are as ever against the poor publican.'

'The sufferings of the poor publican are well

'known,' said John. 'You are an example to us all, Neville.'

'Hm,' said Neville and went on his way to polish glasses.

'Let's go and sit over there,' said John, indicating a discreet corner. Jim followed him across, placed his ale and jammy sandwich on the table and sat down.

'I'm drinking this and eating this and then I'm going home to bed,' said Jim. 'This is one day I do not wish to prolong any further.'

'Come on, Jim. You can't quit the game when there's so much to play for.'

'There are no cards on the table to play with, John. The scrolls have probably gone to dust a hundred years ago. The whole idea is absurd. Why don't you just admit it?'

'Stuff and nonsense. Look upon this as a holy quest. Like *Raiders of the Lost Ark*.'

'Although it has been remarked that I do bear a striking resemblance to Harrison Ford, I have no wish to waste my time on any such foolish venture. Now allow me to eat and drink and go my way.'

'You have a wicked sense of humour, Mr Pooley. So how do you feel we should best go about this? Hire a couple of metal detectors, bring in a dowser—'

'No.' Jim shook his head, wiped breadcrumbs from his chin, finished his ale and rose to his feet. 'I am not interested, John. I want nothing to do with it. I am going home. Goodnight.' And he turned away and left the Flying Swan.

'Then I woke up', Old Pete was heard to say, 'and

my big toe was missing. There was just this little note stuck into the stump which said, "Gone to market".'

John Omally had another pint, then he too left the Flying Swan. Whatever was the matter with that Jim Pooley? he wondered as he wandered aimlessly down the Brentford streets. Had he lost all his spirit? Or was he simply getting on in years?

Omally came to a sudden halt. Why had *that* thought entered his head? *Getting on in years?* He and Jim were the same age. And they were only— Omally stroked his chin. It was hardly *only* any more, was it? It was, well, *as much as*.

Omally paused and, finding himself beside Pooley's favourite library bench, sat down upon it. He and Jim had certainly enjoyed an adventure or two in the past. They'd got drawn into some really terrible stuff, but they'd always come out of it with their heads held high, even if their pockets remained empty. This Brentford Scrolls business was right up their street. An adventure if ever there was one. Tracking down the valuable artefacts, no doubt pursued by some evil maniac bent upon snatching them for himself. Life and death struggles, thrills, risks . . .

Omally gave his chin another scratch. Perhaps Jim was right. Perhaps the whole thing was stupid. The scrolls were probably lost for ever anyway. And even if they were to be found, would the Millennium Committee really hand over the dosh to a pair of Brentford louts who had come across a bit of old parchment?

'I am *not* a lout,' said Omally, startling a solitary cyclist.

'And I am not a transvestite,' the other called back. 'So I like to cross-dress once in a while, but who doesn't, eh?'

Omally let that pass. And then he looked down at his wrist to the place where, had he worn a watch, he would have worn it. 'Half past eight,' said John Omally. 'So, what shall I do? Knock up old Jim and try to change his mind? Take a walk over to Professor Slocombe and ask him what he knows about the Brentford Scrolls? Go back to the Swan for another pint? Go home to bed?'

A wry smile appeared upon the face of John Omally. He might perhaps go to someone else's home and go to bed. And half past eight just happened to be the time when Jack Bryant began his night shift. And Old Pete, that observer of the incubus, was ensconced in the Swan.

Omally rose from the bench, stretched, tucked in his shirt, ran his fingers through his curly hair and set off to the bus stop with a whistle.

Jim Pooley's kettle didn't whistle. It was an electric one and those lads never whistle, they just sort of switch themselves off. Well, most of them do. Jim's didn't, because it was Jim's and it was electric and Jim and electric appliances didn't get on. And even if Jim's kettle had been meant to whistle, it wouldn't have been able to now, because it was full of baked beans.

Jim lifted the lid and peered in at the bubbling

brew. 'Nearly done,' said he. The slice of bread that was destined to become toast rested perilously upon the protective grill of the two-bar electric fire. Both bars were on, because the switch that isolated one of them just happened to be broken. Jim turned the bread over, scorching his fingers as he did so. 'Ouch,' said Jim, the way you do.

But Jim had a whistle left in him. All right it had been a pretty bum day, but there was always tomorrow. It was beans on toast for now and then an early night. Perhaps he might even be able to break the dreaded cycle of up-and-out-the-bookies-then-the-pub-the-pub-then-the-bench-the-bench-then-home-for-tea—

Well, he *might*.

'I shall start anew tomorrow,' said Jim. 'I might even go down to the Job Centre and see what's doing.' He froze and glanced around. And then he shook his head. 'No one heard me say that, did they? No,' he concluded. 'Now, let's get stuck into these beans.'

Knock, knock, knock, came a knocking at Pooley's front door.

Knock, knock, knock, went John Omally at Mrs Bryant's kitchen door. The light flicked on and through the frosted glass John could see the lady of the house approaching. That silhouette, back-lit by the reproduction coach lamps on the kitchen wall, never failed to stir something in John Omally.

'Who is it?' called Mrs Bryant.

'The man of your dreams,' whispered John.

'Jim, I told you only to come on Thursday nights.'

Jim? Omally's jaw dropped open. *Thursdays?* Didn't Pooley always leave the Swan early on a Thursday night with talk about some gardening programme he had to watch on TV? But, *Pooley?* Surely not.

'It's *John*,' called John.

'Oh, John. Oh, ha, ha, ha.' (the sound of hollow laughter). 'Just my little joke. Come in.'

Mrs Bryant opened the door and Omally grinned in at her.

'Your husband's not about, is he?'

'No, he hasn't come home this evening. I'm getting rather worried.'

'Should I go away and come back another night?'

'Are you kidding?' Mrs Bryant took John by the jacket lapels and hauled him into the kitchen.

Knock, knock, knock, knock, went the knocking again at Pooley's front door. Jim dithered about, trying to hook his toast off the bar fire and pull the plug from the kettle at the same time. 'Hold on,' he called. 'I'm coming.'

Knock, knock, KNOCK.

Pooley tossed the toast from hand to hand, blowing onto each in turn and performing a rather foolish dance as he did so.

Knock, knock, KNOCK!

'Oh, stuff it.' Pooley flung the toast over his shoulder and stalked along the passage to the front door. Dragging it open he shouted, *'What do you want?'*

'I know what *you* want,' purred Mrs Bryant, blowing into John Omally's ear.

And of course she did. But John paused for a moment, taking stock. Certainly he wanted a shag. But then he always wanted a shag. Most men want a shag most of the time. Most men would drop whatever they happened to be doing at a moment's notice in the cause of a shag. But did he, John Omally, really want this? Sneaking into a married woman's house for a cheap thrill? It was pretty tacky stuff when you came right down to it. Not that he felt any guilt about old Jack Bryant. Jack was an amiable buffoon. But then, what did this make *him*? A lout?

'I am *not* a lout,' said John Omally.

'I never said you were. Shall I get out the ice cubes?'

'Oh yes please,' said John. 'And—'

WHACK! went Pooley's front door as it burst open and whacked against the passage wall.

'Hey, hang about,' went Jim, as hands were laid upon him. 'Stop this,' he continued, as the hands thrust him back along the passage.

And WHACK! went the front door one more time as other hands slammed it shut.

Mrs Bryant left the fridge door open.

Although this may sound incredible to the reader, there are still some folk left in the world who do not recognize the fridge for the sexual treasure house it is. You may scoff, but it's true. These tragic, un-enlightened beings open up their fridges and see food. Food and drink and nothing more.

Certainly they may have a comprehensive range of marital aids stored away in the bedside cupboard, for after all, who doesn't? But when it comes to the fridge, they just see food and drink.

The connoisseur of kitchen copulation, however, sees the contents of the fridge in all its naked splendour.

The erotic possibilities of the fruit and vegetable section are of course well known. Who in their right mind could fail to be moved to arousal by sight of all those corn cobs and parsnips, bananas and cucumbers? But the connoisseur disdains the obvious and passes on to savour the exquisite pleasures of the half-squeezed lemon and the fiendish red-hot chilli pepper, here a pinch and there a dab. Moving upwards, he views the shelf of lubricants and creams and lotions: the butter and the margarine, the tub of lard, the mayonnaise, the extra virgin olive oil, the salad dressings and the HP Sauce.

And then to the preserves. Did you know that if you take ten small pickled onions and thread them onto a string, you can gently push them . . .

'Don't push me about,' cried Jim. 'What's going on here? Let me go.'

'Mr Pooley? Mr James Arbuthnot Pooley?' A large hand held Jim firmly by the throat and pushed his head against the passage wall.

Pooley glared into the face of his tormentor. It was

an impressive face. A face that had seen a bit of service. A face with a flattened nose and a beetling brow, its mouth bound by tightly corded muscle, its chin unshaven. It was a face that said, 'Don't mess about with me,' without actually having to speak.

'Who are you?' Pooley asked. 'And what do you want?'

'Police,' said the mouth on the impressive face.

Jim viewed the head and body that went with it. Equally impressive. Big and burly. Two more such big and burly men lurked in Jim's passage.

'Police?' said Jim in a timorous tone. 'But I haven't done anything wrong.'

'We have come to search the premises.'

'Ah,' said Jim. 'Ah. I don't suppose you have a warrant.'

'I don't suppose we do.'

'No problem,' said Jim. 'Only might I just ask one favour?'

'You might ask it, yes.'

'Well, you see, mistakes can happen. No one wants them to, but sometimes they just do. Sometimes, by mistake, a policeman will have in his pocket some piece of incriminating evidence. A cache of illegal drugs, say, or even a weapon of some kind. And whilst searching the premises of an innocent party, who has been mistakenly earmarked as a suspect, this piece of incriminating evidence might fall out of the policeman's pocket and land, say, under a mattress, or behind a water pipe, and the policeman, in all innocence, picks it up and exclaims, "Well, well, well, so what do we have here?"

and the next thing you know, the innocent party is being charged with—'

WHACK! went that sound again.

But this time it was not the front door slamming.

WHACK! went the celery. WHACK! WHACK! WHACK!

'Would you like some chocolate powder sprinkled over it?' asked Mrs Bryant.

'Yes please,' said John.

Mrs Bryant brought over John's cappuccino and sat down beside him at the reproduction olde worlde kitchen table.

WHACK! went the celery one more time into the bowl of salt.

'It's always a pleasure to see you, John,' said Mrs Bryant. 'Are you enjoying your salad?'

'Very much indeed, thank you.'

'Need any more ice cubes in your Perrier water?'

'No thanks, it's perfect. Very kind of you to make me a meal.'

'You need a woman in your life. To look after you, John.'

'What a man needs and what a man wants rarely coincide,' said the Irish philosopher.

'Does that explain the bulge in your trousers?'

'Oh, this.' Omally fished out Pooley's book. 'Nothing of consequence, only a history book.'

'Just hand over the book,' said the policeman with the face, hauling Pooley to his feet and hitting him again. 'We can break the place up if you want and we can break you up too. Why not spare yourself the pain? Where is it?'

'I don't have it.' Pooley flinched as another fist went in. 'I don't, honest I don't.'

'We found this, sarge,' said the second policeman.

'It's not mine,' wailed Jim, 'whatever it is.'

'It's got your name and address on it,' said the face. 'It looks to be the packaging of a book.'

'I haven't got it, honestly I haven't.'

'You had it earlier when you turned up at the office of the late Mr Compton-Cummings.'

'How do you know *that*?'

'Never mind how. Are you going to tell us where it is, or do we have to—'

'Where's your teapot?' asked the third policeman.

'Aaaaaaagh!' went Pooley.

'Mmmm,' went Omally, releasing the lower buttons of his waistcoat. 'That was a splendid repast.'

Mrs Bryant was leafing through the pages of Pooley's book. 'What is auto-pederasty?' she asked.

'You really wouldn't want to know.'

'I really would.'

John whispered.

'That's not possible, is it?'

'I understand that it has its own special page on the Internet. Although I don't exactly understand what an Internet is.'

'I think it's a type of stocking worn by female employees on British Railways.'

'Well, you live and learn,' said John. 'So, what shall we do next?'

Mrs Bryant thought for a moment. 'Why don't we have a shag?' she suggested.

'Why don't we all just relax?' said the face. 'Mr Pooley is going to tell us exactly what we want to know, aren't you, Mr Pooley?'

'I don't have a teapot,' moaned Jim from the kitchen floor.

'This looks like one,' said the third policeman, holding up a chipped enamel job that had served the Pooley dynasty for several generations.

'I think that's a watering can.' Jim gagged for breath as a boot went in.

'A pathological fear of teapots by the sound of it,' said the second policeman. 'Inspired by what, I wonder.'

'A pathological fear of death,' mumbled Pooley. 'Please don't kick me again.'

'The book,' said the face.

'I threw it away.'

'Not good enough.'

'I gave it away, then.'

'To who?'

'It's to *whom*, sarge.'

'It's too late for that, lad.'

'Sorry, sarge?'

'If there was going to be a running gag about grammar, it should have been introduced right at the beginning of the scene.'

'Oh, yeah, you're right, sarge, sorry.'

'That's all right, lad. Now, where was I?'

'I think you were going to kick Mr Pooley again.'

'Ah yes.'

'Oh no,' wailed Jim. 'I *did* give it away, honest.'

'To *whom*?'

'To . . .' Jim shook his trembling head. 'I don't remember. A bloke in the pub.'

'Not good enough.' And the boot went in again.

John Omally went in, stayed there for quite a while, and finally came out.

Mrs Bryant looked up from the bed. 'You've been a very long time washing your hands,' said she. 'I was about to start without you.'

John made a strange croaking noise. His face was as white as an albino kipper.

'Are you all right, John? You look a bit—'

'Call the police,' croaked Omally. 'Call the police.'

'Oh, it's role playing, is it? What do you want me to be, a nurse?'

'It's not role playing and it's not a joke. There's something in your bathroom. Some*one*. All shrivelled up and dead. It's horrible. I think it might be your husband.'

Mrs Bryant fainted.

'He's out cold, sarge,' said the second policeman, lifting Pooley's head, then letting it fall back with a dreadful clunk onto the kitchen floor.

'Stubborn fellow, isn't he?' said the face. 'Now why do you think he would be that stubborn?'

Policemen two and three stood and shrugged. Policeman two was still holding the teapot. 'I suppose he won't be wanting the cup of tea now,' he said.

'Just answer the question, lad.'

'We don't know, sarge.'

'Because he's protecting someone, isn't he? Someone he cares about. Someone he does not want to get a similar hammering.'

'Oh yeah.' The second and the third policemen nodded.

'So what do we have on known associates?'

Policeman two rooted out his regulation police notebook and flicked through the pages. 'Just the one,' he said. 'John Vincent Omally of number seven Mafeking Avenue.'

'Well then, I suggest we all go off to the pub for a drink.'

'Why, sarge?'

'Because Omally is an Irish name, isn't it? And Irishmen are all drunken bastards, aren't they? So we won't expect Mr Omally to get home until after the pubs close, will we?'

'Surely that is a somewhat racist remark, isn't it, sarge?'

'Not if it's said by an Irishman.'

'But you're not Irish, sarge.'

'No, lad. I'm a policeman.'

Several police cars slewed to a halt before Mrs Bryant's front door. Sirens a-screaming, blue lights a-flash. In the kitchen Mrs Bryant pushed Omally towards the door.

'Just go,' she told him. 'Leave all this to me.'

'I can't leave you like this.'

'You must, John.'

'Then call me. No, I'll call you, I'm not on the phone. Look, I'm so sorry about this. I don't know what to say.'

'Don't say anything, just go.'

Mrs Bryant kissed him and John Omally went.

He managed to leap onto a 65 bus at the traffic lights and dropped down onto one of the big back seats. He closed his eyes for a moment but a terrible image filled his inner vision. A twisted, shrivelled thing that had once been a man, slouched over the bathroom toilet. John caught his breath and opened his eyes.

'Ah,' said the bus conductor. 'I remember you, you got off this morning without paying.'

John paid up a double fare. It was home for him and bed. This day had been a wrong 'un from the beginning. He should have been a wise man like Jim Pooley, who was probably now sleeping the sleep of the innocent.

'This day is done,' said John Omally.

But it wasn't.

Oh no, no, it wasn't.

8

John stepped down from the 65, crossed over the Ealing Road and stood on the corner outside Norman's paper shop. It was nearly eleven o'clock. Last orders time. He could make it to the Swan for a swift one.

'No,' said John. 'I'm going home to the safety of my bed.'

He turned up his tweedy collar, thrust his hands into the pockets of his similarly tweedy trousers, and trudged off down Albany Road and into Mafeking Avenue.

And he was just putting his key into the lock when he heard it.

A click, a thud and a cry of pain.

Omally spun round.

A groan.

Omally glanced towards the dustbins.

A bloody hand waved feebly.

Omally leapt over to the dustbins and flung them aside. 'Pooley,' he gasped. 'Jim, what's happened to you?'

'Get us inside. Quickly.'

Omally struggled to raise his friend. He dragged Jim's arm about his shoulder and hauled the rest of him with it.

'Bolt the door,' groaned Jim. 'Stick some chairs against it.'

'What's happened to you? Who did it? I'll paste them.'

'Policemen, John.'

Omally helped Jim into the kitchen. It bore an uncanny resemblance to Pooley's – the same un-emptied pedal bin and everything. 'Sit down,' said John. 'Carefully now.'

'Just bar the front door.'

'Leave it to me.' Omally left the kitchen, dragged a heavy armchair from the front room and rammed it up against the door before returning to his wounded friend. He ran cold water onto a dishcloth and bathed Jim's head with it. 'Why did they beat you up? What did you do?'

'I didn't do anything. They wanted the book.'

Omally stared at Jim. He knew his closest friend would never turn him in to the police.

'What makes you think they're coming here?' he asked.

'They had your name in a notebook as my known associate. I pretended I was unconscious. I heard them say they were going for a drink and they'd come back here after closing time.'

Omally dabbed at Pooley with the dishcloth, and Jim responded with winces and groans.

'You took a terrible pounding,' said Omally.

'You've two black eyes now. Any bones broken, do you think?'

'Most if not all.'

'Big lads, were they?'

'Very big.'

'Then we'll have to get out. This isn't a fortress.'

'Where will we go? Oh, ouch.'

'Sorry. I don't know, somewhere safe. Somewhere the police won't come looking.'

John looked at Jim. Jim looked at John. 'Professor Slocombe's,' they said.

That both John and Jim should have named one man with less than a moment's thought might appear strange to anyone who lives beyond the sacred boundaries of the Brentford Triangle. But for those who dwell within this world-famous geomantic configuration (formed by the Great West Road, the Grand Union Canal and the River Thames), there could be no other choice.

John and Jim had known the Professor for more years than they had known each other. He was Brentford's patriarch, exotic, enigmatic, yet part of the vital stuff from which the borough was composed.

Once, long ago, he—

KNOCK, KNOCK, KNOCK, came a dreadful knocking at Omally's door.

'Aaaagh! They're here!' Jim lurched to his feet and began to flap his hands wildly and spin round in small circles, for such was his habit during moments of extreme mental anguish.

'Stop that,' commanded John, halting Pooley's

gyrations by means of a headlock. 'It's the back way out for us.'

'I can't go on, John. I'm not up to it.'

'Get a grip, man.'

'Get a grip? Look at the state of me.'

KNOCK, KNOCK, KNOCK, came that knocking again.

'Run, John. Leave me here.'

'We go together. You won't need to run.'

'I won't?'

Omally pushed Jim out through the kitchen door and into the tiny ill-tended yard at the back. The moonlight offered it no favours. Against the kitchen wall, shrouded beneath a tarpaulin Omally had borrowed from Old Pete, stood *something*.

'Behold the engine of our deliverance,' stage-whispered John, flinging the tarpaulin aside to reveal—

'Not *Marchant*!' groaned Jim.

But Marchant it was.

And Marchant was a bike.

Those who have read the now legendary Flann O'Brien will know all about bicycles. Flann's theory was that in Ireland, during the days in which he wrote, most men owned a bicycle. And the constant jiggling and joggling on bumpy roads over an extended period of years made certain atoms of bicycle and certain atoms of man intermix, so that the man eventually became part bike and the bike part man. He cited an extreme case of a policeman who was so much bike that he had to lean against something when he stopped walking, to avoid toppling over.

In Omally's case this did not apply, but a rapport

existed between himself and his bicycle which had about it an almost spiritual quality.

Almost.

'Onto the handlebars, Jim,' said John. 'We take flight.'

'It never flies now, does it?'

'A figure of speech.'

John helped Jim onto the handlebars, seated himself upon the sprung saddle, placed one foot on a pedal and they all fell sideways.

'Oh no you don't.' John put his foot down to halt the descent. 'Now come on, Marchant, this is an emergency. My good friend Jim is injured and so will I be if you don't assist us.'

'If the police don't kill me, this bike of yours will,' moaned Jim.

'If you behave yourself you can spend tomorrow afternoon in the bike shed behind the girl's secondary school.'

'How dare you!'

'I was talking to my bike.'

KNOCK, KNOCK, KNOCK, came sounds of further knocking, followed by a most distinctive CRASH.

'Hi-o, Marchant!'

Out of the backyard and along the narrow alley they flew, Omally forcing down on the pedals and Jim clinging to the handlebars. It was a white-knuckle, grazed-knuckle ride. Happily it wasn't dustbin day.

Omally swung a hard right at the top. The only way to go was down the short cobbled path and back into Mafeking Avenue.

'Hold on tight,' said John as they shot over the pavement and into the road.

'There, sarge,' came a shout. 'On a bike, and that Pooley bloke's with him.'

'We're doomed!' cried Jim.

'Oh no we're not.'

There came sounds of running police feet, car doors opening and slamming shut and an engine beginning to rev. But they were not heard by John and Jim, for they were well away down Moby Dick Terrace and heading for the Memorial Park. As they swept past, the ever-alert Omally made a mental note to add the John Omally Millennial Bowling Green to his list.

'Have we lost them, John?' cried Jim.

John skidded to a halt, which is not altogether a good thing to do when you have someone riding on the handlebars.

'Ooooooooooh!' went Jim as he sailed forward through the air. 'Aaaagh!' he continued, as he struck the road.

'Sorry,' said John, wheeling alongside the tragic figure. 'But I think we've lost them, yes.'

SCREECH, came the sound of screeching tyres.

'Or perhaps not. Quick, Jim, up and away.'

'I'm dying,' Jim complained.

'Come on, *hurry*.'

'Oh, my giddy aunt.' Jim dragged himself to his feet and perched once more on the handlebars. Omally put his best foot forward and away they went again.

Inside the police car, three policemen laughed

with glee. They do that sometimes. Usually when they're about to perform something really sadistic on a suspect in an interrogation. And while they're doing it. And afterwards, if it comes to that. In the pub. Of course, American policemen do it better. Especially those in the southern states, good ol' boys with names like Joe-Bob. Really manic laughers, those lads.

'Stop that manic laughing, Constable Joe-Bob,' said the face. 'And run those two bastards off the road.'

'I certainly will, sarge,' and Constable Joe-Bob put his foot down.

'Faster,' cried Pooley. 'They're gaining.'

'Of course they're gaining, they're in a car.'

'Then get off the road.'

'Be quiet, Jim. I'm trying to think.'

'At a time like *this*?'

'I'm trying to think of an escape route, you buffoon.'

'Sorry.'

John took a sudden left that nearly dislodged Pooley and headed down towards the canal. To the sounds of further tyre-screeching, the police car did likewise.

'This is a dead end,' wailed Jim. 'We're doomed.'

'Hold on tight, Jim.' Omally tugged on the brakes and Marchant slewed to a standstill.

'What now, John?'

'Put your hands up, Jim.'

'What?'

The headlights hit them and the police car swept forward.

'Put your hands up, Jim.'

'Are you turning me in?'

'Just do it.'

Onward came the police car, gaining speed.

Jim stuck up his hands. 'They're not going to stop.'

'I hope not.'

'What?'

Roar of engine, onward-rushing car.

Cut to Pooley's frightened battered face. Cut to manic policeman behind wheel. Cut to long shot of car rushing forward. Cut to John's face, Jim's face, policemen's faces. Bonnet of car, spinning wheels – then—

'Jump!' Omally pushed Jim to one side and flung himself to the other.

Slow-motion shots now, the two men rolling to either side, the car bumper smashing into Marchant. Then a shot from below of the car passing slowly overhead, pushing the bike before it. And going down and down and down—

Into the canal.

Great plumes of spray, and spouts and splashes. Then fade to black.

'Sandra's crotch,' said Jim.

'You're not wrong there,' said John.

9

Omally climbed slowly to his feet, then helped Jim
to his. Pooley's knees offered little support and the
lad sank down onto his bum. 'What do we do now,
John?'

'Make our getaway, that's what.'

'But they'll drown. They might be rogue policemen but we can't let them drown.'

'What do you take me for, Jim? The water's only
two feet deep.'

'But they might be seriously injured.'

'Then we'll phone for an ambulance.'

Sounds of coughing and spluttering and cursing
now issued from the darkness below.

'Let's go,' said Jim.

John gazed into the black. 'Poor Marchant,' he
said.

From the canal bridge to the Butts Estate is a
pleasant five-minute stroll. But it's a long twenty
minutes when you're limping. Omally helped his
chum along the broad oak-bordered drive towards
the Professor's house. From tree to tree the two men

lurched, keeping to the shadows. They passed the door of Dr Steven Malone, but as yet they did not know it.

Ahead, lit by the golden haze of gaslight – for so remain the street lamps of the Butts – there rose the house of the Professor. A glorious mellow Georgian job, the Slocombe clan had owned it since it was built. High casement windows, chequered brick, a tribute to the mason's craft.

They halted at the garden gate, and waited a moment. Neither man knew why, but it was something they always did before they went inside. Then, taking up a breath apiece, they entered.

And stepped as through a veil that separated one world from another.

The moonlit garden was a thing of rare beauty. The heady fragrances of night-blooming orchids burdened the air. Chrysanthemums, like brazen hussies, swayed voluptuously, while snowdrops peeped and gossiped. Ancient roses showed their faces, craning for attention. Everywhere was colour, everywhere was life.

Ahead light showed through the great French windows and the fragile form of the Professor could be seen from behind, bent low over some ancient book upon his desk.

'Come on, Jim,' said John, hoisting his sagging companion. 'We're here now and we're safe.'

As John reached out a hand, the French windows opened of their own accord and the Professor swung round in his chair. 'Welcome, my friends,' said he.

John waggled the fingers of his free hand. Jim managed a lopsided smile.

The Professor's face took on a look of concern. Blue twinkling eyes narrowed, the nostrils of the slender nose flared, the merry mouth turned down at the corners. 'Set him into the chair beside the fire, John,' said the ancient. 'I will ring for assistance.'

His mottled hand took up a small brass Burmese temple bell and jingled it. John helped Jim onto the chair and then himself onto a Persian pouffe.

Firelight danced in the grate. The Professor's study, with its tall shelves crammed with leathern tomes, its lifeless creatures under high glass domes, its noble furniture and priceless rugs, was silent and was safe.

Presently the Professor's aged retainer, Gammon, appeared, clad in antique livery and bearing a silver tray. On this reposed a ship's decanter containing brandy, three glasses and a small medicine chest.

'Please see to our wounded friend, Gammon,' said the Professor.

'Certainly, sir,' the other replied.

Jim squawked and moaned as Gammon tested limbs, felt ribs, cleaned wounds and applied Band Aid dressings. 'Superficial, sir,' said Gammon as he left the room.

'What does *he* know?' grumbled Jim.

'A very great deal,' said the Professor, pouring brandy.

'Thanks very much,' said John, accepting his.

'And thank you too,' said Jim. 'And say thank you to Gammon for me. I really appreciate this.'

The Professor settled himself back behind his desk and viewed his visitors through his brandy glass. 'I feel you have a tale to tell,' said he.

'And then some,' said John.

'A bit of a bar fight, nothing more,' said Jim.

John looked aghast.

'Difference of opinion,' said Pooley. 'You should see the other bloke.'

Professor Slocombe shook his head, his mane of silky hair white as an albino bloater. 'Come, come, Jim,' he said. 'That is not what your aura says.'

'My aura is probably drunk. I certainly wish I was.'

'Jim got beaten up by the Garda,' said John. 'And all on account of a book.'

'A book?'

'*Brentford: A Study of its People and History*.'

'By Mr Compton-Cummings.'

'You know of it?'

'Indeed, I did a small amount of research for it. And I had him suppress certain passages.'

'Not nearly enough,' said Jim, holding out his empty glass.

'You mean he left in that bit about you and the great wind from the East? I told him to delete it.'

'Oh,' said Jim, as the old man gave him a refill. 'Well, thank you very much.'

'It was another passage entirely,' said John. 'One about . . .' He looked furtively around before whispering words into the Professor's ear.

'*Idrophrodisia?*'

'You don't want to know what it means.'

'I know exactly what it means.'

111

'I don't,' said Jim.

'The publishers called in all the copies of the book and pulped them,' said John. 'Except Jim got one in the post. The police were very anxious to get it back.'

'Exactly how anxious?' the Professor asked.

'They were prepared to kill us,' said John.

'They killed John's bike,' said Jim.

'Somewhat over-zealous. But I suppose, considering the nature of the allegations . . .'

'There're photos as well.'

'Oh dear, oh dear. But you got off lightly.' The Professor pointed towards John's shiner.

Omally fingered his eye. 'That was Jim. We had a slight contretemps over a theological matter.'

'I see.'

'Actually,' said John, 'while I'm here, there's something I wanted to ask you.'

'Ask away.' Professor Slocombe refilled John's glass, then his own.

'Mine too,' said Jim, as his was somehow empty again.

'The Brentford Scrolls,' said John. Jim groaned.

'The Brentford Scrolls?' Professor Slocombe laughed. 'I have spent nearly two hundred years, ahem, I have spent *a very long time* searching for *those*. They are somewhere in the borough, I can sense it. But where, I do not know.'

'Told you, Jim,' said John.

'But what exactly is your interest in the scrolls?' Professor Slocombe raised his glass and tasted brandy.

'Purely historical,' said John.

'Aura,' said the Professor.

'John thinks he's found a way of making millions of pounds from the Millennium Fund,' said Jim. 'There's more than eight hundred Days of God owing to Brentford, so Brentford is entitled to celebrate the millennium two years before the rest of the world. We could celebrate it this year, on New Year's Eve.'

Professor Slocombe threw back his old head and laughed.

And laughed.

And laughed some more.

'Priceless,' he said, when he was able. 'And you're perfectly right. If the scrolls could be discovered and of course if the papal bull was never revoked.'

'I'm sure it wasn't.'

'I can easily check that, John. Hand me', the ancient pointed, 'that large green volume, second shelf up at the end next to the shrunken head.'

Omally hastened to oblige. He tugged and wrestled with the book but could not draw it from the shelf.

'Oh, my apologies.' Professor Slocombe made a mystic pass with his right hand. Omally toppled backwards clutching the book. He crawled over to the desk and set it down upon the tooled-leather surface.

'Sorry about that,' said Professor Slocombe. 'The books are, as always, protected.'

'No problem,' said John, crawling back to his pouffe.

The Professor flicked through the pages, his long

thin fingers tracing lines. Presently he closed the book. 'You would seem to be in luck,' said he.

'*Yes!*' said John, raising a fist.

'But of course you'd have to find the scrolls, and if *I* can't, well . . .'

'Two heads are better than one,' said John.

'Not necessarily.'

'Three, counting Jim.'

'No, count me out.' Jim folded his arms painfully.

'He's had a rough day. He'll be all for it tomorrow.'

'Oh no I won't.'

'Oh yes you will.'

'Won't.'

'Will.'

'Gentlemen.' Professor Slocombe raised a calming hand. 'Whether you will or whether you won't, you have pressing business to attend to first.'

'We do?' asked John.

'The police.'

'Ah.'

'But I think I can sort that out for you. Chief Inspector Westlake of the Brentford Constabulary is a good friend of mine. We are both members of the same lodge. If I were to ask him a personal favour, he would not refuse it.'

'You're a saint,' said John.

'Not yet. But I am also a good friend of the present Pope.'

'Say hello from me next time you see him.'

'I certainly will. But in order to smooth things over with the police, it will be necessary to give them

114

Jim's book. Do you have it about your person?'

'I do.' Omally fumbled at his trouser pocket. 'Oh, no. I don't.'

'He's lost it.' Jim threw up his hands. 'Ouch.'

'No, I haven't lost it. I . . .' John's thoughts returned to an hour before. To a terrible hour before. To the kitchen of Mrs Bryant. In all the horror and madness, he had left the book upon the reproduction olde worlde table.

'Oh dear, oh dear,' said John Omally.

The newly widowed Mrs Bryant was not at her reproduction olde worlde table, but huddled on a chair at the Brentford Cottage Hospital. Outside the mortuary.

Within this cold and dismal room the duty physician was filling in Jack Bryant's death certificate.

'The subject died through lack of blood caused by excessive straining on the toilet, leading to acute rectal prolapse and arterial rupture.'

At the bottom of the death certificate the duty physician signed his name: Dr Steven Malone.

And having signed, he turned and pointed in profile to a wrinkled naked thing which lay upon the mortuary block just off the page. 'Bung that in a drawer,' he told a nurse.

10

A golden dawn came unto Brentford. The flowers in the Professor's magical garden hid their faces as the borough's denizens began to stir.

Omally hadn't slept at all. While Pooley mumbled and snored in one of the Professor's guest bedrooms, John paced the floor of another. Until the book was recovered from Mrs Bryant's and handed over to the police, he and Jim could not return to their homes, nor set out upon their quest. But what of Jack Bryant? What had happened to him? Omally shuddered at the recollection of that hideously shrivelled body. It had looked as if all the blood had been drained from it. And what could do *that* to a man? A vampire? In Brentford? That was nonsense, surely. But was it? And what if it came back to feast upon Mrs Bryant?

And then there was Marchant. Poor, poor Marchant. The trusty iron steed that had served John for more years than he cared to remember. Marchant would have to be recovered from the canal and lovingly restored. And that would take money and John didn't have any money, unless he could find those Brentford Scrolls.

Omally's thoughts went round in a circle like an unholy mandala. Or perhaps more like some hideous black vortex that just kept sucking more dark thoughts into it. The death of Compton-Cummings now seemed more than suspect. Folk were dropping like flies hereabouts.

By the coming of the golden dawn John had resolved on a course of action. He would go as soon as possible to Mrs Bryant's, offer what comfort he could and recover Jim's book, which he would then deliver to Professor Slocombe. When matters were straightened with the police, he would sneak along to the canal and rescue Marchant.

And then with Jim's help, or without it, he would seek the Brentford Scrolls.

Which should take him up to lunchtime and a pint or two of Large in the Flying Swan.

Omally left a note for the Professor, thanking him for sanctuary and promising to return by breakfast with the book, and set off across Brentford to catch a 65.

There were no police cars outside Mrs Bryant's. But why should there have been? The chances were that the lady wouldn't even be there. She would be staying with a relative for the night, or might possibly be under sedation in a hospital bed.

John went round to the back and knocked gently at the kitchen door. No answer. Should he force the lock? Omally, not by nature one to dither, dithered.

Come back later, was that the best? No, he was here now, do it.

John turned the handle and gave the door a shove.

It opened before him.

Magic.

John slipped inside, closed the door behind him and strode over to the reproduction olde worlde table. Jim's book was not on it.

'Damn!' said John.

'Eeeeek!' screamed Mrs Bryant, who'd been coming down the hall.

'Oh, sorry.' John put out his hands to catch her as she swooned away. He helped her to a kitchen chair and poured a glass of water.

'I thought you were a burglar, John.'

'I'm so sorry. I wanted to see if I could do anything to help. Sip this.'

'Thank you. I'm all right. It was a terrible shock, though.'

'It was certainly that.'

'But one must look on the bright side.'

'Yes, I'm sure one must.'

'It was the way he would have wanted to go.'

'It was?'

'To die like the King.'

'The who?'

'Not The Who, the King.'

'I'm sorry,' said John. 'You've lost me here.'

'The King,' said Mrs Bryant. 'Elvis. Jack died like Elvis.'

'Oh, I see. Yes, I suppose he did. What did he die of, if you don't mind me asking.'

'A massive haemorrhage. He was straining too hard and something burst.'

A small but clear alarm bell rang in John Omally's head. The image of the defunct Jack Bryant would probably never leave him. Every detail was indelibly etched. But if Jack Bryant had died while taking a dump, then he, John Omally, was a clog-dancing Dutchman. For one thing, although Jack may have been seated on the toilet, the lid was down. And for another, unlike Mr Compton-Cummings, Jack Bryant had died with his trousers up.

'How very strange,' said John.

Mrs Bryant sniffed and sipped her water. 'According to the duty physician it's quite common, just not the kind of thing people like to talk about. They always say "he died peacefully in his sleep".'

'Yes, I suppose they would. Now is there anything I can do to help?'

'No, thank you. My brother's coming down from Orton Goldhay. He'll sort out the funeral arrangements. I may move back up there.'

'I'll miss you,' said John.

'And I shall worry about you. Get yourself a good woman, John. Sort your life out.'

'I'll try.' John Omally kissed her lightly on the forehead. 'Oh, just one thing,' he said. 'Can I have that history book back? I left it here on the table.'

'History book?' Mrs Bryant stiffened. 'It's hardly a history book, is it? What is *sacofricosis* anyway?'

'You really wouldn't want to know.'

'No, I suppose I wouldn't.'

'So, can I have it back?'

'Well, you could,' said Mrs Bryant, 'but I'm afraid I don't have it any more.'

'What?'

'I must have left it in the waiting room at the Cottage Hospital.'

When John left Mrs Bryant's he caught the 8.15 bus. Bill got thrown off again for fondling a schoolgirl and a lady in a straw hat told John all about her husband, who had once sprayed deodorant on his beard and gone to a fancy dress party as an armpit.

Omally got off at the Cottage Hospital. More bad thoughts were now being sucked into the black vortex in his head.

A very pretty nurse stood at the reception desk.

'Good morning, ms,' said John. 'I wonder if you might help me?'

'Are you ill?'

'No. My name is,' John paused, 'John *Bryant*.'

'Oh yes? How's Fergie doing?'

'Sorry, I don't quite understand.'

'Sorry, it just slipped out.' The nurse gave a Sid James chuckle.

John made a mental note to return at a later date and ask her out. 'My brother was brought here last night,' he said. 'Jack Bryant. He died.'

'Oh yes, Mr Bryant. Tragic way to go.'

'But just like the King.'

'I thought the king said "bugger Bognor" and died in his bed.'

'I wonder if I might have a word with the doctor who was on duty at the time.'

'I'm afraid not,' said the nurse. 'He's not here at the moment, and I can't give out any information at all.'

'I see. It was Dr Pooley, wasn't it?'

'Dr Malone.'

'Ah yes, old *Jim* Malone.'

'Dr *Steven* Malone.'

'Of course. Does he still live in Hanwell?'

'No, he lives in Brentford now.'

'That's right, in Mafeking Avenue.'

'In Kether House on the Butts Estate.'

'Won't be the same chap, then. I'm sorry you couldn't help me. Oh, just one other thing: my sister-in-law left a book of mine in the waiting room. *Brentford: A Study of its People and History*.'

'Oh, *that* book,' said the nurse, giving out with another Sid James.

Oh dear, thought John. 'Might I have it back?'

'The doctor on duty took it home with him.'

Dr Steven Malone was enjoying his breakfast. He was also enjoying Jim's book. 'Well, well, well,' he went, as he munched on kedgeree and swallowed orange juice. 'Whoever would have thought it? Whoever would have thought that a Brentford corner shopkeeper would be the first man to wade across the Channel?' He turned another page and glanced at a photograph. 'And whoever would have thought *that*?'

KNOCK, KNOCK, KNOCK, came a knock-knock-knocking.

Dr Malone got up and answered the door.

Upon the step stood John Omally, notebook and biro in hand.

'Dr Malone?' he asked. 'Dr Steven Malone?'

'I am he.'

Omally viewed the monochrome medic. 'Has anyone ever told you that you bear an uncanny resemblance to—'

'Many times,' said Dr Steven. 'And although it has never been a curse, it's never been a big bird-puller.'

'Well, my name's Molloy,' said John. 'Scoop Molloy of the *Brentford Mercury*. I came as soon as I could.'

'Excuse me?'

'Tip-off,' said John. 'From an inside source at the Cottage Hospital.'

'I have no idea what you're talking about. Would you kindly leave?'

'Be pleased to, as soon as you give me a quote. We don't get a story as big as this very often.'

Dr Malone began to close the door. John stuck his foot in the gap. ' "VAMPIRE CLAIMS FIRST VICTIM",' he said in a very loud voice. ' "ALL BLOOD DRAINED".'

'You'd better come in,' said Dr Malone.

'Ah, come in, Jim,' said Professor Slocombe, looking up from his desk. 'And how are you feeling this morning?'

'Still a bit shaky, sir, as it happens. My head aches something wicked.'

'That might perhaps have something to do with the half a bottle of brandy you consumed.'

'No, it will be the concussion.'

'Breakfast?'

'Oh yes please.'

Professor Slocombe rang his small brass bell.

'Would you care for some breakfast?' asked Dr Malone.

'No thanks,' said John. 'Deadlines to keep, you know how it is.'

'Indeed I do,' the doctor smiled.

John Omally didn't like that smile. In fact he didn't like anything about Dr Steven Malone. With his pale gaunt features he looked every bit the vampire. Such a brazen approach, although calculated to gain entry, had not perhaps been the wisest of moves. If he was now inside the lair of a genuine undead, was he all that likely to get out again?

'Did you come alone?' asked the doctor.

'Ah, no,' said John. 'Three of my colleagues are waiting outside in the car.'

'Well, I'm sure we can clear this up between the two of us.'

'I'm sure we can.' Omally sat down in a chair with his back to the wall and placed his notebook on the dining table. 'Between you and me,' he said, 'I think this whole thing probably has a simple explanation.'

'It certainly does.'

'But who cares about that, eh? Give the readers what they want, blood and guts. This one should run and run.'

Dr Steven's pale gaunt features turned a whiter shade. 'Listen,' he said. 'There is no story here. Jack

123

Bryant died from a haemorrhage whilst evacuating his bowels.'

'I heard he was naked,' said John. 'And the words NUMBER ONE were written in his blood on the wall.'

'He was not naked and there were no words on the wall.'

'So you were there, then? You can swear to that?'

'I was there. I arranged for the removal of the body. He was sitting on the toilet with his trousers down.'

'Trousers down you say?' John made a note. 'Just the trousers?'

'Just the trousers.'

'And no holes in the neck?'

'No.'

'What about holes anywhere else?'

'*What?*'

'Just trying to keep one step ahead of the *Sunday Sport.*'

'Newspaper, Jim?' asked the Professor, across the breakfast table.

'No thanks, I never read them.'

'You're probably wise.'

'Probably. Oh, see if there's anything in there about Mr Compton-Cummings.'

'A book review? I think that most unlikely.'

'No, about his death.'

'His *what*?'

'His *willy*,' said John. 'No holes in his willy?'

'Absolutely not!'

'Well, it looks as if I have no story here at all. What a shame.'

'You have my sympathy.'

'No, I mean, what a shame I'll have to write it up anyway.'

'*What?*'

'My bonus depends on it. If I don't hand in a story today, I won't get my bonus. And if I don't get my bonus, I won't have enough to buy my dear little white-haired old mother her stairlift.'

'And how much is this bonus of yours worth?'

'How does fifty quid sound?'

'You sound shocked,' said Jim. 'But then I suppose you are.'

'Compton-Cummings dead and you didn't think to mention it?'

'It somehow slipped my mind. I'd had a rough evening.'

'Compton-Cummings dead,' said the Professor. 'Compton-Cummings dead.'

'Just one more thing before I go,' said John Omally, turning at the open front door. 'There was another chap died yesterday, a Mr Compton-Cummings. His body must have been brought into the Cottage Hospital. Did you examine it?'

'There was no other body in the morgue.'

'But anyone who dies locally would be brought to the Cottage Hospital, surely.'

'They would. But I know nothing about any Compton-Cummings.'

'Perhaps there's a story there,' said John.

'Forget it,' said Dr Steven Malone, closing the front door upon him.

John set off across the oak-lined street, whistling. Inside his waistcoat pocket he now had ten nice crisp five-pound notes. The day had hardly begun and already he was ahead.

Dr Steven Malone bolted the front door and shook his pale head. Compton-Cummings? Who was Compton-Cummings? The name sounded strangely familiar. Ah yes, of course, it was the name of the author of that book on his dining table.

Dr Steven Malone returned to examine the book. He was more than a little peeved to find it wasn't there.

'Hi-de-ho,' said John Omally, breezing in through the Professor's French windows.

'Hi-de-nothing!' said the old man, rising from his desk. 'Why did you not tell me about the death of Compton-Cummings?'

'It somehow slipped my mind,' said John. 'I'd had a rough evening.'

The Professor glared at John and then at Jim. Jim winced.

'But I'll tell you what,' said Omally. 'There's something very strange going on around here. The body of Mr Compton-Cummings never made it to the morgue at the Cottage Hospital.'

Professor Slocombe raised an eyebrow. 'And how do you know that?'

'I've just been speaking to a Dr Steven Malone.'

'The geneticist, lives in Kether House?'

'Geneticist he may be, bloody liar also.'

'Sit down,' said the Professor. 'Sit down and tell me everything that happened last night. And I do mean *everything*.'

John Omally sat down.

An hour later a police car arrived at Professor Slocombe's house. In it was Chief Inspector Westlake. He and the Professor exchanged a certain handshake and Jim's book was taken into police custody.

John and Jim were made to sign copies of the Official Secrets Act and issued with very stern warnings. When the Chief Inspector left, Professor Slocombe glared once more. 'Am I supposed to settle this?' he said, waving a piece of paper.

'What is that?' asked Omally.

'It is the bill for a police car. A police car that ran into the canal last night. Something else you forgot to mention.'

'I'll deal with it,' said John.

The Professor didn't wish them well as he closed the garden gate upon them. 'Get out and stay out,' were the words he used.

'I've never seen him angry before,' said Jim as they trudged away. 'He was very upset about Mr Compton-Cummings.'

'Brothers under the apron,' said John. 'But we came out on top, didn't we?'

'On top? Are you jesting?'

'Slate wiped clean. No longer on the police hit list. And we've turned a profit.'

'What profit?'

John dug four crisp five-pound notes from his waistcoat pocket. 'Hush money from Doctor Death. This is your half.'

'I don't want that,' said Jim. 'That's tainted, that is.'

'Well, please yourself. I'll keep it.'

'Oh no you won't.' Jim snatched the fivers from Omally's mitt. 'I owe it to myself to come out of this with something.'

'Share and share alike,' said John. 'That's our way, isn't it?'

'Always has been,' said Jim.

'In triumph or adversity.'

'I'll drink to that.'

'Let's shake on it instead.'

'All right, let's.'

The two men shook hands.

'So,' said John. 'Your share of the cost of the new police car is eight and a half thousand pounds. Do you want to give me cash, or a cheque?'

John ducked the flying fist and helped Jim up.

'Eight and a half thousand?' Jim's knees were all wobbly again, his hands beginning to flap. 'Where could I get eight and half thousand?'

'Take it out of your salary.'

'What salary?'

'The one you will be getting as a director of the Brentford Millennium Committee.'

Jim groaned.

'Unless you have another means of earning it.'

'I don't.'

'Then, Jim, as the sun shines down upon us, let luck be a lady and the devil take the hindmost, we set out upon a holy quest. To search for the Brentford Scrolls.'

'Should we have a pint before we do?'

'Let's have two,' said John Omally. 'Just to be on the safe side.'

11

They strolled along the thoroughfares of Brentford.

'All right,' said John. 'My plan is this—'

'*Your* plan?' Jim put up his hand. 'I thought all this was to be a fifty-fifty deal.'

'You have a plan of your own you would like to discuss?'

'Not as such.'

'Well, until you do, perhaps we might try mine.'

'Fair enough. I just felt it needed saying.'

'Quite so.'

'Thank you.'

'Might I continue?'

'Certainly.'

'My plan is this. I go now to the canal and attempt to recover Marchant. You go to the Memorial Library, dig out all the ancient maps of the borough you can find and photocopy them. Can you manage that?'

'Don't patronize me, John.'

'My apologies. Bring the photocopies and meet me in the Swan at, say,' John looked down at his naked wrist, 'precisely twelve noon, that's an hour and five minutes from now.'

'John,' said Jim.

'Jim?' said John.

'I hope you get your bike back OK.'

'Thanks. I'll see you later, then.'

'So there's this Eskimo,' said Old Pete. 'And his snowmobile breaks down, so he hauls it to the garage. And the mechanic has a look at it and says, "I think you've blown a seal, mate," and the Eskimo says, "No I haven't, it's just frost on my moustache." '

There was a moment's silence in the Flying Swan before the lunchtime patrons took in the enormity (and indeed the genius) of this particular joke. And then there was a great deal of laughter.

'Surely,' said Small Dave the postman, 'that is somewhat racist.'

'Not if it's told by a policeman,' said Old Pete.

John Omally entered the bar, sighted Jim in a far and private corner and squelched over.

'You're squelching,' said Jim, looking up.

'I had to wade.'

'But you got Marchant back?'

'What's left of him. I carted the old boy around to Norman at the corner shop. He has agreed to rebuild him for me.'

'That will cost a bob or two.'

'Not a penny. I have offered Norman a seat on the board of the Brentford Millennium Committee. He was happy to accept.'

'Did you mention to him that all depends upon us finding the Brentford Scrolls?'

Omally tapped his forehead. 'It somehow slipped my mind.'

Pooley grinned. 'I've got you a pint in.'

'Cheers. Are those the copies of the maps?'

Jim spread the photocopies before him. 'There's not a lot to go on, but we have to start somewhere.'

Omally sat down, tasted ale and joined Jim in perusal.

'The Professor must have been through all these,' said Jim.

'The Professor is a scholar, Jim. A magus, an illuminatus.'

'And we're a couple of louts.'

'I am *not* a lout. What I mean is, his approach to a problem differs from ours. We are free spirits, we think differently.'

Jim swallowed ale. 'I know exactly what you mean. It's always been like that for me. I could never be one of the gang. When everyone else was being a mod, I was being a beatnik.'

'I was a mod,' said John. 'I had a Vespa. Now that was a fanny-magnet.'

Pooley thought *Sandra* and said, 'Well, we're certainly not part of the herd, whatever we are.'

'We are individuals, Jim, and *you* are a character, sir.'

'So does this mean that we can find the scrolls in a couple of days, when it's taken the Professor God knows how long not to find them at all?'

'It means that if we set about the task and do it *our* way, we'll succeed.'

'So, where are the scrolls hidden, John?'

'Good question.'

John gave the maps further perusal. 'Which is the earliest one?'

'This one. It's dated 1580.'

'About the right period, then. So what's on it?'

'Very little really.' Jim swallowed more ale. 'A few tracks, some farms. A tavern, right here, Ye Flying Swanne, a manor house, and a few rude huts.'

'Why do they call them *rude* huts, do you suppose?'

'Because of the *arse-ends*, I think.'

'The *what*?'

'*Arse-ends*, wooden trusses that support the roof.'

'Fascinating. Anything else on the map?'

'Only the monastery.'

'Not a lot to go on. But I suppose we should check the obvious places first.'

'Absolutely,' agreed Jim. 'And where might those be?'

'Well, if you were a monk, where would you hide something precious?'

'In my boots.'

'In your boots! Very good, Jim. And there was I thinking that monks wear sandals.'

'Oh yeah. Do monks wear underpants, do you think? Or are they like Scotsmen with kilts?'

John drummed his fingers upon the table. 'I will ask the question again. If you were a monk, where would you hide something precious?'

'I know. In the monastery.' Jim gave John the old thumbs up.

John gave Jim the old thumbs down. 'No,' he said. 'Not in the monastery. In the pub.'

'Eh?'

'When you're really pissed—'

'Which I can rarely afford to be.'

'But when you are, what is the last thing you say before you leave the pub?'

'Goodnight?'

'No, you say, "Neville, please mind my wallet." '

'Do I?'

'You do.'

'Oh yes. And the next morning I wake up and I can't find my wallet and I get all depressed and I'm really hung over, so I gather up some pennies and halfpennies for a hair of the dog and I come into the Swan and Neville says, "You left your wallet here last night," and I get really cheered up.'

'Exactly. So if you were a monk and you'd just come back from this pilgrimage to Rome and you were really proud of yourself because you'd pulled off this great deal with the Pope and you wanted to get a skinful for celebration, where would you go?'

Jim pointed to the map. 'I would go to Ye Flying Swanne.'

'And so would I. So let's check here first.' John finished his ale, took up the two empty glasses and went over to the bar.

'. . . the Irish Uri Geller', said Old Pete, 'rubbed a spoon and his finger fell off.'

'You old bastard,' said Omally.

'Who are you calling *old*? That's an ageist remark. There should be a law about people making comments like that!'

John held the glasses out to Neville. 'Two of similar, please.' And the part-time barman did the business.

'Neville,' said John. 'Do you have a lost property cupboard?'

'Certainly do. It's a priest hole, been there since the pub was built.'

'Really?' said John, in a casual tone.

'It's got stuff in it going back years.'

'Really?' said John once again.

'Oh, yes. Umbrellas, packs of cards, a couple of top hats, some flintlock pistols, even a monk's satchel.'

Omally tried to say 'Really?' but the word wouldn't come.

'I should have a clear-out, I suppose,' said Neville. 'But I never seem to find the time.'

'I wouldn't mind doing it for you,' said John, in a curious strangled kind of whisper.

'Something wrong with your voice, John?'

'No.' John cleared his throat. 'Lead me to it. I'll clear it out right now.'

'Oh, I wouldn't put you to the trouble.'

'It's no trouble, I assure you. Consider it my good deed for the day.'

'Well, if you really want to.'

John rubbed his hands together.

'No, it doesn't matter,' said Neville.

'Oh, it does, it really does.'

'Well, please yourself,' said Neville. 'But there's nothing of value down there.'

'I never thought there was.'

'Oh, good,' said Neville, 'then you won't be disappointed when you don't find the Brentford Scrolls.'

John returned to Jim's table with the drinks. 'Why is everyone up at the bar laughing?' Jim asked. 'And why have you got a face like a smacked bottom?'

'Never mind,' said John, in a bitter tone.

'Am I to assume that we will be continuing our search elsewhere?'

'You are. Let's have another look at those maps.'

'I don't think it will help. Look here, I photo-copied a present-day map of the borough. The whole place has been built over. See what stands on the site of the old monastery?'

John saw. 'The police station,' he said.

'We're not going to find it from maps.' Jim sipped some ale. 'How many people must have tried before us?'

'At least two dozen in here, apparently,' said John through gritted teeth.

'What was that?'

'Never mind. All right, throw away the maps. Let us apply our wits.'

'You're not hoping for an early result then?'

'If the scrolls exist, we will find them. Trust me on this.'

'Oh, I do. But we'll have to come up with some-thing pretty radical.'

'Necromancy!' said John.

'Yes, that's pretty radical. What are you talking about?'

'Calling up the spirits of the dead.'

'Get real, John, please.'

'Spiritualists do it all the time.'

'I got thrown out of a spiritualist church once,' said Jim.

'Did you? Why was that?'

'Well, I went along because they had this guest medium, Mrs Batty Moonshine or someone, and she kept saying, "There are spirits here, I can see them all around, they're trying to communicate," and then she said, "I'm getting a message for someone called John." '

'Yes,' said John, 'curiously enough they always say that.'

'And she did and there's Johns all over the church putting up their hands. So I called out "Ask the spirit for John's surname," and they threw me out.'

'I'm not surprised.'

'I was only trying to be helpful. But I don't think it works really, do you?'

'Probably not. But if it did and we could speak to the monk directly . . .'

'The only way you could do that is if you had a time machine.'

Omally laughed.

But Pooley didn't. 'That's it,' he said.

'That's what?'

'A time machine.'

'Did you suck a lot of lead soldiers when you were a child, Jim?'

'No, I mean it. That's how we do it. Travel back in time.'

'Travel back to the bar and get some more drinks in.'

'No, John, I'm not kidding. I've been doing these mental exercises for months. Trying to travel forwards in time through the power of the mind.'

'In your search for the winning lottery numbers. I've tried hard not to laugh.'

'But I can only travel backwards. I relive my childhood over and over again.'

'That's not time travel, Jim. You recall your childhood memories because they *are* memories. Just memories.'

'I could do it. I know I could.'

'Away into the night with you.'

'I *could* do it.' Jim made a most determined face.

'You're not kidding, are you?'

'No, I'm not.'

'I'll get these in,' said John, taking up the glasses. 'And we'll speak some more of this.'

At a little after lunchtime closing, John and Jim were to be found once more strolling the thoroughfares of Brentford.

'All right,' said John. 'We'll give it a go. Where do you want to do it?'

'I've always done it on the bench outside the Memorial Library.'

'It's a bit public there. Do it in the park.'

'Okey-dokey.'

John and Jim strolled down to the park. There

138

were few people about, a dog-walker or two, a pram-pushing mum.

Jim sat down with his back against a tree.

'What exactly do you do next?' John asked.

'I just sort of go to sleep.'

'Oh dear, oh dear.'

'But it's not a real sleep. It's an altered state.'

'Are you usually sober when you do this?'

'Sometimes.'

'Is there anything I can do to help?'

'You could make a noise like a road drill.'

'Why?'

'Well, they've been digging up the road near the library and I find the noise seems to help.'

'Brrrrrrrt!' went John Omally, trying to keep a straight face.

'Curiously that sounds just like a Vespa.'

'Raaaaaaaa!' went John.

'Not bad, but can you do it in A minor?'

'A minor,' said John. 'That takes me back.'

'It takes me back also, but why does it take *you* back?'

'A minor. Blues harmonica. I had a Hohner. It was in A minor. The blues are always in A minor.'

'Perhaps that's significant. Go on then, do it in A minor.'

Omally did it in A minor.

A lady in a straw hat walked by. 'Shouldn't be allowed,' she said.

John continued in A minor as Pooley settled back against the tree and readied for the off. He took deep breaths and closed his eyes.

And soon the dreaming mind of Jim went once more on its walkabout.

Lottery balls went pop, pop, pop and the *Blue Peter* bloke-who-wasn't poured out the same old spiel. Jim saw himself in the audience again with his left foot bandaged up. Then there it was again, the breakfast-then-the-bookies-the-bookies-then-the-pub-the-pub-then-home-for-tea—

'Back,' commanded Jim. 'Go back.'

'Mmmmmm,' went John Omally.

Back went Jim. To his teenage years, the Blue Triangle Club and Sandra of the rhyming slang. Then back to the childhood holidays and school and the headmaster's room.

'Go back.'

To nursery school, the cradle, the maternity ward, then—

WHACK!

And it wasn't the sound of a door on a wall. It was a WHACK of a different persuasion.

'I'm going,' whispered Jim. 'I'm off and going now.'

'Then go with God, my friend,' said John, for this seemed the right thing to say.

And so Jim drifted back.

Streets of houses rose up before him and fell away behind, women in mop caps with babies on their hips, gentlemen with high wing collars, splendid in their sideburns. Hansom cabs and broughams, horses and pony traps, then dandies in coloured waistcoats, fops and dollymops, ladies with pompadours, hoop skirts and silken drawers—

Back.

Jim felt heat upon his face. Where was he now? It was hot here. In the distance rude dwellings. Jim thought himself closer. Phew! What a stink! So that's why they were called rude. But who's this?

Jim saw him marching over a hill, his robes blowing about him. Brown robes, knotted at the waist, bare legs and sandals. He was clutching something to his chest, something wrapped in a velvet cloth.

The monk marched ever closer.

Jim could see his face now. It was the face of an Old Testament prophet. Noble-browed, wild of eye, with a great beak of a nose, a chin thrust forward.

And on he marched. Right past.

'Hold on,' cried Jim. 'I want a word with you.'

But the monk didn't turn.

He didn't see Jim.

But who was this?

A hooded rider was coming out of the East, as though borne on the wind. He rode towards the monk, reigned in his horse and dismounted.

'Ho there, holy father,' he cried.

'Out of my way, villain.'

Rather harsh words for a monk, thought Jim, but he stared in awe at the rider. For the rider had now pulled back his hood and his face could clearly be seen.

'I go with God,' declared the monk. 'Do not stand in my way.'

'But I am God's messenger, or rather the

messenger of his messenger.' The rider smiled wickedly. 'I have something to deliver.'

'I want nothing from you, odorous one. I smell the breath of Satan on you. The sulphur of the pit.'

'Your words are unappealing, monk. What have you in your bundle?'

'I have the Days of God. And God will not be denied them.'

'God may not be denied his days. But I deny you yours.'

'Stand aside, Antichrist.'

'Your days are numbered, monk. Your end is now.'

'Stand aside.'

'Recommend yourself to your maker.'

And then a blade flashed in the sunlight and the searing wind and drove in again and again.

And then Jim saw more. Much more. Horror piling on horror.

And then he awoke with a scream.

Omally was shaking him. 'Are you all right, Jim? You're white as a sheet.'

'I'm OK. I'm OK.'

'You've a terrible sweat on you.'

'I'm not surprised.'

'Did you see him? The monk, did you see him?'

'I saw him all right. I saw everything. It was terrible, John. Terrible.'

'Do you want to tell me about it?'

'It was the stuff about me in Compton-Cummings's book. "Surely this is the breath of

Pooley." An assassin came out of the East with the wind and the assassin was me.'

'*You?*'

'One of my ancestors. One of my ancestors murdered the monk.'

'Holy Mary!'

'He was sent by the Pope. You see, the Pope couldn't rescind the papal bull. Those things are supposed to be inspired by God. And God isn't noted for changing his mind. So the Pope called in an assassin to murder the monk and destroy the Brentford Scrolls.'

'And this assassin was one of your blokes?'

'He looked just like me.'

'And did he destroy the scrolls?'

'No. He tried to blackmail the Pope. Demand piles of gold for the scrolls.'

'So what did the Pope do?'

'He sent an assassin to assassinate the assassin.'

'Bastard.'

'Too right. That assassin was a Mr Sean Omally.'

'God's teeth and trousers.'

'So then the assassin of the assassin tries it on with the Pope and the Pope gets another assassin to assassinate him. And then this assassin—'

'Does this go on for very long?'

'For years.'

'So who fetched up with the scrolls in the end?'

'One of my blokes.'

'And did he destroy them?'

'No, he buried them.'

'Where, Jim? Did you see where?'

'I saw exactly where.'

'So do you know where they are now?'

'I know exactly where they are now.'

'Tell me.'

'It's so weird,' said Pooley. 'I mean, the thing must have been locked into my genes. Part of some ancestral memory, perhaps. Passed down from father to son from generation to generation.'

'Go on.'

'I must have known all along. It's the place I always go to, you see. My kind of spiritual haven. I'm drawn to it whenever I want to be at peace and think. I never knew why, but something inside always told me to go there.'

'So where is it, Jim?'

'The bench outside the library. The scrolls are buried in a casket underneath.'

12

'Would you look at that?' said John Omally. 'Did you ever in your life see a bench more firmly cemented into the ground than this lad?'

Jim Pooley shook his head. 'But I suppose if it wasn't, it wouldn't be here for long.'

'True enough. But how are we going to get it up?'

Jim stroked his chin. 'All right,' said he, 'considering that we have got this far by doing it *our* way, I suggest we apply our unique talents and effect a speedy and successful conclusion.'

'Well said,' said John. 'Go on then.'

'Go on what?'

'Apply your unique talents.'

'Right.' Jim looked the bench up and down and around and about, scuffed his heels upon its mighty concrete base and then stood back with his hands upon his hips and his head cocked on one side. 'We will just have to blow the bugger up,' said he.

'Blow the bugger up?' Omally flinched.

'Easiest solution. No messing about.'

Omally sighed. 'Jim,' he said. 'Exactly how deep in the ground are the scrolls?'

'I give up,' said Jim. 'Exactly how deep?'

'I have absolutely no idea. But we can't blow up the bench in case we blow up the scrolls also.'

'Controlled blast. You know all about explosions, John.'

'Not so loud.' John put sshing fingers to his mouth. 'It's a bad idea. And don't you think that the sound of an explosion might just attract the attention of passers-by?'

'We could do it at night, when everyone's asleep.'

John let free a second sigh. 'Do you have any more inspired ideas of a unique nature?'

'Yes,' said Jim. 'I do. We could tunnel under.'

'Tunnel under?'

'Like in this film I saw. *The Wooden Horse*, I think it was called. These prisoners of war built this vaulting horse and they went out every day and exercised with it. But there was a bloke inside with a spoon and a bag and he dug this tunnel and—'

'Wasn't Trevor Howard in that one?'

'He might have been. I think John Mills was.'

'Didn't Anton Diffring play the Nazi officer?'

'With the long leather coat?'

'Yeah. Didn't you always want a coat like that?'

'I still do.'

'I'll buy you one when we get our first pay cheque.'

'Thank you very much, John. Now what exactly were we talking about? I think I've lost the plot here.'

'You were just telling me that we should build a vaulting horse and carry it out into the library garden every morning so that while I exercise on it you can be underneath with a spoon tunnelling to the bench.'

Jim nodded enthusiastically. 'I have to say', he said, 'that when you put it that way, it comes across as a really stupid idea.'

'Doesn't it though.'

'So,' said Jim, 'that leaves us with Marchant.'

'Marchant?'

'Once he's restored to his former greatness, we'll hitch him to the bench with a length of chain and—'

John was shaking his head.

'You're shaking your head,' said Jim.

'I am,' said John.

'All right then, I give up. I've offered you three perfectly sound suggestions and you've pooh-poohed every one. It's your turn.'

John offered up another sigh. 'There has to be some simple way to shift it,' he said. 'Let's go and discuss it somewhere else. The sound of all these road drills in A minor starting up again is giving me a headache.'

And John looked at Jim.

And Jim looked at John.

And then they both smiled.

And Early the Very Next Morning

'And what do you think you're doing there, my good man?' asked the official-looking gent with the bowler hat, the big black moustache and the clip-board.

'Me, guv?' asked the bloke down the hole.

'Yes you, guv.'

'Cable TV,' said the bloke. 'We're laying the cable.'

'Does anyone in Brentford actually want cable TV?'

'I shouldn't think so. It's all crap, isn't it? Presented by a lot of has-beens, like that *Blue Peter* bloke who had that spot of bother with the—'

'I believe I read of it in the *Sunday Sport*. But if no one actually wants cable TV, what's the point of all this digging?'

The bloke down the hole grinned. 'Now you're asking,' he said, 'and I'll tell you. You see, I drill the hole and then my mate here takes this big saw and cuts off the important roots of the roadside trees.'

'But won't that kill them?'

'It certainly will. Within two years from now there won't be a single tree left in any town or city in the country.'

'But surely that's a *very bad thing*?'

'Depends whose side you're on, I suppose. It will be a bad thing for us, but not for the alien strike force drifting secretly in orbit around the planet.'

'*What?*'

'Well, this is only my personal theory, and I may be well off the mark, but I believe that the cable television network is run by space aliens bent upon world domination. And they're seeing that all the trees get cut down so the atmosphere on Earth changes to one more suitable for themselves.'

'Great Scott!' said the official-looking gent.

'Nah, only kidding,' said the bloke down the hole. 'The truth is that we only do it because we're stupid. Blokes who dig holes in the road are all working class and all the working class are stupid.'

'Surely that is a somewhat classist remark.'

'What does "classist" mean?'

'You really wouldn't want to know.'

'But who are you, guv? You look a bit of a toff. Should I call you "your honour" rather than "guv"?'

' "Guv" will be sufficient. I am from the Department of Roads.' The official-looking gent flashed an official-looking ID.

'Gawd luv a duck,' said the bloke. 'That has me fair impressed.'

'And so it should. Now I want you to stop digging there at once and start digging over there instead. I will supervise.'

'Whatever you say, guv. Where exactly do you want us to dig?'

'Right there.' The official-looking gent pointed to the bench outside the Memorial Library.

Now, the other chap who did a lot of pointing hadn't been heard of for a while. But he had been busy and he was up to absolutely no good whatsoever. Dr Steven Malone wasn't lecturing this morning, nor was he putting in any time at the Cottage Hospital. He was working alone in his underground laboratory at Kether House.

You might well suppose that as a chap who looked the dead Kennedy of Paget's Holmes, in black and white, Dr Steven would have had one of those Victorian Mad Scientist's laboratories. You know the kinds of jobbies, all bubbling retorts and brass Bunsen burners, with squiddly-diddly glass pipes and red rubber tubing. There would be a lot of early electrical gubbinry also, sparking coils and polished spheres and a heavy emphasis on the switchboards with the big 'we belong dead' power handles.

But not a bit of it.

Because, let's face it, nobody would have a laboratory like that nowadays. In fact nobody really had a laboratory like that in those days. Laboratories like that were invented by Hollywood. And although we are all eternally grateful for the way Hollywood has rewritten history for us, this is *not* Hollywood.

This, thank God, is Brentford.

And we do things differently here.

Dr Steven Malone's laboratory was a living hell. Anyone who has seen photographs of Ed Gein's kitchen, or Jeffrey Dahmer's bathroom, will be able to form an immediate impression. Somebody once said that 'psychos never comb their hair'; well, neither do they wash their dishes. And Dr Steven Malone was a psychopath, make no mistake about that. Although he did comb his hair, and wash his dishes.

For the record, it is possible to trace the precise moment when the genetic engineer stepped out of sanity and entered loony-doom. The day five years before when he changed his name from Stephen to Steven.

It came about in this fashion. Dr Steven had been introduced to a certain writer of Far-fetched Fiction at a party in Dublin. This writer showed Dr Steven his pocket watch. The numbers on the face had been erased and replaced by the letters of the writer's name. Twelve letters, six for the Christian name and six for the surname. Dr Steven viewed this preposterous vanity and, unlike others who have viewed it and responded with certain gestures below waist level, Dr Steven was intrigued and he knew that he must own one. The effect upon him was profound, because he realized that the name Stephen Malone has thirteen letters. And thirteen is an unlucky number.

And the man who would change the world would not have thirteen letters in his name.

There was some kind of Cosmic Truth in this, albeit one of a terrible madness. The body of the writer was pulled from the river the following day. His pocket watch was never seen again.

Except by Dr Steven Malone.

So back to his laboratory.

It smelt bad down here. Bad, as in fetid. Bad, as in the stench of death. There were Dexion racks down here, poorly constructed. Glass jars stood upon these racks, glass jars containing specimens. Human specimens. Pickled parts, suspended in formaldehyde. Here a tragic severed hand, its fingertips against the glass, and here some sectioned organ, delicate as coral, wafer thin as gossamer. And all around stared human eyes, unseeing yet reproachful from within those tall glass jars.

On the floor was litter. Crumpled cartons, empty bottles, discarded cigarette packs (for most psychos smoke), and magazines and books and newspapers and unopened letters and flotsam and jetsam and filthy rags and tatters. And there were bloodstains on the walls and on the ceiling and on the litter. And on the hands of Dr Steven Malone.

And on further Dexion racks, where stood six zinc water tanks. Each filled with a sterile solution and each containing a naked human torso. The arms, legs and head had been neatly and surgically removed from each, the wounds tightly stitched, plasma drips inserted. Electric implants caused the hearts to beat. And within each swollen female belly something moved.

Something living.

Something newly cloned.

Dr Steven walked from tank to tank, examining his evil handiwork. And smiled upon it all.

What a bastard!

'This could be a bit of a bastard,' said the bloke from the hole as he viewed the concrete base of the library bench. 'Now what we usually do when faced with a situation like this is go off to breakfast for a couple of hours.'

'In keeping with your working class stereotype?'

'I wouldn't be at all surprised. So we'll see you later, eh?'

'I think not,' said the official-looking gent. 'Let us

cast convention to the four winds this day. Let us tear off the woollen overcoat of conformity, lift the grey tweed skirt of oppression and feast our eyes upon the golden G-string of egalitarianism. Take up your pneumatic drill and dig.'

'Gawd stripe me pink, guvnor. If that weren't a pretty speech and no mistake.'

'Just dig the damn' hole.'

'What's going on?' asked a casual passer-by, whose name was Pooley.

'We're digging a hole,' said the bloke who had been digging, but now was mopping his brow. 'It's for cable TV. This official-looking gent says we're to dig it here.'

'Mind if I just stand and watch?'

'Don't you have any work to go to?'

'Well,' said Jim. 'I used to be an unemployed, but now I'm a job seeker.'

'Oh, you mean a layabout.'

'No, I don't.'

'Well, stand back and don't get in the way. This pneumatic drill is a fearsome beast. Mind you, it's a joy to use. It drills in the key of E.'

'Surely it's A minor,' said the official-looking gent.

'No, E,' said the bloke. 'Like in the blues. The blues are always in E.'

'The blues are always in A minor,' said the official-looking gent. 'I used to have a harmonica.'

'It was a Hohner,' said Jim.

'How do you know that?' asked the bloke.

'Just a lucky guess.'

'Well, the blues are always in E, take it from me.' The bloke returned to his drilling.

A lady in a straw hat peered into the hole and nodded her head to the rhythm of the drill. 'That's C, that is,' she shouted above the racket.

'E,' shouted the bloke, without letting up.

'A minor,' shouted the official-looking gent.

'A minor,' Jim agreed.

'C!' shouted the lady. 'My husband used to play with Jelly Roll Morton, and he invented the blues.'

The bloke switched off his pneumatic drill. 'Jelly Roll Morton did not invent the blues,' he said. 'Blind Lemon Jefferson invented the blues.'

'He never did,' said the lady.

'Nobody did,' said the official-looking gent. 'The blues go back hundreds of years to the time of slave-trading.'

'No they don't,' said a young fellow with a beard who'd stopped to take a look at the hole. 'The blues are a form of folk music which originated amongst Black Americans at the beginning of the twentieth century.'

'With Jelly Roll Morton,' said the lady.

'Blind Lemon Jefferson,' said the bloke.

'There is no specific musician accredited with beginning the blues,' said the bearded fellow. 'But the form *is* specific, usually employing a basic twelve-bar chorus, the tonic, subdominant and dominant chords, frequent minor intervals and *blue notes*.'

'What are *blue notes*?' Jim asked.

'A flattened third or seventh.'

'But always in A minor.'

'In any key you like.'

'Are you a job seeker too?' asked the bloke in the hole.

'No, I'm a medical student,' said the bearded fellow.

'Another layabout.'

'Would you mind if we just got back to the drilling?' asked the official-looking gent, consulting a wrist that did not have a watch on it. 'The day is drawing on.'

'Yeah, dig your hole,' said Jim.

'Listen, mate,' said the bloke. 'Just because I dig holes for a living doesn't mean I'm stupid.'

'I thought you said it did,' said the official-looker.

'I was being ironic. All right?'

'Socrates invented irony,' said the lady in the straw hat.

'Bollocks,' said the bloke.

'No, she's right,' said the beardie. 'As a means of exposing inconsistencies in a person's opinions by close questioning and the admission of one's own ignorance. It's called Socratic irony.'

'How would you like a pneumatic drill up your fudge tunnel, sunshine?' asked the bloke.

'Come now, gentlemen,' said the official-looking one. 'We all have our work to do.'

'He doesn't,' said the bloke, pointing at Pooley. 'Blokes like him are just a drain on the country's resources.'

'I resent that,' said Jim, who did.

'Punch his lights out,' said the lady in the straw hat.

'Do me a favour,' said the bloke. 'Look at the state of him. He's got two black eyes already. Wanker!'

'Come on now,' said he of the official looks. 'There's work to do.'

'You keep out of this,' shouted the bloke. 'Bloody jumped-up little Hitler.'

'I resent that.'

'Oh yeah, do you want to make something of it?'

'Excuse me,' said the bloke's mate, who had been quietly digging away with a spade throughout all this. 'But I think I've found something here. It looks like a treasure chest.'

'Let me take a look at that,' said he of looks official.

'No chance!' said the bloke. 'If my mate's found something, then we're keeping it.'

'If I've found something, *I'm* keeping it,' said the mate.

'It could be an unexploded bomb,' said Jim, in a voice that sounded unrehearsed.

'Bollocks!' said the bloke and the mate of the bloke.

'It could be,' said the lady in the straw hat. 'They used to drop all these booby traps in the war. Disguised as tins of Spam and packets of cigarettes and electric vibrators and—'

'We'd better cordon off the area,' said the OLG. 'You two chaps out of the hole and away to a safe distance. I will take charge of the bomb.'

'Good idea,' said Jim. 'Come on, everyone, back, back.'

'Did someone say "bomb"?' asked Old Pete, who had been passing by.

'Move along please, sir.'

'Why are you wearing that daft moustache, Omally?'

'What's all this about a false moustache?' asked the bloke in the hole, climbing out of it.

'Just a deluded old gentleman,' said John Omally. 'Come on now, all of you, clear the area.'

'What's your game?' shouted the bloke, taking a swipe at Omally and tearing off his false moustache.

'Oooooh!' said the lady in the straw hat. 'It's the weirdo from the park who makes road drill noises in A minor while his mate here goes to sleep.'

'His mate here?' The bloke turned upon Pooley.

'I've never seen this official-looking gent before in my life,' said Jim, crossing his heart and hoping not to die.

'Who's in charge here?' said someone else, pushing through the nicely growing crowd.

'I am,' said John.

'You bloody aren't,' said the bloke.

'Well, someone better be. What have you done to my bench?'

'*Your* bench?' said John.

'I'm the chief librarian,' said the chief librarian.

'He is,' said Jim.

'Oh, it's you, is it?' said the chief librarian. 'I should have known. You're always dossing about here. I knew you were up to something.'

'Bloody layabout,' said the bloke.

'Right,' said Jim, rolling up his sleeves. 'That does it.'

'Right,' said the bloke, punching Jim on the nose. 'It does.'

'Stop all this,' cried Omally, stepping forward to grab the bloke, but tripping over his mate who was climbing out of the hole.

'Fight!' shouted the lady in the straw hat, stamping on the chief librarian's foot.

'Sandra's crotch!' yelled the chief librarian, hopping about like a good 'un.

And then the crowd gave a bit of a surge and the fists began to fly.

Omally got his hands on the treasure chest, but the mate, who wasn't giving up without a struggle, head-butted him in the stomach, knocking him into the hole. The lady in the straw hat began to belabour all and sundry with her handbag. The young man with the beard, whose name was Paul and who knew not only about the blues and Socratic irony but also Dimac, brought down the bloke who was kicking Pooley with a devastating blow known as the Curl of the Dark Dragon's Tail.

And as if on cue, for always it seems to be, the distinctive sound of a police car siren was to be heard above the thuds and bangs and howls of the growing mêlée.

Omally clawed his way up from the hole. 'The mate's getting away with the chest, Jim,' he shouted. Jim, now in the foetal position, responded with a dismal groan.

The police car swerved to a halt and three police-men leapt from it. One had a face to be reckoned with, another rejoiced in the name of Joe-Bob.

'Let's give those new electric batons a try,' said the one with the face.

And things went mostly downhill after that.

13

'No,' said Professor Slocombe. 'No, no and again no.' He gestured to the muddy casket on his desk. 'Impossible! Ludicrous!'

'I'm sure it's the real deal,' said Jim.

'Oh, I'm quite sure it is. But I have been searching for the scrolls for years – decades – and you . . . you . . .'

'Found them,' said John. 'We're quite proud of ourselves really.'

'Ridiculous! Absurd!' Professor Slocombe shook his head.

'We thought you'd be pleased,' said Jim.

'Oh, I am. I am.' The Professor peered at Pooley. 'Why is your hair sticking straight up in the air like that?'

Jim made a very pained expression. 'I was doubled on the ground and this policeman came up behind me with an electric truncheon and stuck it right up my—'

'Quite!' The Professor waved his hands in the air. 'I don't think we want to go into that.'

'Exactly what I screamed at the policeman. But it didn't stop him.'

The Professor fluttered his fingers. 'Just sit down,' he told Jim.

'I'd rather not, if you don't mind.'

Professor Slocombe sighed and fluttered further.

'Go on,' said John. 'Open the box. You know you want to.'

'Of course I want to.' The Professor sat down at his desk. 'But it's all so . . .'

'Impossible?' said Jim.

'Ludicrous?' said John.

'Those, yes. How *did* you find the scrolls?'

'We've Jim to thank for that.' John patted his companion on the shoulder. 'Jim put himself into a mystical trance and travelled mentally back in time.'

'There's no need to take the piss,' said Professor Slocombe.

'I'm not. That's exactly what Jim did.'

Professor Slocombe shook his head once more. 'You two must have done something good in a former lifetime,' he said.

Two heads shook.

'Quite the opposite,' said Jim.

'Well, you must tell me all about it.'

'There was this monk,' said Jim, 'and he—'

'At some other time.' Professor Slocombe ran his fingers lightly over the casket. 'Have you opened it already?'

'Ah, no,' said Omally. 'You see, we couldn't run and open at the same time.'

'I don't think I quite understand.'

'There was a bit of bother,' said Jim. 'A minor fracas.'

'Hence the policeman with . . .' Professor Slocombe made the appropriate wrist movements.

'Amongst other things. Two yobbos nipped off with the library bench, you see, and the chief librarian ran amok with a pneumatic drill.'

'They had to restrain him in a straitjacket,' said John.

'But not before he'd destroyed the police car,' said Jim.

'Was that before or after he fractured the gas main?' John asked.

'After,' said Jim. 'Remember, you were being beaten up by the hole-bloke's mate when you smelt the gas.'

'So it wasn't the chief librarian who set off the explosion?'

'No, it was the policeman's electric truncheon. We were both running away by then.'

'Most people were running away by then.'

'Well, they would, what with all those blokes abseiling down from the helicopters and everything.'

'And the tear gas,' said John. 'And the horses.'

'That hole-bloke's mate gave you a right seeing to,' said Jim.

'Yes. I loved every minute of it.'

'*What?*' said Professor Slocombe.

'The hole-bloke's mate was an eighteen-year-old college girl on work experience,' Jim explained.

'She was fast, too,' said John. 'She outran the police dogs.'

'But a marksman brought her down with a rubber bullet.'

'I thought it was the fellow on the water cannon.'

'Gentlemen,' said Professor Slocombe. 'Gentlemen.'

'Yes?' said John and Jim.

'Will you both shut up!' He rang his little brass bell.

Presently Gammon arrived with a bottle of champagne and three glasses.

'Fetch a glass for yourself, Gammon,' said the Professor. 'We should all celebrate this together.'

'I'll be fine, sir,' said the retainer, taking a swig from the bottle. 'Oh, do excuse me. I had a bit of trouble getting back from Budgens, what with the army having closed off most of the streets and declaring martial law—'

'And everything,' said Jim.

And Everything

The champagne glasses clinked together, toasts were called and soon the bottle emptied.

Professor Slocombe sat down at his desk and placed his hands upon the casket. 'Before I open this,' he said. 'I am going to ask you to close your eyes for a moment of silent prayer.'

Jim looked at John.

And John looked at Jim.

'Something serious is coming, isn't it?' said Jim.

'Something very serious. Just humour me.'

Sunlight streamed in through the French windows. And outside in the magical garden the birds ceased their singing. As the four men closed their eyes and held their breath, the air within the study seemed to offer up a sigh. And just for a second, or two, or was it ten, or was it a lifetime of seconds and minutes and hours and days, there was absolute peace and tranquillity.

Absolute.

And then the moment passed. Each man exhaled and somehow felt embarrassed and uncomfortable. As if they had lain themselves utterly bare. And had experienced something so special and so moving that it physically hurt.

'Something happened,' said Jim, clutching at his heart. 'Something wonderful happened. What was it?'

Professor Slocombe smiled. 'Gentlemen,' he said. 'Something wonderful is just beginning.' He put his hands to the casket's lid and lifted it. And then the study air filled with the scent of lilacs.

John Omally crossed himself. 'The odour of sanctity,' he whispered.

'Correct, John, the perfume that issues from the incorruptible bodies of the saints.' Professor Slocombe spoke the Latin benediction, reached into the casket and took out something wrapped in a red velvet cloth. And this he laid upon his desk. Gently turning back the covering he exposed the scrolls. Latin-penned, embossed with the papal seal.

'Oh yes,' said Professor Slocombe. 'Oh yes indeed.'

'It *is* them, isn't it?'

The snow-capped scholar looked up at the man with the electric hair-do, the two black eyes and the bloody nose. 'You have been through quite a lot for these, haven't you, Jim?' he said. 'But do you really know just what you've found?'

'The Brentford Scrolls,' said Jim, proudly.

'The Days of God,' said Professor Slocombe. 'Jim, you may very well have altered the entire course of human history through your discovery.'

'Sandra's—'

'No,' said John. 'No, don't say *that*.'

Professor Slocombe spoke. 'When Pope Gregory changed the calendar from the Julian to the Gregorian, he did it for purely practical reasons. There was nothing mystical involved. But, you see, the precise date of Christ's birth had never been known for certain. The coming millennium, the year 2000, is only an approximation. The Pope wasn't aware that when he signed the papal bull authorizing the Days of God, he would be creating the wherewithal for someone in a future time to ensure that the millennium was celebrated on the correct day of the correct year.

'But does that really matter?' Jim asked.

'Oh, absolutely, Jim. If you had studied the science of magic for as long as I have, and practised it with, dare I say, some moderate degree of success, you would understand that precision is everything. For a working to be successful, each magical building block must be precisely aligned. If one is missing or out of place, the entire metaphysical edifice collapses. But if all are precisely fitted together, the seemingly impossible becomes possible. "Natural" laws are transcended, higher truths imparted, wisdoms revealed. If the exact day of the exact year on which the millennium should be celebrated passes by without the appropriate ceremonies, *its* magic will not become manifest.'

'But what magic is this? You're not talking about Armageddon or the end of the world, or dismal stuff like that, are you?'

'On the contrary. If the ceremonies are performed on the correct day of the correct year something marvellous will occur. Something unparalleled. Something that will change the world for ever.'

'Oh,' said Jim. 'And what might that be?'

'What did you feel just now, when you closed your eyes in prayer?'

'I don't know exactly.' Jim shook his head. 'But it was something wonderful.'

'Imagine feeling like that all the time. Imagine a state of heightened awareness and understanding. Of inner peace, of tranquillity, of love, if you like. Yes, love would be the word.'

'And you're saying that if the millennium is celebrated on the correct day of the correct year, everyone will experience that?'

'It is the next step,' said Professor Slocombe. 'The next evolutionary step. The next rung up the ladder. Or, more rightly, a further turning of the wheel. The holy mandala that takes us nearer to godhead by returning us to it. All was born from THE

BIG IDEA, all will ultimately return to it.'

Jim opened his mouth. 'I'm speechless,' he said.

'Just one thing, Professor.' John put up his hand.
'I have been listening carefully to all you have said.
And you said that the precise date of Christ's birth
had never been known for certain.'

'That is precisely what I said, John, yes.'

'Does that mean it is known now?'

'It does.'

'And you know it?'

'I do, yes.'

'Then tell us,' said Jim.

Professor Slocombe smiled that smile of his, and
spoke some more. 'When you came to me the night
before last, asked me about the scrolls and told me of
your plan to have Brentford celebrate the millennium two years before the rest of the world, you will
recall that I laughed. I did not laugh because the
idea was preposterous, I laughed because, whether
through luck (perhaps) or judgement (perhaps not)
or fate, you had it right. Right upon the nose and the
button. The correct date is December the thirty-
first. The correct year, this very one.'

It was teatime, or thereabouts, when John and Jim
left the Professor's house. Martial law had been
lifted and but for the occasional burned-out car or
shattered shop window there was nothing to suggest
that things were not as they always had been in
Brentford.

But they were not.

And John and Jim knew that they were not.

John and Jim knew that something very big was about to happen, something very big indeed. And it scared them not a little, though it thrilled them also.

They spoke few words as they strolled along, hands in pockets, heads down, kicking the shell of a CS gas canister, whistling discordantly. Outside the Flying Swan they stood a while in silence.

And then John took a breath. 'And so,' said he. 'We have heard all that the Professor had to say. We have dwelt upon it. We are mystified, we are bewildered, we are fearful, we are rapt in wonder. But, are we not men?'

'We are Devo,' said Jim.

'We are John and Jim,' said John. 'Occasionally daunted but never done for.'

'I assume all this bravado is leading somewhere.'

'It is leading to this. The Professor may be correct in all that he said. On the other hand, it might turn out to be a load of old blarney. But whatever the case, *we* found the scrolls. And the scrolls *are* authentic. And in celebration of this, I suggest we up our salaries as directors of the Brentford Millennium Committee.'

'I'll drink to that,' said Jim. 'Let's double the blighters.'

'Let's do that very thing.'

And so they did.

'What did St Patrick say when he drove all the snakes out of Ireland?' asked Old Pete.

The patrons at the bar shook their heads. Corner-shopkeeper Norman Hartnell said, 'I don't know.'

'He said, "Are you all all right in the back there?" '

Old Pete awaited the hilarity.

None, however, came.

'Surely,' said Norman, 'that's a somewhat surrealist joke.'

'The elephant's cloakroom ticket,' said Old Pete.

'Two pints of Large please, Neville,' said John Omally. 'Jim's paying.'

'Am I?'

'The least you can do. Considering your inflated salary.'

'And two whisky chasers, Neville,' said Jim.

'What's all this?' asked Old Pete. 'Got yourself a job, Pooley? I thought you were registered at the Job Centre as a snow-shifter's mate.'

'Such days are behind me, Pete. John and I are to be men of substance. There are great times ahead for Brentford, and we are the men you will be thanking for them.'

'I'll drink to that,' said Old Pete. 'Very kind of you.'

Neville did the business. 'So, John,' said he, with a grin upon his face. 'I assume this means you found the Brentford Scrolls.'

The patrons erupted into laughter. Norman Hartnell slapped his knees and croaked and coughed.

'Easy, Norman,' said Old Pete.

Norman straightened up. 'Sorry,' he said. 'But "Are you all all right in the back there?" Brilliant.'

Neville wiped a tear of mirth from his good eye. 'Come on, John,' he said. 'Only joking.'

Omally shrugged. 'No problem at all. But I have not found the Brentford Scrolls.'

'Tough luck,' said Neville.

'Jim has found them.'

Further hilarity. 'Very good,' said Neville. 'Very droll.'

'They're with Professor Slocombe,' said John.

'Well, they would be, wouldn't they?'

'No,' said John. 'They really *are* with Professor Slocombe. Jim *did* find them.'

'Were they lost, then?' asked Norman. 'Only when you said about me getting a directorship on the Brentford Millennium Committee, you led me to understand—'

Omally whispered figures into Norman's ear.

Norman whistled. 'That's a most substantial salary. I will be able to buy that particle accelerator I wanted now.'

'Hold on. Hold on.' Neville put up his hands. 'A joke is a joke, John. But Jim has *not* found the Brentford Scrolls.'

'Have too,' said Jim.

'Has too,' said John.

'As if,' said Neville, sauntering off to polish glasses.

'What do you want a particle accelerator for?' Jim asked Norman.

'To accelerate particles, of course. What did you think?'

Jim shrugged. 'Are you currently in inventor mode, then?'

'I am building a de-entropizer.'

170

'Ah,' said John. 'One of those lads, eh?'

'It's for the sweeties,' said Norman informatively.

'I give up,' said Jim. 'Whatever are you talking about?'

'Well.' Norman sipped ale. 'You know what entropy is, don't you?'

Jim made a thoughtful face and then he unmade it.

'Exactly,' said Norman. 'Well mimed. Entropy is how everything falls apart into chaos rather than order. Eventually culminating in the heat death of the universe when everything that can be burned up will have been burned up and there's nothing left. I am working on a device to de-entropize. Reverse the process. It's for the sweeties, as I said. My shop is full of jars of old sweeties. They're quite inedible but I can't bring myself to part with them. Old folks come in and wistfully look at them and remember the good times.'

Old Pete made a wistful face that was quite out of character. Then, in keeping with the law of entropy, he said, 'Bollocks.'

'My device', Norman continued, 'will de-entropize my sweeties. Reconstitute them. Break them down to their atomic substructure then rebuild from the nucleus up. I hope to have it on-line by the end of the week. Then I shall produce sweeties the way sweeties used to taste, because they will be those very sweeties.'

John Omally grinned. 'Perfect,' he said. 'Ideal for the millennium. Sweeties the way sweeties used to be.'

'Any chance of doing it with beer?' Jim asked.

'I heard that,' said Neville.

'No offence meant,' said Jim.

'Once the process has been perfected, then I suppose I could do it with anything.' Norman sipped further ale. 'Beer, wines, spirits.'

John Omally took out a little notebook and wrote the words *The John Omally Millennial Brewery* at the top of an empty page.

Scoop Molloy, cub reporter for the *Brentford Mercury*, now entered the bar. His head was bandaged and his left arm in a sling. John and Jim turned away. As no mention had been made so far of the riots and mayhem, especially by Old Pete, who now had a nice library bench in his back garden, low profiles were the order of the day.

Scoop limped up to the bar and ordered a half of shandy.

Neville, who abhorred such abominations, and cared not for members of the Press, topped it up from the drip tray. Scoop downed it in one. 'Same again,' he said.

'Been in an accident, Scoop?' asked Old Pete, trying to keep a straight face.

'A spot of bother, yes.'

'You do have an exciting time of it. Nothing ever happens to folk like us.'

'There was a riot,' said Scoop. 'Stone-throwing mobs, baton charges, special forces helicopters.'

'Really?' Old Pete stroked his grizzled chin. 'My pension day. I must have missed it.'

'And I missed it too.'

'Then what happened to you?'

'Bloody mad doctor.' Scoop swallowed further drippings as Neville looked on appreciatively. 'I got word that something weird had happened at the Cottage Hospital the night before last. And I go around to see the duty physician, Dr Steven Malone. And I say, "Hello, my name is Scoop Molloy from the *Brentford Mercury*." And he puts me in an armlock and throws me down his front steps.'

'Occupational hazard,' said Old Pete.

'Yeah, well, I accept that. But I missed the bloody riots and now I don't have a story for tomorrow's paper.'

John Omally turned.

And so did Jim.

'Oh yes you do,' they said.

14

Now we've all heard about the Corridors of Power. But their exact location is not altogether certain. Are they in Westminster, or in Whitehall? Or are they perhaps underground corridors, where the real rulers of our country, those beloved of conspiracy theorists, edge and sidle in a low light? And why Corridors of Power anyway? What goes on in corridors, for pity's sake? Don't these people, whoever they are, who do whatever they do in these corridors, have rooms to do whatever it is in? Chambers of Power, that's what they should have.

But maybe they do. And all this talk of corridors is just to throw us off the scent.

Fascinating, isn't it?

No?

Well check this out.

This corridor was big and broad and high of ceiling. One wall was dressed with enormous canvases, framed in heavy gilt. Biblical scenes most seemed to be. All very Judgement Day.

John Martin's *Fallen Angels Entering Pandemonium*

was there, which was odd, because it should have been in the Tate. And Goya's terrifying *Saturno*, which should have been in the Prado, Madrid. And *La Chute des Anges* by Frans Floris definitely should have been in the Koninklijk Museum, Antwerp. And so on and so forth. Evidently whoever had clothed the walls of this particular corridor with the robes of fine art had ACCESS. And they also had sense enough to keep the curtains drawn on all the windows in the wall opposite. The light was low in this corridor. And it was gentle and the temperature was regulated. This *had* to be a Corridor of Power!

And so it was.

Two figures appeared through a doorway at the end of this corridor. They were a good way off. A very long corridor was this. The two figures marched forward. In step. Determined. They wore identical grey suits and, given the preponderance of art here, it might have come as no surprise to find they were none other than Gilbert and George.

But they were not. They were just two anonymous-looking blighters you wouldn't have thought to look at twice.

They stopped before a mighty door. Straightened clothes that didn't need straightening. Then one or other of them knocked.

KNOCK, KNOCK, KNOCK, went this knocking as had knockings previous. Although these KNOCKS really echoed. K-N-O-C-K they went.

'Come,' called a voice from within.

And those without pushed upon the mighty door and entered.

The room within revealed itself to be nothing less than a Chamber of Power. There could be no mistake. The furniture, the fixtures, the fittings. The Fabergé, the *famille*, the Fantin-Latours. The ferns, the fiddle-backs, the finery. This was one effing Chamber of Power.

And furthermore.

With his feet up on the fender and a flat cap on his head sat a fleabag of a fellow by the name of Fred.

Fred was filing his filthy fingernails with a piece of flattened flint.

'Friends,' said Fred.

'Fred,' said the friends, fondling their forelocks.

'Forget the forelock-fondling,' said Fred. 'Fetch over that form and fill me in the facts.'

One of the anonymous duo fetched over the form and both of them sat down upon it (which must have meant that it was a bench, rather than a piece of paper).

'There's been a flipping foul-up,' said the form-fetcher.

'Foul-up?' said Fred.

'Foul-up,' said the fellow who hadn't fetched the form.

'Foul-up?' said Fred.

'Foul-up,' said the first fellow. 'Not to put too fine a point on it.'

'Hm,' said Fred. 'What are you feckless furtlers on about?'

The form-fetcher unfolded a newspaper and displayed its front page.

and it's official

'Fuck me!' said Fred, and fell off the fender.

The duo hastened to his aid.

'Get off me. Just give me that frigging newspaper.'
Fred snatched away the copy of the *Brentford Mercury*
and began to pace up and down, reading as he
paced. Words all beginning with the letter F spilled
from his mouth but, what with the law of diminish-
ing returns and everything, they will remain
unrecorded.

'No!' cried Fred. 'No! No! No!'

'I'm afraid it's yes,' said one or other of his
visitors.

'If I say it's no, then I bloody well mean it.' Fred
tore the newspaper to shreds and flung the pieces all
about. 'We've worked too long and hard on this,'
Fred shouted. 'How could it happen? Tell me how?'

'One of Compton-Cummings's books escaped
the pulping. It fell into the hands of this Pooley chap
and somehow he and another chap called Omally
located the Brentford Scrolls.'

'I wasn't speaking to *you*.'

'Sorry, Fred.'

'Don't you Fred me, you bastard. I want this
sorted and I want it sorted now. Don't you realize
the gravity of this?'

'Well, I do, sir, yes. But it might be helpful if you
were just to run through it all one more time.'

'To clear up any confusion that might exist,
sir.'

'Which one of you said that?'

'I did, sir.'

'Are you sure it wasn't him?'

'No, but I was thinking it, sir.'

'Right,' said Fred. 'One more time and try to pay attention. First question. Where are we now, at this precise moment?'

'In the Chamber of Ultimate Power, sir.'

'Correct, not just any old Chamber of Power, you will notice. But the Chamber of *Ultimate* Power. And who am I?'

'You are our worst nightmare, sir.'

'Correct again. And why am I this?'

'Because you are a jumped-up, talentless uncharismatic little nobody who, driven by ruthless ambition, has managed to claw his way to the top of the tree and now occupies the position of absolute control, literally holding our very lives in the palm of his grubby unwashed hand, sir.'

'Correct once again. And how did I achieve this?'

'Popular opinion would sway towards the belief that you sold your soul to Satan, sir.'

'And popular opinion would, upon this rare occasion, be right on target there, wouldn't it?'

'It certainly would, sir, yes.'

'And so, bearing all this in mind, what exactly do you think I would be up to now?'

'You would be furthering the hideously evil schemes of your unspeakable master, sir.'

'Which are?'

'Too numerous to mention, sir.'

'Yes, well, I do try to keep myself busy. But within

178

the parameters of the present discussion, would you care to clarify my position?'

'You represent, indeed embody, the nexus of power behind the millennial celebrations. It is your job to see that these do *not* take place on the correct day of the correct year, as he of the cloven hoof would be dead miffed to have peace and love breaking out all over the world.'

'Wouldn't he just! Go on.'

'And so you, and others before you, have striven to see that the Brentford Scrolls are not recovered and the Days of God are not used to ensure that—'

'Yes, well, that's pretty much all of it. But somebody has fouled up, haven't they?'

'I think we're all agreed on that,' said the form-fetcher, or it might have been the other one, it doesn't really matter.

'So,' said Fred. 'What are you going to do about it?'

'He means you,' said the form-fetcher.

'He doesn't,' said the other one. 'It's you he means.'

'Oh well. If it's me,' said the form-fetcher, 'I think I'll just panic and run around like a headless chicken, if that's all right by you.'

'It's fine by me,' said Fred. 'So what are *you* going to do about it?'

'Me?'

'You.'

'Could I just run about like that too?'

Fred shook his head.

179

'Then I suppose that I must put certain wheels into motion.'

'I like the sound of that. Would you care to be a little more specific?'

'Not really.'

'Then I shall tell you both exactly what you are going to do.' Fred took up a fire-iron from the fender and struck the chap who was running around like a headless chicken a blistering blow to the skull. 'Firstly I want Brentford sealed off from the outside world. I do not want the media getting in and I do not want the scrolls to get out. What I do want is a professional team in position, to buy off whoever can be bought off and dispose of anyone who can't. Who has the scrolls now?'

'Professor Slocombe, sir.'

Fred drew a finger across his throat. 'He gets *this*,' he said. 'As for the rest of them, use your discretion.'

'I don't have any discretion,' said the fellow with the dented head. 'In fact, I'm a God-damn crazy ape-shit one-man killing machine when I get going.'

'Fine. I'll put you in charge of the disposing side of it, then.'

'Thanks a lot, sir.'

'Call me Fred.'

'Cheers, Fred.'

'But listen now and hear me well. I want this thing done quickly. Quickly and quietly and efficiently.' Fred stood with his back to the fireplace and rose upon his down-at-heels. And Fred began to tremble. A terrified look appeared on his face and it stayed. A tortured look it was, as of one tormented from within. Muscles twitched and spasmed. Eyes bulged from their sockets. Sweat broke from the pores. 'I want those scrolls,' cried Fred in a voice no longer his. 'I want them here to rip them and to burn.' The voice was a growl, an atavistic growl, a real bowel-loosening bed-wetter of an atavistic growl. And the lips of Fred turned blue and the tongue of him grew black. And that tongue darted from the mouth and curled all around and about. 'Bring the scrolls to me, and bring me more. Bring me the heads of Pooley and Omally.'

The anonymous two were prostrate now, their faces pressed against the cold marble floor. And the floor trembled and shook to the sound of that hideous voice.

That terrible voice.

That eldritch voice.

That voice of the Evil One himself.

'This world is mine!' The voice boomed and echoed. 'Mine for another thousand years and I will not be denied it. Nothing and no one will stand in my way. Nothing and no one, do you understand?'

'Oh, we do. We do.' And cowering and trembling, the minions of Fred crawled to the mighty door, clawed it open, pushed on through, flung it shut and ran.

Ran and ran along that Corridor of Power. And the voice came after them, rushing like a great and fiery wind. Ripping at the curtains and tearing at the gilt-framed canvases.

And the two men ran before it.

Ran and ran.

'Nothing and no one.' Howl and shriek and scream.

And howl and shriek and scream.

In another chamber of some power, in Brentford, something small and pink and soft and shiny howled and shrieked and screamed.

And Dr Steven Malone wrapped it in a towel and held it to his chest. 'Just two alive,' said he, 'but two will do nicely for my purposes. And nothing and no one will stand in my way.' And Dr Steven laughed aloud.

And howl and shriek and scream.

15

Howl and shriek and scream.

'Will you please turn off that appalling racket?' asked Professor Slocombe.

Brentford's mayor, the worshipful Puerto Rican Don Juan Lopez Carlos de Casteneda, switched off his ghetto-blaster. 'That is *not* a racket,' he said. 'That is my favourite band, the Hollow Chocolate Bunnies of Death.'

'And highly derivative they are too,' said the Professor. 'I detect the influence of both Slayer and Deicide.'

'Huh,' said the mayor, chewing on a small cheroot.

They sat at the big table in the council chamber of Brentford Town Hall. Curtains of sunlight wavered from upper windows. Rich oak panelling shone with a mellow patina, smoke hung in the air.

John and Jim were there, with several members of the council, hastily gathered, the secretary of the late Mr Compton-Cummings (who knows why?) and Scoop Molloy with his notebook.

'This is all so much shite,' said the mayor, cuffing

his copy of the *Brentford Mercury*. 'I am woken from the arms of my lover by a march-past. Peons in the streets are hanging balloons from the lamp posts. Someone has passed word around that I have declared today a public holiday.'

John Omally, up since dawn and busy with it, rolled himself a cigarette.

'Yesterday riots and today we have dancing in the streets.' The mayor threw up his hands and made excitable gesturings. 'It is all too much.'

'My dear Don Juan,' said Professor Slocombe, 'I will agree that events have proceeded with some alacrity. More alacrity, in fact, than I might have wished for.' He waggled the fingers of his gloved hand beneath the table and John Omally's roll-up fell to pieces. 'But we are gathered here to discuss what may be done and how it may be done.'

'Such as this?' The mayor snatched up a piece of foolscap and took to the cuffing of it. 'Proposal to construct the Hanging Gardens of Brentford on the site of the allotments, to be called the John Omally Millennial Tower.'

Professor Slocombe curled his lip. John grinned painfully.

'Beauty Pageants and Beer Festivals, a rock concert in the football ground, who the hell are Devo anyway?'

'Please remain calm.' Professor Slocombe raised a calming hand.

'And I tell you this.' The mayor screwed up the foolscap and flung it aside. 'These scrolls that make all this possible. That make these two gringos here',

184

he shook a fist at John and Jim, 'think that they can run all this. These scrolls were dug up on council property. I should take these scrolls.'

'The scrolls were located by Mr Pooley. Under the Finders Keepers law—'

'And what is that?'

'It's a tradition, or an old charter, or something. But under it, the scrolls belong to Mr Pooley.'

'He didn't find them. A young woman dug them up.'

'Under his instruction.'

'On council property. And who will pay for a new library bench?'

'That will be included in the budget for the new library,' said John. 'The John Omally Mil—'

'Shut your mouth, home boy!'

'Make a note of that, Jim,' said John. 'Dock the mayor a week's pay.'

'*What?*'

'Gentlemen,' said the Professor. 'Nothing is ever achieved through acrimony. We must act as one or we will not succeed.'

'I'll dock him two weeks,' said Jim. 'Just to be on the safe side.'

'You think to make fun of me, huh?' The mayor smote his chest. 'You think I am some stinking wet-back?'

'Surely that's a somewhat racist remark,' said Scoop Molloy, writing it down.

'Your mother!' said the mayor, thumbing his teeth.

'Gentlemen, please.'

'I tell you this,' said the mayor, all pointing fingers now. 'No one will swallow this shite. Who will swallow it, huh? The real Millennium Committee? The Prime Minister? The Queen? The world? Who?'

'I will swallow it.'

Faces turned towards the new speaker.

'And who the hell are you?' asked the mayor.

'Celia Penn. I was secretary to the late Mr Compton-Cummings.'

'And you will swallow, will you?'

'I will swallow with pleasure.'

Here we go again, thought Jim. Carry on up the Council Chamber.

'Call out the mariachi bands,' said the mayor. 'The day is saved.'

'If you will just let me speak.'

'Speak on, lady. Be my guest.'

'Thank you. I represent certain interested parties who are determined that the millennial celebrations go ahead on the correct day of the correct year. The Professor knows what I am talking about.'

'I do, but how—'

'SUCK,' said Celia Penn.

'Oh dear,' went Jim Pooley.

'SUCK,' said Professor Slocombe. 'The Secret Unification for the Coming King, an occult organization dating back to before the Knights Templar. Keepers of the Great Mystery.'

'Protectors of the Brentford Scrolls,' said Celia Penn. 'It was I who encoded the location of the scrolls into Mr Compton-Cummings's book. And I

186

who sent the last remaining copy to Mr Pooley. I knew I had the right man.'

'Eh?' went Jim. 'But I never—'

'Aha!' went the mayor. 'Oh yeah, I get this. Another one looking for a handout. What do you want, lady? A new car, is it? Well you can SUCK my—'

Click went the Professor's fingers. *Lock* went the jaw of the mayor.

And KNOCK KNOCK KNOCK came a knocking at the council chamber door. And duck for cover went John and Jim.

'Come out,' called the Professor. 'It's only the tea trolley.'

The door opened and in came the woman with the tea trolley. She was wearing a straw hat and she trundled over to the mayor. 'Coffee, your holiness?' she asked.

'Grmmph mmph,' went the mayor, clutching his jaw.

'Only what you see on the trolley, I'm afraid.'

'Excuse me,' said a councillor with a mean and hungry look. 'But as the mayor seems to be experiencing some difficulty in speaking, perhaps I might take the chair.'

'Certainly,' said Professor Slocombe.

The councillor got to his feet, took the chair and left the chamber.

'The old ones are always the best,' said Jim. 'Although this hardly seems the time.'

'Excuse me,' said a councillor who was old and rough and dirty and tough. 'But as the mayor is incapacitated and Councillor Cassius has gone off with the chair, perhaps I might put in my threepenny-worth.'

'Certainly,' said the Professor.

And the councillor placed three pennies on the table.

'Where do you think this is leading?' Jim asked.

'Excuse me,' said a third councillor, this one cool as a mountain stream, yet as corny as Kansas in August. 'But as the mayor is incapacitated, Councillor Cassius has gone off with the chair and Councillor Starguard of the Galactic Brotherhood has put in his threepenny-worth, perhaps I might just ask a question.'

'Go ahead,' said Professor Slocombe.

'Why does a brown cow give white milk when it only eats green grass?'

'Is it just me?' asked Jim. 'Or have things taken a distinct turn for the weird?'

'Would you like an octopus in your tea?' the lady in the straw hat asked Omally. 'I've a camel outside that will go four days if you brick it.'

'Cover your faces,' cried Professor Slocombe.

'Don't you start,' cried Jim.

'Cover your faces quickly and make a run for the door.'

'My husband once made a run for the chickens,' said the lady in the straw hat. 'But then he was a Jesuit.'

'Talking of eggs,' said Celia Penn. 'There was this sausage and this egg in a frying pan. And the sausage said "My, it's hot in here" and the egg said "Eeeek!

A talking sausage." ' Celia Penn began to laugh and the lady in the straw hat began to laugh and Scoop Molloy began to laugh and Councillor Starguard began to laugh. And then they all began to cry and to shout and to hit one another.

'Mmph grmmph,' went the mayor.

'Out,' cried the Professor. 'John, Jim, out, quickly.'

'What is going on?' asked John. 'And who brought that horse in here?'

'Jim, help Ms Penn and hurry.' Professor Slocombe tugged at Pooley.

'I love you, Suzy,' said Jim. 'Let me show you the trick with the ice cubes.'

'Hurry, Jim.' Professor Slocombe tugged again at Pooley and Pooley tugged at Celia Penn.

'Fly with me to my plantation,' he crooned. 'There may be snow on the roof but there's a beaver in the basement.'

'Hurry, Jim. Come on, John.'

'Everybody conga,' said Omally, kicking up his legs.

And pushing and shoving in a bumbling line, Jim followed John, Ms Penn followed Jim and the Professor followed all of them and thrust them through the door.

Along a corridor which had no power at all, and out into the car park.

'Sit down, stay still and take deep breaths.' Professor Slocombe forced them to the tarmac, where they sat giggling foolishly.

Binding, the scrofulous attendant, issued from his

189

sentry box. 'They can't sit there,' he complained. 'They don't have official permits.'

'Bring water quickly,' commanded the Professor.

'I can't go giving out water to any old Tom, Dick and Hari Krishna, it's more than my job's worth.'

Professor Slocombe fixed the car park attendant with a certain stare.

'I'll bring three cups,' said Binding, hurrying off at the double. 'And a glass for your good self.'

Jim Pooley was struggling to his feet. 'I will fight for the woman I love,' he shouted. 'Bring on your best guitarist.'

Professor Slocombe looked both ways, then felled Jim with a nifty uppercut. 'I'm sorry about that,' he said. 'But you'll thank me for it later.'

'Thank you,' said Jim, somewhat later. 'But what exactly happened?'

'Someone drugged us, didn't they?' Omally held his head.

Professor Slocombe nodded his. 'I had Binding drive us here in the mayor's low-rider. A charming fellow, Binding, when you get to know him.'

Pooley sat once more in the Professor's fireside chair. Celia Penn lay unconscious upon the chaise longue. 'Is she going to be all right?' Jim asked.

'She'll be better sleeping it off.' Professor Slocombe placed a hand upon the young woman's forehead. 'She's running a bit of a temperature. I'll have Gammon fetch an ice-pack.' He returned to his desk and rang his little bell.

'Who did this to us?' Jim rubbed his face. 'And

who punched me? My chin's bruised too now.'

Professor Slocombe decanted sherry and passed a glass to Jim. 'I wondered how it was that I remained unaffected. I suspect it must have been due to these.' He pointed to his leather gloves upon the desk. 'I always wear them, as you know. The skin of my hands is sensitive to sunlight.'

'So we touched something?' Jim sniffed at his fingertips.

'I have scrubbed your hands. But that I think must have been it. I placed my gloves beneath the microscope and lo and behold.'

'Lo and behold what exactly?'

'A rather lethal cocktail of mescaline, peyote and amphetamines.'

'What about the councillors? The lady in the straw hat and everyone?'

'I called an ambulance, and they've been dealt with. No fatalities.'

'But how?'

'How was it done? Remarkably simple. The drug was mixed with furniture polish in an aerosol can and sprayed onto the council table.'

John Omally shook his aching head. 'But why?' he asked.

'I would have thought that was obvious. To sabotage Brentford's plans to hold the millennial celebrations two years early.'

'But who?' asked Jim.

'Whoever was responsible for the pulping of Mr Compton-Cummings's book. Ms Penn will tell us more, I trust, when she awakens.'

'But how?' asked Jim.

'We did "But how?", Jim.'

'No, I mean how did they act so fast? To prepare this drug and spray it on the table just before we got there. They don't mess around, this lot, do they?'

'Binding informed me that an unmarked van entered the car park an hour before we arrived. Two "cleaners" in grey suits. He couldn't describe them, said they looked totally anonymous.'

'But fish?' asked Jim.

'Pardon me?' said the Professor.

'Nothing,' said Jim. 'I don't think the drug's quite worn off yet.'

'Hang about,' said John. 'The lady in the straw hat never touched the council table.'

'The lady in the straw hat is barking mad anyway,' said Jim.

'Oh, right. But if I can ask one more question, Professor. How did these would-be assassins know that we'd all be at the council meeting this morning?'

'I doubt that they did. They were just being thorough. There would have to have been a council meeting to discuss matters sooner or later. They were simply putting themselves ahead of the game, as it were.'

'Well, they're messing with the wrong lads here,' said Omally, flexing his shoulders. 'This is Brentford and we have right on our side. Let them try it again and see what happens.'

Gammon knocked and entered with an ice-pack

on a tray. 'I'm sorry to trouble you, sir,' said he. 'But I think you'd better take a look outside. The military gentlemen of yesterday have returned and this time they are erecting what seem to be barricades and border posts.'

16

'People of Brentford,' came the voice through the electric loudhailer. It was a military voice. Educated. Authoritative. 'People of Brentford, return to your homes, go about your businesses.'

'Boo!' went the people of Brentford. 'Boo and hiss!'

'These barricades and crossing points have been erected for your own welfare, to protect you from an influx of undesirables.'

Beyond the barricades, undesirables in the shape of news crews buffed up their lenses and went 'one two' into their microphones.

In Professor Slocombe's study the ancient scholar bolted his French windows. 'They will certainly come for the scrolls,' he said. 'You must take them to a place of safety.'

'He means you, John,' said Jim.

'I mean both of you,' said Professor Slocombe.

Jim's hands began to tremble as they always did prior to a flap.

'Easy, Jim,' said John. 'Where shall we take them, Professor?'

'To Buckingham Palace, perhaps. Or Ten Downing Street.'

'There's a priest hole at the Flying Swan,' said Jim. 'We could take them there.'

'Perhaps the British Museum,' said Professor Slocombe, 'or the Bank of England.'

'I rather like the sound of the priest hole,' said John.

'Or perhaps they should be taken directly to Rome and delivered to my friend the Pope.'

'The priest hole has it then,' said Jim.

'My good friends,' said the Professor, 'without the scrolls we have nothing. They must be authenticated by a panel of experts. And a panel that has not been compromised. I must confess that sending you both on a pilgrimage to Rome does have a certain charm. The possibilities for picaresque adventures are endless. But I doubt whether either one of you even possesses a passport.'

'I had one once,' said Jim. 'But I lost it on my travels.'

'You've never been on any travels.' John Omally laughed. 'You get airsick travelling on the top deck of a bus.'

'I never do.'

'You do. And you get a nosebleed.'

'It's the altitude. And I have travelled. I've been to Margate.'

'Gentlemen, please. Take the scrolls to a place of your own choosing. I hate to say protect them with your lives—'

'Then don't,' said Jim.

'But we will,' said John. 'But what of you, Professor, and Ms Penn? They will come here looking for the scrolls, and will not treat you kindly.'

'I am well aware of that. I will make my own arrangements and contact you at the earliest opportunity.'

'Hold on,' said Jim.

'What is it, Jim?'

KNOCK KNOCK KNOCK, came a knocking at Professor Slocombe's front door.

'It's *that*,' said Jim. 'I'm beginning to develop a sixth sense when it comes to *that*.'

'Out of the kitchen door then and away.'

'You're sure you'll be all right?' asked John.

Professor Slocombe made a mystic pass and vanished in a puff of smoke.

'I think he'll be just fine,' said Jim.

They arrived at the Flying Swan just in time to see Old Pete being stretchered into a waiting ambulance.

John hurried over to the fogey. 'What happened to you?' he asked.

Pete looked up with a dazed expression on his face. 'What would you reckon the chances were of there being a one-legged lesbian shot-putter in the pub when I happen to be telling a joke?' he asked.

'Two pints of Large please, Neville,' said Jim, rooting in his pockets for the last of his small change. 'And would you mind sticking this casket in your priest hole?'

'Not at all,' said Neville. 'That would be the now legendary Brentford Scrolls we've been hearing so much about, I suppose.'

'It certainly would,' said Jim.

'Get out of my pub,' said Neville. 'You're barred.'

'What?'

'See who that is over there?' Neville pointed.

'A one-legged lesbian shot-putter?'

'No, next to her.'

'Oh my God.' Jim fell back in alarm. 'It's Young Master Robert.'

'Correct, damnable issue of the Master Brewer's loins. Blight of my life. Bane of my existence. Would-be despoiler of my—'

'So what's he doing here?'

'What does he always do here?'

'He tries to renovate the pub,' said Jim in a doomed tone. 'Turn it into a theme bar or something equally hideous.'

'Exactly, and thanks to you he's back on the case.'

'So what is it this time? No, let me guess, the Millennial Eatery, snacks in a space-age styrofoam bucket.'

'Nothing so tasteful. Here, peruse this before you take your leave.' Neville pushed a scribbled plan across the bar counter.

'Afternoon, Neville,' said Omally, breezing up. 'Jim getting them in, is he?'

'Jim is just leaving,' said Neville. 'And you with him.'

'What?'

'Peruse.' Neville pointed to the plan and John perused.

'By all the holy saints,' said John. 'Where is he?'

'Over there,' and Neville pointed once again. 'Next to the one-legged—'

'We can't have this.' Omally plucked up the plan and stalked across the bar. 'Good afternoon, my friend,' he said, extending a hand for a shaking.

Young Master Robert looked up from his light and lime. 'Oh, it's you, is it?' he said. 'I remember you.'

'And I you.' Omally thrust his unshaken hand into his trouser pocket. With the other he waved the scribbled plan about. 'I see you've been busy again. Brilliant stuff. I take my hat off to you.'

'You don't wear a hat and even if you did I wouldn't want you to take it off.'

'Is this bloke bothering you, Bobby?' asked the Young Master's burly monopedal companion.

'No, Sandra. The gentleman is just leaving.'

'Sandra?' said Omally. 'Sandra, it's you.'

'Omally, it's you!' Sandra hopped to her foot and gave Omally a bone-crunching hug. 'After all these years and you haven't changed a bit. Apart from looking so much older.'

'Nor you,' said John, 'apart from—'

'The leg?' grinned Sandra. 'I got fed up with it. So I had it amputated. Did it myself with a chainsaw.'

'It suits you,' said John.

'Thanks. It's a great bird-puller. You should have one of yours done.'

'I'll give that some thought.'

Young Master Robert made agitated finger flutterings. 'I hate to break up this happy reunion, but will you please bugger off, Omally.'

'But I want to talk to you about your plan for the Swan's renovation. The Road to Calvary, England's first religious theme pub. Well, I say first, but there's the one along the road of course, and two in Ealing, and—'

'Forget it,' said Young Master Robert. 'The Road to Calvary it will be.'

'We'll speak more on this. Farewell, Sandra, splendid to see you again.'

'And you, John, and if you ever fancy having any body parts removed, you know where to come.'

'I certainly do.' And John Omally returned to the bar.

'Well?' said Neville.

'Sorted,' said John.

'What?'

'Well, almost sorted. Give me time. You can't just rush at these things.'

'That little bastard can. You will have to do something, John. I hold you and Jim directly responsible for this.'

'Trust me,' said John. And Neville served the drinks.

'That woman with Young Master Robert looks strangely familiar,' said Jim.

'It's Sandra.'

'Sandra? No. But surely she used to have—'

'She cut one off. It's a fashion statement or something. Big birdpuller, she says.'

'Bird-puller? Dear oh dear.' Jim shook his head. 'That's put your rhyming slang all to pot.'

'Yours remains unaffected, however. Cheers.' John raised his glass.

'To the future,' said Jim.

'Have you really got the Brentford Scrolls in here?' Neville asked.

'True as true,' said John. 'Want to take a look?'

'Yes please.'

John turned the casket towards Neville and lifted the lid. The part-time barman took a peep inside.

'Oooooooh!' he went.

'Pretty impressive, eh?'

'Staggering,' said Neville. 'Truly staggering.'

'Jim found them,' said John. 'I told you he did.'

'And there was I not believing you.'

'You are forgiven.'

'And which emperor did you say they belonged to?'

'Not an emperor, a monk.'

'No, I'm sure it was an emperor.'

'Monk,' said John.

'Emperor,' said Neville.

'Monk.'

'Emperor.' Neville reached across the bar and snatched John's glass from his hand. 'The one with the new clothes. Get out of my pub, you're barred for life.'

'What?' John swung the casket round and looked inside. 'Aaaaagh!' he went.

'What's happening, John?' Jim Pooley took a look. 'Aaaaagh!' he agreed.

'Out,' cried Neville. 'The both of you, out.'

'No, Neville, no.' Jim's hands began to flap.

Omally's did likewise.

'They're gone,' cried Jim. 'My God, they're gone.'

'And for best actor nomination in *Farewell my Scrolls*, we have James Pooley and Jonathan Omally. Get out!' shouted Neville. 'Never darken my drip trays again.'

'No, Neville, this is serious. Deadly serious.'

Neville reached for the knobkerrie he kept beneath the bar. 'Out, Jim,' he shouted. 'Or know the wrath of my displeasure.'

Jim snatched up the casket. 'What do we do? What do we do?'

'We go back,' said Omally. 'To the Professor's. Unless you think they might just have fallen out while you were carrying them here.'

'No, I don't think that.'

'Nor me. Come on, let's go.'

They went at the trot.

'Oh dear,' wailed Jim, while trotting. 'Oh doom and gloom.'

'Be silent, man. There must be some simple explanation.'

'They were nicked. While we were all at the town hall.'

'*Too* simple,' said Omally. 'Though all too possible.'

'But no one can sneak into the Professor's. There's magic all over the place.'

'Perhaps these lads have magic too.'

'I don't like the sound of that.'

'Come on, let's run faster.'

By the time they reached the Professor's, Jim was half doubled up with a stitch. 'Leave me here to die,' he croaked.

'Let's go in.' John pushed upon the garden gate.

The garden gate refused to budge.

'But it's always open. Come on, I'll give you a leg up over the wall.'

'No way.' Jim shook his head fiercely. 'Remember that time we saw a tom cat trying to climb over the wall and he sort of—'

'Ah, yes. Horrible smell of frying. Put me off beefburgers for a week.'

'So do you want me to give *you* a leg up?'

'I don't think so. No.'

'What shall we do, then?' Jim clutched at his side and did deep breathing.

'Round to the front. But slowly. Take a little peep.'

'I'm right behind you.'

'Come on, then.'

John crept along the garden wall.

Jim put down the empty casket and followed.

John reached the corner and took a little peep around it.

'All clear,' he whispered. 'A couple of soldiers over the other side of the square having a fag, but they're not looking over here.'

'It could be a trap. Perhaps we should come back later.'

'Poltroon,' said Omally. 'Let's knock at the front door. See what happens.'

'OK. I'll stay here as look-out.'

'Good idea.'

'Why, thanks very much.'

'I was joking. Come on, let's do it.'

John marched up to the front door and knocked. KNOCK from the outside sounds different from the inside. There's not quite so much of it. KNOCK went Omally again, KNOCK KNOCK KNOCK.

'All right,' called the voice of Gammon. 'I'm coming.'

'It's Gammon,' said John.

'And he's coming,' said Jim.

Gammon put his eye to the little spy hole. 'Are you alone?' he asked.

'I am,' said John. 'What about you, Jim?'

'Yes, I am too.'

'All right, come in.' Gammon pulled upon numerous bolts and turned several keys in heavy locks. 'Hurry, now. They're back, Professor,' he called.

'Send them in then.'

Gammon hustled the pair towards the study.

Professor Slocombe sat at his desk, quill pen poised above a sheet of vellum. 'I didn't expect you back,' said he.

'We came at once,' said Omally. 'As soon as we could.'

'Very good. And you put the scrolls somewhere very safe?'

Jim Pooley groaned.

'Why are you groaning, Jim?'

'The casket was empty.'

Professor Slocombe laughed. 'A most convincing ruse, you will agree.'

'What?'

'An illusion,' said Professor Slocombe. 'A little magical camouflage. It obviously had you convinced. Let's hope it does the same should anyone else take a look in the casket. So where did you put it? In the priest hole?'

John looked at Jim.

Jim looked down at his empty hands. 'Aaaaaagh!' went Jim.

The garden gate opened without difficulty from the inside. Jim plunged through it and out into the street. And stared down at the place where he had put the casket.

'Aaaaaagh!' went Jim again.

17

'Aaaaaagh!' went Professor Slocombe behind him. 'You fool, Jim. You craven buffoon.'

'How was I to know? The casket looked empty. You should have told us.'

'Yes.' Professor Slocombe nodded. 'I suppose I should. Professional vanity got the better of me again. The watchword of magic is secrecy. The magician never divulges his knowledge.'

'We wouldn't have cared *how* you did it,' said John. 'Only that you *had*.'

Professor Slocombe shook his head sadly. 'Well, we will now have to see what we can do about recovering the scrolls.'

'There was no one about,' said Jim. 'Not a soul.'

'You might well have been followed.'

'I'm sure we weren't.'

'I could have followed you,' said the Professor. 'You wouldn't have seen me.'

'John said he thought these lads might have magic too. What do you think, Professor?'

'I think it more than likely. These are not just

205

businessmen we're dealing with. These people kill without pity.'

'It's the dark side of the force then, is it?' Jim asked.

Professor Slocombe raised an icy eyebrow.

'Sorry,' said Jim. 'But what are we going to do?'

Professor Slocombe shook his head sadly. 'I wish I knew,' said he. 'I really wish I knew.'

Dr Steven Malone had a smile upon his face. It was a big smile, a broad smile, a real self-satisfied smugger of a smile. No normal fellow could have pulled off a smile like that. It takes a real mad bastard to do the job properly.

And now he chuckled. Like they do. And then he laughed. (Joe-Bob wasn't in there with a chance.) And then he tapped his fingers on the item that lay before him on his dining table.

And that item was, in case you might not have already guessed it, Pooley's casket.

What a joke. By sheer chance he'd been looking out of the window and seen that Irish lout who had stitched him up for fifty quid go running by with his mate. And his mate had put down the casket. And Dr Steven had crept out and filched it away.

Dr Steven examined the casket. He lifted the lid. Empty, but evidently a thing of great age. An antique and in good condition. There were jewels on this casket. They looked real enough. Dr Steven laughed again.

And then he took the lid in one hand, put his knee

206

upon the casket, applied pressure and ripped the lid right off.

And then he laughed again.

And then he left the room.

And then he came back again, carrying something wrapped in a towel. 'Here you go, little one,' he said. 'Away in a manger, no crib for his bed.' And he placed the baby in the casket.

A soft and golden glow surrounded the child as it stirred from its sleep. Its eyes flickered open and stared up at the gaunt figure all in black and white.

The eyes were golden, shining as though lit from within.

And the child's mouth moved. A gurgle and a little cough.

'Dada,' said the baby.

'Yes, that's right,' said Dr Malone. 'I am your dada. Go to sleep now.'

'Good night, dada.'

'Good night, little boy.'

'Good afternoon,' said Fred. 'Any progress to report? Teatime looms; I trust you have everything under control.'

'We do,' said anonymous fellow one.

'We don't,' said his companion. 'But we're getting there.'

'Hm,' said Fred. 'I like not the sound of this. Where are the scrolls?'

'Where indeed,' said the first anonymous fellow.

'I have the fire stoked up,' said Fred. 'I can add you to it. I'm not at all bothered.'

'We do have the situation under control,' said number two. 'Which is to say that we are certain the scrolls are still in Brentford.'

'But you don't actually have them.'

'Not as such, no.'

'All right,' said Fred. 'Tell me all about it.'

'Well,' said number two. 'Derek here—'

'Who's Derek?'

'I'm Derek,' said Derek.

'Oh,' said Fred. 'I didn't know you actually had a name.'

'Oh yes,' said Derek. 'I've had it since I was christened.'

'Don't use that language in here. And I suppose you're going to tell me that you have a name too.'

'I just did,' said Derek. 'It's Derek.'

'Not you. Him.'

'Clive,' said Clive.

'Derek and Clive.'

'Live,' said Derek and Clive.

'Go on then,' said Fred. 'Tell me it all. And then I'll decide which of you I throw on the fire.'

'Derek here', said Clive, 'drugged the council chamber. It was a real hoot. I was looking in through the window. A lady in a straw hat got bonked by these stoned councillors. One of them stuck his—'

'What about the scrolls?'

'Couldn't find them,' said Clive. 'Went round to the Professor's house, donned the old cloak of invisibility the way one does and had a good shufty about. The casket was there but it was empty. Later the two louts took it round to the local pub.

Probably to sell it. We jacked it in then and came back here.'

'Didn't you forget something?'

'No, I don't think we did.'

'Their heads!' shouted Fred. 'What about their frigging heads?'

'Ah now, we thought about that,' said Derek. 'And we considered it a bit previous. Better to let the louts lead us to the scrolls, we thought. Then cut off their frigging heads.'

'So what exactly are you doing back here?'

'Dunno,' said Clive. 'What are we doing back here?'

'Money,' said Derek. 'We want lots of money.'

'For what? You haven't done anything yet.'

'For bribery and corruption. Set friend against friend. Break the community spirit. They're thick as pus from a weeping wound, these Brentonians, they all club together. A bung here and a bribe there will set them at each other's throats.'

Professor Slocombe stoked up the fire. 'What I should have done', said he, 'was to cast a spell of return over the scrolls. Then, wherever they were, all I'd have had to do was summon them.'

'Things always seem so simple when you look back at them, don't they?' said John.

'Urgh!' went Jim. 'Urgh! Uuh! Argh!'

'I do so agree,' said John. 'An advanced form of Esperanto is this, or what?'

'No, I've got it, I've got it.'

'Well, don't get any on me.'

'The old ones aren't always the best,' said the Professor.

'No, I really have got it,' said Jim. 'Things always seem simple when you look back at them. John's right.'

'Go on.'

'Look back at them,' said Jim. 'Don't you get it?'

'No,' said the Professor. 'I don't.'

Jim sighed. 'It's so simple. I should have thought of it at once. Go back. In time. I can do that. I go back in time and see who pinched the casket.'

'Give that man a big cigar,' said John Omally.

Dr Steven puffed upon a big cigar, the way proud fathers do.

On the dining table lay the casket, in this lay the golden child. Upon the floor lay the lid and in this lay the other one.

Dr Steven stooped and peered. There was something not quite right about the other one. Only two had survived the terrible zinc tanks and they had both been cloned from dried blood from the Turin Shroud. But they were by no means identical.

The golden child exuded warmth and joy.

But this one.

Dr Steven blew cigar smoke into its face.

The features twitched. Dark they were. Swarthy. The hair was black, the eyebrows and the lashes. But there was an all-over blackness about this child. A little shell of darkness seemed to surround it. A palpable thing. Whenever Dr Steven fed it with the bottle he felt his fingers growing cold. There was something far from right about this baby.

The fact that everything about all of this was far from right eluded Dr Steven.

'What exactly are you?' asked the genetic engineer.

The baby's dark eyes opened and they focused.

'Dada,' it said, in a deep dark tone.

'Does it need to be dark?' asked Professor Slocombe. 'Should I switch off the lights?'

'No problem.' Jim settled himself on the chaise longue. 'Where did Celia Penn go?' he asked.

'She went home,' said Professor Slocombe. 'We had a chat. I won't bore you with the details.'

'Secrets again.'

'Indeed. Yes.'

'And whoever knocked upon your door? Did they give you any trouble?'

Professor Slocombe winked.

'*You* did that. To get us off on our way.'

'I'd like to get you off on your way now, if you don't mind.'

'No problem, Professor.' Jim closed his eyes. 'Do the road drill, John.'

'Do I have to?'

'Yes, you do.'

'Brrrrm,' went John.

'In A minor.'

'That *was* A minor.'

'That was B flat,' said Professor Slocombe. 'Like the blues. The blues are always in B flat.'

'Just do it like you do it, John.' And Jim drifted off. 'Om,' he went, drifting backwards.

'What is Om?' Omally asked.

'The Universal note,' said Professor Slocombe. 'In Hinduism, the sacred syllable that typifies the three gods, Brahma, Vishna and Shiva, who concern themselves with the threefold operation of integration, maintenance, and disintegration. Birth, life and death. Om as a symbol is more powerful than the pentagram or cross. It represents love and love of life, without fear of death. To give and to receive this symbol is an act of love.'

'Why is Jim Omming?' Omally asked.

'I haven't the faintest idea,' said Professor Slocombe.

'Om off to Alabama with a banjo on my knee,' sang Jim Pooley.

A long black car with blacked-out windows drew up outside the Professor's house. At the wheel sat a chauffeur, whistling.

'Shut up the bloody whistling,' said Clive.

'I can whistle if I want to.'

'And I can rip your fucking heart out,' said Derek (him being the God-damn crazy ape-shit one-man killing machine of the partnership).

The chauffeur stopped whistling.

'So what happens next?' said Clive.

'We wait 'til they come out. Follow them and nab the scrolls.'

'Fair enough,' said Clive.

'Now I'll tell you what I want,' said Derek.

'What you really, really want?'

'What I really, really want is a Zigger cigar.'

212

'And what is that, exactly?'

'I haven't the faintest idea. But I really, really want one.'

'Actually I had one once,' said Clive. 'But it wasn't all it was cracked up to be. Hey, hang about. Are they coming out?'

'No,' said Derek. 'They're not.'

'You're not doing it properly, are you, Jim?'

'I'm sorry, John, I can't seem to get in the mood.'

'Should I Brrrrm some more?'

'I don't think it will help.'

'I could put you under hypnotically,' said Professor Slocombe.

'No thank you,' said Jim. 'I can manage on my own.'

'I don't think that's altogether true.'

'Look, it's my magic, let me do it on my own.'

'I'm sorry. Go ahead then.'

Jim closed his eyes and drifted back. And then Jim opened his eyes and he screamed very loudly.

'Jim, are you all right?' Omally hastened to his side.

'John, it was terrible. Terrible.'

'Not the murdering of the monk again?'

'Far worse. Bodies all cut to pieces. In tanks. Women's bodies.'

'Holy God,' said John.

'Tell me exactly what you saw.' Professor Slocombe looked Jim deeply in the eyes.

'In a basement,' said Jim. 'The bloke who took the casket. He's got a basement full of dismembered bodies. Floating in tanks. Pregnant bodies without arms and legs. It's the most disgusting thing I've ever seen in my life.' Jim lurched to his feet, flung himself through the open French windows and threw up all over the garden.

'That won't please my roses,' said Professor Slocombe.

At length Jim returned, pale-faced, to the study. 'Weirdest thing of all,' said Jim. 'This bloke. The murderer. He was really strange. There was no colour at all to him. He was all in black and white.'

'Ah,' said John Omally. 'Then we have the bastard.'

18

Do dah. Do dah. Do dah. Do dah went the police cars.
And *Weeeeeeeeeeeeeeeeeeee*.

Chief Inspector Westlake stood in the Professor's study. 'You are absolutely certain about this?' he asked. 'There can be no mistake?'

'Jim?' said the Professor.

'I saw it,' said Jim. 'It was real.'

'Absolutely certain,' said Professor Slocombe.

'If it's true,' said the Chief Inspector, 'it will clear up a lot of unsolveds. Not murders, but bodies going missing from morgues. We've had eight in the last eight weeks.'

'The chap's the duty physician at the Cottage Hospital,' said John Omally.

'Dr Malone?' The Chief Inspector shook his head.

'Genetic engineer,' said Professor Slocombe. 'I've never met the fellow but I know of his work.'

'So do I,' said Jim. 'Go and arrest him.'

'All in good time, sir. His house is surrounded. We do things softly softly here.'

*   *   *

'What are they doing now?' asked Clive.

'They've got one of those big battering ram things,' said Derek. 'I think they're going to smash down the door.'

'Oh, goody. Do you think it's all right for us to stay here? We shouldn't have the chauffeur drive us somewhere else?'

'I just killed the chauffeur,' said Derek. 'The bastard was whistling again.'

'Things are working well for us. But what do you think all this police presence is about?'

'I haven't the foggiest. Ah, here come the louts.'

'You just leave all this to the professionals,' said Chief Inspector Westlake.

'My pleasure,' said the Professor. 'My only wish is to recover a casket that I believe is in the doctor's house.'

'Something of yours, is it?'

'A family heirloom.'

'Oh, I've always wanted to see one of them. They actually weave real hair, do they?'

'By the yard,' said Professor Slocombe.

'Makes you proud to be English,' said John.

'But you're . . .' Professor Slocombe paused. 'Yes, I know exactly what you mean.'

'I don't,' said Jim.

The battering ram didn't go KNOCK. It went BASH. And then it burst right through. Uniformed constables stormed into Kether House, electric truncheons drawn, hopes of their use growing fiercely.

Constables toppled into the hall, constables

rushed into the ground-floor rooms, constables pelted up the stairs. Constables pelted down other stairs. These constables saw things that would later waken them screaming from their sleep. Many of these constables did as Jim had done in the Professor's rose garden.

Chief Inspector Westlake wiped a handkerchief across his mouth and stared about the basement hell. 'Bastard,' he said. 'Mad bastard. Where is he?'

'Gone,' said a chalk-faced constable. 'No trace. But, Chief Inspector, there's worse over here. Far worse.'

'What is that, constable?' The Chief Inspector looked.

The constable turned back a length of tarpaulin, exposing four tiny twisted dead things.

Chief Inspector Westlake turned away. 'Holy Mother of God,' he whispered.

In the dining room Professor Slocombe patted Jim upon the shoulder. 'Well done,' he said.

Jim looked down upon the empty casket. 'Are they in there? I still can't see them.'

'They are there. Well done.'

'I'd like to go now, if you don't mind. This place turns my stomach. There's evil here.'

'Yes, there is.' The Professor stroked the Om he wore about his neck. 'Great evil, so close to my own home, yet I never knew.'

'How did he get out?' asked John. 'This place was completely surrounded.'

'Tunnels, probably. These houses are very old.'

'I'll have to ask you to clear the house, please,

Professor,' said the Chief Inspector, who looked like death. 'We'll need the forensic boys in here. This is very bad, Professor. Very bad indeed.'

'I would like to help you with the forensic examination, if I might.'

'You are eminently qualified. I would appreciate it.'

Professor Slocombe offered the policeman a certain handshake. 'Upon the square and beneath the arch,' he said.

'Should we take this back to your place, Professor?' John Omally lifted the casket.

'Best to. I will be along presently.' Professor Slocombe made mystical finger-motions over the casket and spoke certain mystical words.

'Goodbye, then.'

'They're coming out,' said Derek. 'They've got the casket. Although it hasn't got a lid on any more.'

'But the bloody thing's empty.'

'Are we absolutely sure of that?'

'Well, it wouldn't hurt to take a look.'

'No, it wouldn't.'

Jim stopped to take deep breaths. 'I can't believe all that stuff in there,' he said. 'What was that all about?'

'Madness,' said John. 'Plain and simple.'

'Plain and simple? I don't think so.'

'Perk up, Jim. You got the scrolls back. You're a genius, my friend.'

'I suppose the Professor wouldn't mind if we had

218

a drink or two at his expense while we were waiting, to celebrate as it were.'

'I'm sure he wouldn't.'

'Good. Because I certainly need some.'

The limousine backed up really fast. An electrically driven window drove down and a hand reached out to snatch the casket.

'We'll take that,' said a voice behind the hand.

'No you bloody well won't.' Jim drew back.

'Run,' was John Omally's advice.

And Jim took it.

'After them,' shouted Derek.

'No need to shout,' shouted Clive. 'Which way are they going? How could the bloody chauffeur see through this tinted windscreen?'

'I think he wore dark glasses.'

'Oh, that would be it, then.'

'Run, Jim.'

'I'm running. I'm running.'

'Take the scrolls out of the casket. It's less to carry.'

'I can't see them.'

'You can feel them, though.'

'That's right.' Jim groped in the casket. Drew out the invisible scrolls, which reappeared as he did so. 'Clever,' said Jim. 'Very clever.'

'Run,' said John.

'I'm way ahead of you.'

*   *   *

'Up that way.'

'I can see them. I've got the glasses on now.'

Derek had a great big gun on his lap. He began to push great big shells into the breech. 'Nine-gauge auto-loader,' he said.

'Phase plasma rifle in a forty-watt range?'

'Only what you see on the shelves, buddy.'

'God, I love those movies.'

'They're running that way. After them!'

'I'm on it.'

'Are we going to make for the canal again?' Pooley puffed.

'No, you can only pull off a trick like that just the once. Down here.' Omally ducked into an alley-way.

Jim joined him, huffing now, as well as puffing. 'Well, they can't drive down here.'

'You can't drive down there,' shouted Derek. 'Stop the car, we'll chase them on foot.'

'In the movies they turn the car on its side to go down alleyways.'

'Yeah!' said Derek. 'They do, don't they?'

'Aaaaaagh!' went Jim, as the limo swerved onto its side and shot along the alley, making glorious showers of sparks.

'Run faster.'

'I'm running. I'm running.'

★   ★   ★

'You know,' said Clive, as he clung to the wheel, 'I much prefer this kind of job to all that farting around in the Corridors of Power.'

'Oh yeah.' Derek fed another shell into his gun. 'This definitely has the edge on accountancy.'

'We're coming to the end of the alleyway now. When I bump the limo back down onto its wheels, what say you lean out of the window and let off a few rounds?'

'Spot on.'

John and Jim ran out into Moby Dick Terrace.

'John,' Jim huffed and puffed and gruffed, 'pardon me for asking a really stupid question, but why didn't we just run back into Dr Malone's house, where we would have been surrounded by police-men?'

John said nothing and the two ran on.

The limo smashed down into the terrace and Derek bashed out a back window with his gun butt.

'You only had to press the button, Derek.'

'Yeah, but it's much more exciting this way.'

Now, you'd have thought that there would have been someone around. Someone, or lots of someones, what with the army cordoning off streets and setting up border posts and everything. But there wasn't, because the army had, as usual, ballsed it all up. They *had* cordoned off a road here and there, and set up a border post here and there, but the plucky Brentfordians, rather than engage in another riot, had simply decided to ignore them. They had taken to skirting the roadblocks by going down alleyways, or through people's houses and out of their back gates. And as few folk in the borough actually drove motor cars, there weren't any traffic build-ups either.

So that explains that, really. In case you were wondering.

They were not making particularly good progress up Moby Dick Terrace. Dustin Hoffman may have done all that stuff in *Marathon Man*, but this is John and Jim here. The limo soon caught up and cruised in pace with the pavement runners. Derek stuck his head out of the shattered window. And he stuck his gun out also.

'Do you want to stop?' he called to Jim. 'Or should I just shoot your face off?'

Jim clutched the scrolls to his bosom. 'All right. All right,' he gasped. 'I give up, don't shoot.'

'You too, asshole.'

'Me too,' said John.

'OK, now get into the car.'

Derek moved across the back seat as John and Jim climbed in beside him. 'Close the door,' said Derek. John closed the door.

Clive struck a match on the dead chauffeur's head and lit up a Zigger cigar. 'Where to?' he asked.

'Round to Fred's,' said Derek. 'And burn a bit of rubber on the way.'

19

From a bedroom window in Moby Dick Terrace, Dr Steven Malone watched as the black limousine roared off in a cloud of smoking rubber. 'And bloody good riddance to them,' he said.

He had left very little to chance. He had known of the secret tunnel when he bought Kether House and he had later bought this one, where the tunnel emerged in the back garden shed. The occupants of this house, an old couple with no living heirs, hadn't wanted to sell. Their death certificates said *natural causes*. Dr Steven had signed them himself.

The mad and monochrome medic turned away from the window and smiled at the two little babies on the bed.

'All right, my boys?' he said.

'All right, dada,' said the golden one.

The dark one only growled.

'All right, boys,' said Fred. 'Wheel 'em in.'

Derek and Clive pushed John and Jim from the Corridor of Power into the Chamber of the same persuasion.

223

'Superb,' said Fred, eyeing up the arrivals. 'And do I spy the Brentford Scrolls?'

'You certainly do,' said Derek.

'And do I spy a nine-gauge auto-loader?'

'You certainly do, sir, yes.'

'And you walked through this building, carrying that?'

'Er,' said Derek.

'Twat,' said Fred. 'But very well done all the same.'

'I picked up this machete on the way,' said Clive, brandishing same. 'Do you want Derek to chop their frigging heads off now?'

'Ooh, yes please,' said Derek.

'All in good time. What exactly is that prat doing?'

'He's flapping his hands and spinning round in small circles, sir.'

'Well, make him stop.'

Derek clouted Pooley in the ear.

Jim ceased his foolish gyrations, and collapsed in a heap on the floor. John clenched his fists, but there was nothing he could do.

Fred's feet were up on the fender. 'Drag him over here. And pick up those scrolls. Valuable items, they are. We wouldn't want any harm to come to them, would we?'

'Wouldn't we, sir?'

'Of course we would. I was being ironic.'

Derek picked up the scrolls and handed them to Fred.

'Right,' said Fred. 'So, here we are then. The Brentford Scrolls.' He held them up and gave them a good looking over. 'Pretty fancy, aren't they? Good quality parchment. I suppose I should savour this moment, but I don't think I'll bother. I'll just toss them on the fire.'

'No.' John took a step forward. Derek barred his way.

'What are you no-ing about?' Fred asked.

'Don't burn them. You can't.'

'That's a rather foolish remark to make, isn't it?'

'All right. So you can. But why do you want to burn them? And who are you anyway?'

'He's your worst nightmare,' said Clive.

'I don't think so,' said John. 'After what I've seen during the last few days he doesn't even come close.'

'But he is,' Clive insisted. 'He's a jumped-up little nobody who's clawed his way to the top of the tree and—'

'Clive,' said Fred.

'Fred?' said Clive.

'Shut up.'

'If you're going to burn the scrolls and kill us both,' said John, 'you could at least have the decency to tell us why.'

'I could,' said Fred, 'but I won't. I know there is a long and acknowledged literary and cinematic tradition for the villain to make the great explanatory speech to the heroes before he tops them. And then at the last minute, when all seems lost for the heroes, the clever unexpected twist comes and—'

'If you burn the scrolls and kill us,' said John, 'you'll never learn about *The Great Secret*.'

Fred shook his head. 'Nice try,' he said. 'But it's all such a cliché, isn't it?'

'Look out behind you!' shouted Jim.

Nobody moved. Nobody even batted an eyelid (whatever that means).

'Sorry,' said Jim. 'Just thought I'd give it a try.'

'All right,' said Fred. 'So, Brentford Scrolls into the fire and two heads onto the floor. And here we jolly well go.'

Fred took the scrolls in both hands and moved to toss them onto the roaring fire. John turned his face away. Jim closed his eyes.

'Eh?' said Fred. 'What's all this?'

John turned back his face and Jim reopened his eyes.

Fred was struggling with the scrolls. If you've ever seen the act mime artists do with a balloon, where it's in the air and they pretend it's immovable and struggle to shift it, that was pretty much what Fred was doing now.

As Clive had both hands free he took to clapping. 'Very good,' he cried. 'Very good indeed.'

Fred fought to force the scrolls into the fire. But they wouldn't be shifted. He let them go, but instead of falling to the floor they simply hovered there in mid-air (well, not exactly *mid*-air – they were certainly nearer to the floor than the ceiling – but hover they did, none the less).

Fred made a most unpleasant growling sound deep down in his throat and grabbed the scrolls once more. But they wouldn't be shifted, not a smidgen, not a titchy bit, not a lone iota.

'Brilliant,' said Clive, going clap–clap–clap. 'Very impressive.'

'Stop that bloody clapping, you pranny, give us a hand with these.'

'Oh,' said Clive. 'Oh, all right then.'

And Clive took to struggling and forcing and straining and then things got tricky for Clive. The scrolls took a sudden lurch upwards, dragging Clive from his feet.

'What's happening, John?' whispered Jim.

'The Professor,' whispered John. 'Remember he said some words over the scrolls before we left Malone's. It would be that spell of return he told us about.'

'Get me down,' wailed Clive, from somewhere near the high ceiling.

'Shoot the bloody things out of the sky!' shouted Fred.

'But I might hit Clive, sir.'

'As if I give a shit!'

'Righty-ho, sir.' Derek angled up his gun and let off several rounds in a manner which could only be described as indiscriminate.

And down came lots of nicely stuccoed ceiling. Very noisily and heavily.

John and Jim leapt aside as lath and plaster crashed about them.

'Give me that gun, you bloody fool.' Fred snatched the auto-loader from Derek and let off several rounds of his own. Down came much more ceiling and a chandelier.

'Aaaaagh!' went Derek, as the chandelier came down on him.

'Aaaaagh!' went Fred as Clive came down on him.

Lath and plaster, dust and mayhem.

Lots of very bad language.

Fred struggled up, hurling Clive aside and fanning dust and rubble about him. The scrolls now took to zig-zagging backwards and forwards across the ceiling and Fred took to running beneath them, firing and firing again.

Clouds of dust and gunsmoke choked the air, obscuring vision. Flashes of gunfire tore like lightning, thunder followed with smashings and crashings as sections of ceiling hurtled down, flattening furniture, shattering showcases, pulverizing porcelain. With the screams and cries and coughings and croakings and very, very bad language, it all contrived to create a fair facsimile of that evil abode where Fred's employer dwelt.

And then, with a final effing and blasting, Fred ran out of shells.

And there followed a very tense silence indeed.

White with dust and terror to an equal degree, Clive and Derek held their breath as the air slowly cleared to reveal the extent of the devastation. Somehow the Chamber of Power didn't look quite so powerful any more. Rather woebegone, in fact. A battle zone, an indoor wasteland.

Fred stood upon what once had been his desk, bloody about the cap regions and very wild of eye. Most of the windows had been shot out and in the distance could be heard that distinctive on-cue sound of approaching police car sirens.

Fred turned his damaged head from one side to the other.

The Brentford Scrolls were gone.

And so, too, John and Jim.

Having endured several hours of mind-numbing horror at the house of Dr Steven Malone, Professor Slocombe now leaned back in his chair and allowed himself the luxury of considerable mirth.

Before him, on his desk, lay the Brentford Scrolls, pristine and undamaged. Framed in the French windows stood two individuals who looked anything but.

'Would you mind ringing your little brass bell?' Jim asked.

Professor Slocombe rang his little brass bell. 'Come on in,' he said, stifling another chuckle. 'Sit yourselves down and relax.'

The two men slumped into fireside chairs. And then they gazed into the fire, shook their heads and reseated themselves elsewhere. They did not, however, relax.

'And where exactly have you been?' asked the Professor.

'Penge,' said Jim.

'Penge?' Professor Slocombe tugged upon an earlobe. 'I understand that it's a very nice place, although I've never been there myself.'

'Delightful,' said Jim. 'Especially the offices of the Millennium Committee.'

'Ah.' Professor Slocombe nodded. 'Of course. It all falls rather neatly into place.'

'The ceiling didn't,' said Jim, rubbing at a dent in his forehead.

'Then I assume you met Fred.'

'We did.' Omally picked dust from eyebrows. 'And Fred is not a very nice man at all.'

'Fred is your worst nightmare.'

'He's rapidly rising up the chart, yes.'

Gammon entered without knocking.

'Thanks for that,' said Jim.

On Gammon's tray stood three pints of Large. Gammon offered them around.

'Just the job, Gammon,' said Jim, accepting his eagerly.

'Cheers,' said John, raising his glass.

Gammon placed the last pint before the Professor and stood quietly by.

Jim took a large swallow and said, 'My oh my.'

'Oh my,' said John, peering into his glass. 'This is splendid stuff.'

Professor Slocombe took a sip or two. 'I am no connoisseur of ale,' he said, 'but I believe this to be of superior quality.'

'And then some.' Jim did further swallowings. 'I'm sure this is how beer is supposed to taste, not that the ale in the Swan is much less than perfect.'

'Where did you get this?' John asked. 'Did you brew it yourself?'

'On the contrary. It was a gift from Normal Hartnell. He had a bit of a breakthrough this afternoon with his latest experiments and dropped a barrel round to get my opinion.'

'All hail to the scientific shopkeeper.' Jim raised his now empty glass in salute. 'A whole barrel, did you say?'

Professor Slocombe smiled. 'Gammon,' he said.

'Yes, sir?'

'Best roll in the barrel.'

'So go on.' John Omally topped up his glass from the barrel that now stood upon the Professor's desk. 'Tell us what you know about this Fred. The last we saw of him, he and his cohorts were being dragged in handcuffs into a police car. Fred looked far from jovial.'

'Well, I doubt whether he will remain in custody for very long. Fred has many friends in high places. And also in *low places*.'

'Now that would be what is known as a *sinister emphasis*,' said John.

'About as sinister as it is possible to get. Fred is indeed your worst nightmare. Fred is in league with the Devil.'

Pooley groaned.

'Well, what else would you have expected?'

'Not a lot, I suppose. So what do you propose to do about him?'

'Me? Nothing.'

'Don't look at us.'

'No, no.' Professor Slocombe sipped further ale and nodded approvingly at his glass. 'I have not been idle since last I saw you. I have made several calls to certain prominent persons of impeccable character, authorities in their particular fields. A meeting will convene here tomorrow at ten, for the authentication of the scrolls. Carefully chosen representatives of the media have also been invited. Once the scrolls are confirmed as authentic, the world's press will be informed. Fred may squirm and plot as much as he likes after that, but he will not be able to stop the celebrations and ceremonies taking place on the final day of this year. Now it is absolutely necessary that no word of this meeting leak out. This is all strictly Above Top Secret.'

'You can trust us,' said Jim, raising two fingers, boy scout fashion.

'Of that I have no doubt at all. But I hope you will pardon me if I ask you not to leave this house tonight. Please stay here, wine and dine, finish the barrel of Large, taste brandy, smoke cigars. But do not take one footstep out of the door until everything is tied up tomorrow at ten. How does all that sound to you?'

'Sounds pretty good to me,' said Jim. 'Much obliged.'

'Yes, thank you very much.' John raised his glass. 'But then look at it this way, Professor. After all we've been through today, what else could possibly happen?'

20

KNOCK, KNOCK, KNOCK, came a knock, knock, knocking at the Professor's door.

Well, no, actually it didn't.

I mean, don't you just hate all that 'What else could possibly happen?' stuff. It's like those dreadful TV sitcoms, where the lead character says, 'No way! There's absolutely *no way* I'm going to do *that*!' and the scene fades out and then fades in again to reveal that he is doing just *that*. And then the canned laughter machine goes into overdrive. Oh, ha ha ha, very funny indeed!

So there wasn't any KNOCK KNOCK KNOCKing and nothing horrendous whatsoever befell Jim and John for the balance of the night.

All right, so it could be argued that it would have been a lot more fun if something had. But these chaps are only human, you know. And they'd had a very rough day. How much more could they take?

At a little after ten of the morning clock, nearly fifty people stood, sat or generally lounged about in Professor Slocombe's study.

Gammon moved amongst them, dispensing drinks and those Ferrero Rocher wrapped-up chocolate things that are dead posh.

There were Professors a-plenty here. Professors of linguistics, Professors of theology, Professors of history, Professors of this thing, that thing and the other. Learned men were these, who held seats. Seats of this thing, that thing and the other. Media men were much in evidence, Scoop Molloy holding court amongst them. And the Mayor of Brentford had been invited too. He was accompanied by several members of his gang, dubious Latino types with names such as Emilio and Pedro, who favoured sleeveless denim jackets, brightly coloured headbands and impressive tattooing.

And most of the town council were there, and Celia Penn was there, and a lady in a straw hat who had been passing by was there. She was there with her friend called Doris, who had also been passing by. They were chatting with a couple of cabinet ministers, one of whom used to play the blues with John Coltrane. And of course Pooley and Omally were there, and so too was Norman Hartnell.

Fred was *not* there and neither were Derek and Clive.

Professor Slocombe called the meeting to order, made a brief speech regarding the history of the scrolls and the Days of God, and then invited each Professor in turn to view the documents and make their informed pronouncements regarding authenticity.

One after another these scholarly fellows leaned low over the Brentford Scrolls, cocked their heads from one side to the other, smacked their lips and tickled their noses. Then they withdrew into a little cabal in the corner, whispered amongst themselves, turned as one and gave Professor Slocombe the old thumbs-up.

'Gammon, the champagne,' said the Professor.

By two of the afternoon ticker, the champagne bottles were shells of glass and all the dead posh chocolates eaten, farewells had been belched out, hands had been shaken. Professor Slocombe sat down at his desk. John and Jim stood with their hands in their pockets and quite foolish looks on their faces.

'You did it, Professor,' said Jim. 'You did it.'

'*You* did it, Jim,' the ancient replied.

'Well, we *all* did it,' said John. 'But it's done. We've cracked it. Brentford will host the millennial celebrations two years ahead of the rest of the world. *And it's official.*'

'Yes.' Professor Slocombe rolled up the scrolls. 'These will now go, under heavy security, to the Bank of England. And I will prepare myself to perform the ceremonies. We shall triumph, gentlemen. We shall triumph.'

'We certainly shall.' John took out his little notebook. 'Now where exactly should we start, I wonder?'

'With the Jim Pooley,' said Jim. 'Definitely the Jim Pooley.'

Omally nodded thoughtfully. 'Or possibly the John Omally Millennial Massage Parlour.'

'Are we knocking down the flatblocks for Pooley Plaza straight away, do you think?'

'We'll have to give that a lot of thought. I'm not quite certain where the best place to build Omally's will be.'

'Omally's?' Jim asked. 'I don't think you mentioned Omally's.'

'It's a casino. Very exclusive.'

'I bet it's not as exclusive as my one's going to be.'

'How much do you want to bet?'

'Gentlemen?' Professor Slocombe raised a pale thin hand. 'Gentlemen, what exactly do you think you're talking about?'

'How best to spend all the millions from the Millennium Fund,' said John. 'Great care must be taken to do the job properly. You can rely on us.'

'I'm sure that I can. But hate as I do to rain on your parade, what makes you think that the Millennium Fund will contribute one single penny to your schemes?'

'Well, they'll have to now, won't they? What with the scrolls and everything.'

'You really think so, do you?'

'Yes I do,' said John.

'And so you'll be asking Fred personally, will you?'

'Won't Fred have to cough up?' Jim's face took on a look of alarm. 'Won't he be made to?'

Professor Slocombe shook his head. 'I wouldn't think so for one moment. He will not draw attention

236

to himself by actively refusing outright. On the contrary, when interviewed by the media, I expect he will be all smiles and generosity. But, *but*, when it comes to actually handing over any money, he will prevaricate, tie you up in paperwork more tightly than a *Blue Peter* presenter in a cling film codpiece.'

'You mean . . .' John's jaw dropped.

'Not a penny,' said the Professor. 'Not a bean, not a farthing, not an old bent nickel. Zero, zilch. I'm sorry.'

'But . . .' John's jaw hovered in the dropped position.

A small sigh escaped from the lips of Jim Pooley. Though small, it was so plaintive, and evocative of such heart-rending pathos, that had there been a King Edward potato present this sigh would have brought a tear to its eye.

'Don't do that,' said John. 'You've made all the hairs stand up on the back of my neck.'

'But, John, but, oh oh oh.'

'Look at him,' John told the Professor. 'You've made him cry now.'

'I'm not crying. I'm just, oh oh oh.'

'Jim,' said the Professor. 'You mustn't be down-hearted. What you have done by finding the scrolls is something so wonderful that mere money could never reward you. You will go down in the annals of history as the man who changed the world.'

'Will I get a pension?' Jim asked.

'Probably not. But certainly a round of applause. Would you care for one now?'

'Not really.'

'Well, that's that then. So it only remains for me to thank you on behalf of the people of the world. Wish you well in whatever field of endeavour you choose next for yourself. And bid you a fond farewell. I'd offer you a late lunch, but I have much to do and you must be pretty stuffed with all those chocolates you've eaten.'

'Not particularly,' said Jim in a grumpy tone.

'Well, eat all the other ones I saw you sticking in your pockets.'

'So is that it?' John shrugged hopelessly.

'That's it. I must prepare myself for the ceremonies. I have a great deal to do over the coming months.'

'So we'll say goodbye, shall we?'

'Yes. Goodbye, John.'

'Goodbye then, Professor.'

'And goodbye to you, Jim, and thank you very much indeed.'

'Don't mention it.'

'Oh, Jim. Just one thing before you go.'

'What is that?' asked the sorrowful one.

'Only this.' Profesor Slocombe rose from his desk and strode over to Pooley. He stared him deeply in the eyes and nodded thoughtfully. 'One clouted ear, a pair of black eyes, a bloodied nose, a grazed chin and a dented forehead.'

'And a few cracked ribs,' said Jim. 'Not that I'm one to complain.'

'Well, you deserve better than that.'

'On this we're both agreed.'

'Kindly close your eyes.'

Jim closed his eyes.

Professor Slocombe whispered certain words and passed his hands over Jim's face. 'You can open them now,' he said.

Jim opened his eyes. Professor Slocombe held up a small hand mirror. Jim gazed into it.

'I'm cured,' whispered Jim. 'All my bumps and bruises gone.'

'The very least I could do. Farewell to you now, Jim, and may God go with you.'

'Give us another chocolate,' said John.

Jim rooted in his pockets. 'Here you go,' he said. 'And that's the last one.'

'No it isn't.'

'It's the last one you're getting.'

'Oh, I see.'

As the library bench was now in Old Pete's back garden, John and Jim sat on the rim of the hole, their feet dangling down.

'I don't even have a bench to sit on any more,' sighed Jim.

'The scrolls are yours,' said John. 'By the Finders Keepers law, or whatever. You could sell them. They must be worth a few bob.'

'I don't think the Professor would be very happy about that.'

'It's outrageous.' John made fists and shook them in the air. 'After all we've been through, we come out of it with absolutely nothing.'

'So no change there, then.'

'We're not beaten yet.'

'I think I am.'

'Oh no you're not.'

'Oh yes I am.'

'You're not,' said John. 'And neither am I. There must be some way for us to get our hands on all that money. If it wasn't for Fred—'

'We could kill Fred,' said Jim.

'Kill Fred?' Omally shook his head.

'Well, it's not as if we wouldn't be doing the world a favour. He is in league with the Devil, after all.'

'So we should kill him?'

Jim shook *his* head, then lowered it dismally. 'No, of course not. But if he wasn't in charge of all the Millennium money, maybe then we could get a share of it.'

'There's wisdom in your words, Jim Pooley. Perhaps there might be some way to oust Fred and get someone favourable to our cause into his position. Me, for instance.'

'Or perhaps we should just forget the whole damn' thing. Put it down to experience, go off about our business.'

'And what business would that be?'

Jim made grumbling sounds. 'I shall continue with my time travelling. I'll get forward eventually. And when I do . . .'

Omally now sighed, something he rarely did. 'There's a fortune to be made in this millennial celebrating and we are the ones who should be making it.'

'No.' Jim shook his head once more. 'I've had enough, John. We nearly got killed yesterday. And we nearly got killed the day before. And we nearly got killed the day before that. Today no one has tried to kill us. Tomorrow, I hope, will be even better. I'm quitting, John. I've had it. Honestly.'

'Come on, man.'

'No, John, I quit. No more mad schemes. No more risks to life and limb and sanity. I'm going home to bed. I may well remain there for a number of days. If not for ever.'

'Jim, this is a temporary setback, nothing more.'

'I'm sorry, John.' Jim climbed wearily to his feet. 'Enough is enough. Goodbye.'

'No, Jim. You can't go like this, you can't.'

'Look, John, if I call it quits now, at least I can survive this day unscathed. I mean, what else could possibly happen?'

And so saying, Jim turned dismally away, slipped upon the loose soil and fell heavily into the hole.

21

Summer was coming to an end, and with it Jim's stay in the Cottage Hospital. He was out of traction now and the plaster casts were off. There was still considerable stiffness, but he could walk all right with the aid of a stick.

Jim had not spent his time in idleness though. He had written a book. *The Brentford Scrolls: My Part in Their Discovery*.

Well, it had started out with that title anyway. But Jim had favoured later excesses, *Raiders of the Lost Scrolls, Scrollrunner*, and finally, for no apparent reason, other than it sounded good, *The Brentford Chainstore Massacre*.

Although purporting to be a strictly factual auto-biographical account, few who knew Jim personally would have recognized the lantern-jawed, hard-bitten, Dimac-fighting sex machine hero with the devastating wit and the taste for fine wines and pussy-magnet Porsches.

Jim had sent off copies to several major publishers, but was still awaiting replies. He had not sent a copy to Transglobe.

He had quite given up on the time travelling, even though he'd had plenty of time to perfect it. He could only go back. And back didn't seem to be a joyful place to go.

During Jim's months of hospital incarceration, John had made many visits, and Jim had been forced to listen to the Irishman's vivid accounts of great fund-raising ventures. Of whist drives and raffles and pub quiz competitions, of wet T-shirt contests (there seemed to have been many of these) and of guided tours and sponsorship deals. But the millions were as far away as ever, as were too the thousands and the hundreds.

'I have so many expenses,' John told him.

Jim plodded homeward on his stick. The trees in the Memorial Park were taking on their autumn hues, and Autumn Hughes the gardener was sweeping up some leaves. The sun was sinking low now and the air had a bit of a nip to it. Thoughts of a nip turned Jim's thoughts to the Swan. And the optimist in him put what spring it could into his plod.

When Jim reached the Swan, however, the optimist went back to sleep.

A large neon cross blinked on and off and the sign of the Flying Swan no longer swung. The Road to Calvary, spelled out in coloured lights, flashed red, then amber, green, then red again.

Jim offered up a prayer, hung down his head and plodded on.

He settled himself onto the new bench before the Memorial Library. But the new bench, being built entirely from concrete, was uncomfortable. Jim offered up another prayer, hung his head lower still and plodded home.

He turned the familiar key in the familiar lock and sought sanctuary. There were no letters of acceptance from publishers to greet him on the mat; the house smelled damp and dead. Jim sighed. The optimist in him was now in coma.

Jim closed the door and put on the safety chain. A lesser man than he might well have plugged up the gaps and turned on the gas at a time like this, but not Jim. Jim had no change for the meter.

He was just about to turn from the door when he heard the first click. It wasn't loud but, as all else was silent, it was loud enough.

The second click was louder. It was a very distinctive click, the sort of click which, had it been able to speak instead of just click, would have said, 'I am the click made by a gun being cocked.'

And then there was the third click, very loud indeed.

And then the bright, bright light.

Jim pressed back against the door. 'My dear God, no,' he cried.

And then came the noise.

A screaming, shouting, yelling noise.

'Surprise!' screamed Celia Penn.

'Welcome home!' shouted John Omally.

'Happy homecoming!' yelled Norman Hartnell.

Jim stood and stared as the hall about him filled. Professor Slocombe was there, and Old Pete and Small Dave and three young women from the windscreen wiper works (one of whom Jim had always fancied) and Sandra the shot-putting lesbian uniped. And there was the lady in the straw hat and her friend Doris and the medical student named Paul who knew all about the blues. And there was someone else and someone else and even someone else. But these folk were still in the kitchen as you really couldn't get that many people into Jim's hall. Mind you, you could never have got nearly fifty people into Profesor Slocombe's study, but as that seemed to have slipped by unnoticed we'll say no more about it.

'Hip hip hoorah!' went those in the hall. And those in the kitchen. And others still in the front room. The couple making love in Jim's bed would probably say it later.

'Welcome home, old friend,' said John Omally, wringing Jim's hand between his own.

Jim tried to speak, but he just couldn't. There was a big lump in his throat and a tear in each of his eyes.

'For he's a jolly good fellow,' sang the assembled multitude, as John led Jim towards the kitchen and a drink.

Now, as we all know, there are parties, and then there are PARTIES!

At parties, you stand around sipping sherry and making polite conversation with doctors and dentists and architects and women with severe haircuts and halitosis. But at PARTIES! – at PARTIES! you do things differently.

At PARTIES! there is a fight in the front garden,

245

someone being sick in the wardrobe, a couple making love in the host's bed (you see, Jim's had already got off to a good start). There's a bloke who climbs onto the roof and moons at the moon, there's another so well and truly out of it that he tries to tunnel under the garden fence, convinced he's escaping from a prison camp. There are discussions about seemingly ordinary matters that turn into great Zen mind-boggling mystical all-encompassing trips into cosmic infinity, which sadly will never be remembered in the morning. There are ugly women who become tantalizingly beautiful as the night wears on. And ugly men who do not. There is laughter, there is gaiety. There are several visits from the police about turning down the noise. And if you're really lucky there's a woman who takes off all her clothes and dances on the kitchen table. And if you're really, really, really lucky you might just get to meet a blonde choreographer with amber eyes and a fascinating mouth and—

'Nice PARTY, Jim,' said a blonde choreographer with amber eyes and a fascinating mouth.

'Who is *that*?' whispered Jim, as the beauty vanished into the crowd.

'Oh, forget *her*,' said John. 'She's with her uncle Rob.'

'This is some PARTY though, John. Thank you *very* much.'

'Well, I couldn't let you come home to an empty house. Cheers.'

'Cheers.'

The lady with the straw hat said 'Cheers' also, and

then she said, 'That Old Pete bloke is up on your roof mooning at the moon.'

'Magic,' said John. 'Having offended almost everyone on Earth he is now turning his attention to the cosmos.'

'Cheers,' said Jim.

'There's some policemen outside,' said Small Dave. 'They've come about the music.'

'There isn't any music,' said Jim.

'That's what they said, so they've lent us this ghetto-blaster.'

'Magic,' said John, hoisting it onto the unspeakable kitchen worktop and plugging it into the socket.

Howl, shriek and scream.

'It's the Hollow Chocolate Bunnies of Death,' shouted Jim above the cacophony. 'They're beginning to grow on me.'

Professor Slocombe stuck his head round the kitchen door. 'There's some policemen outside,' he shouted. 'They say to turn the noise down.'

'Magic,' said John Omally, turning it down by the merest fraction.

In Jim's back garden, a chap who was well and truly out of it tried to tunnel under the fence. Upstairs someone was being sick into Jim's wardrobe.

'Couldn't you do that somewhere else?' asked the couple who were making love in Jim's bed. It was a different couple.

'You know, John,' said Jim, as John topped up his glass from the dangerous blue vodka bottle, 'you're a good friend to me.'

John consulted his naked wrist. 'It's a bit early in the evening for that kind of talk, isn't it?'

'Yes, you're right. Dare I ask how the fund-raising is going?'

'So-so,' said John, making the so-so gesture.

'Hm,' said Jim. 'Well, cheers anyway.'

And John topped up his glass. 'I think I'll go and see if I can find that blonde choreographer,' he said, turning up the ghetto-blaster.

'Go with God, my friend,' called Jim. And Jim lounged back against his unspeakable worktop, a glass of dangerous blue vodka in his hand, and the Hollow Chocolate Bunnies of Death playing havoc with his inner ears. In the front garden two men fought goodnaturedly and all seemed once more right to Jim with Brentford and the world.

'So God and St Peter are playing golf,' said Old Pete, now down from the roof and in the front room, 'and St Peter's winning. And God takes a swing at the ball and slices it into the rough and this rabbit picks it up in its mouth and races across the fairway, and then out of the sky plunges this eagle and it picks the rabbit up in its talons and soars away into the blue and the next thing this hunter shoots the eagle and the eagle plummets dropping the rabbit and the ball rolls out of the rabbit's mouth and straight into the hole. And St Peter looks at God and says—

' "Do you want to play golf or just fuck about?" '

Two West London Wandering Bishops who had happened by laughed uproariously at this. A woman with a severe haircut and halitosis, who was at the wrong party, said, 'Surely that joke is in very bad taste.'

'Shall I goose her, or will you?' Old Pete asked the bishops.

'Now crop circles,' said Paul the medical student, toking on a joint of Cheech and Chong proportions. 'Crop circles are the stigmata of the Corn God. A visual expression of the agonies of the landscape's Passion, brought on through modern day man's rape of the natural world. Agrichemicals, intensive farming, the land cries out in sorrow and pain. But will anyone listen? Will they?'

'Don't Bogart that joint,' said the lady in the straw hat, snatching it away.

'Anybody here got an acoustic guitar?' asked Paul.

'No!' shouted all within earshot, and those out of earshot also. And Paul was hustled from the party and flung into the street. Acoustic guitar indeed!

'Huh,' said Paul, 'and I can do "Blowing in the Wind" without even looking at my fingers.'

'And *stay* out!'

A well and truly out of it chap ran by shrieking, 'Free, I'm free!'

'Would you like to dance, Jim?' asked the blonde choreographer with the amber eyes and the fascinating mouth.

'Yes I would,' said Jim. 'It's Suzy, isn't it?'

'That's right, but how did you know my name?'

Jim took her most politely in his arms and, as the Hollow Chocolate Bunnies (right on cue) went into a slow and smoochy number, began that slow and dreamy turning round in circles dance that people such as Jim who can't otherwise dance at all always seem to be able to do when holding on to someone really wonderful.

'What were you saying?' asked Jim, who even through the haze of cigarette smoke could smell the beauty's hair.

'I said, how did you know my name?'

'Ah yes. Well, very odd thing. Someone put this hallucinogenic drug onto a council table and I got some on my fingers and started tripping. And I hallucinated you.'

'Was it a good trip, or a bad trip?'

'Oh, a good trip,' said Jim. 'A very good trip.'

'You can hold me a little closer, if you want.'

'Oh. Yes please.'

'You are a very beautiful woman,' said John Omally.

The very ugly woman he was dancing with laughed in a manner that was not unknown to Sid James.

'Now your standard engine,' said Paul, who had crawled back in through a hole beneath Jim's back fence, 'your standard warp-drive engine, functions through the ionization of beta particles creating a positronic catalyst, which bombards the isotope with gamma radiation, giving rise to galvanic variations and the transperambulation of pseudo-cosmic anti-matter.'

'I only asked you what the time was,' said a young

woman from the windscreen wiper works. 'And you start coming out with all this Zen mind-boggling mystical all-encompassing trip into cosmic infinity.'

'That's all right,' said Paul. 'We'll never remember it in the morning.'

'And then I fell into the hole and broke both my legs,' said Jim.

'Incredible,' said Suzy. 'And do you still have the Porsche?'

The Hollow Chocolate Bunnies thrashed back into Death Metal, and two police officers instantly knocked on the front door. 'Turn that bloody noise down,' they said. Upstairs someone else was sick in Jim's wardrobe and yet another couple who were making love told him to do it elsewhere.

'You are a very beautiful woman,' said John Omally.

'Leave it out,' said Old Pete.

22

By three o'clock in the morning the PARTY began to thin. But this *was* three o'clock in the morning of the PARTY's second day, so no one felt too embarrassed about that.

Paul strummed upon an acoustic guitar, but it *was* after three in the morning and he *was* strumming the blues (in A minor), so that *was* permissible.

Professor Slocombe had long said his goodbyes and left with two of the young women from the windscreen wiper works. These would later know such exquisite pleasure as to leave them smiling for a week.

Old Pete was asleep in the shed. And the lady in the straw hat was asleep on the sofa with Suzy's uncle Rob.

Suzy and Jim were nowhere to be seen.

John Omally awoke in Jim's bed to find himself gazing into a face that looked like a bag of spanners. 'Oh dear,' said John. 'Oh dear, oh dear.'

Suzy and Jim sat upon the canal bridge staring down into the moonlit waters.

'You could have made love to me, you know,' said Suzy.

'I know,' said Jim. 'But actually I couldn't. I never can the first time and often not even the second or the third. It puts a lot of women off. But it's the way I am. Too emotional, I suppose.'

'You're a good man, Jim. I like you very much.'

'And you're a very beautiful woman.'

Suzy flicked a pebble into the canal waters. 'What do you want to do with your life, Jim?' she asked.

'Just experience it, I suppose. When I was young I promised myself that I would experience everything I could. Travel the world, see exotic places, take it all in. As much as I could, before time ran out.'

'So, what stopped you?'

'What stops any of us? Habit, I suppose. You get into habits. They're hard to break away from. But what about you? What do you want to do with your life?'

'Something wonderful,' said Suzy. 'I think something wonderful is about to happen. I can feel it in the air. Can't you?'

Jim put his arm about the beautiful woman's shoulder and gazed into the stunning amber eyes. 'Yes,' he said. 'Oh yes, I can.'

The sun rose slowly from behind the windscreen wiper works and two young women crossed the bridge. Both were smiling broadly.

Jim took Suzy in his arms and kissed her fascinating mouth. 'I hope I'll see you again,' he said.

'You will,' said Suzy.

John and Jim munched upon egg and bacon at the Plume Café.

'I thought I might find you here,' said John, thrusting buttered toast into his mouth. 'There's no food left at your place.'

'You look a little, how shall I put this, shagged out, John.'

'I barely escaped with my life. If the woman hadn't tripped over this bloke who was being sick in your wardrobe, I don't think I would have made it.'

'I suppose a wardrobe full of vomit is not too high a price to pay.'

'Someone set fire to your shed. Old Pete, I think.'

'It was only a shed.'

'Sorry about the front windows. The lady in the straw hat woke up and threw Paul out through them. Something to do with key changes, I believe.'

'Windows can be replaced.'

'A cruise missile then demolished the entire house.'

'Such is life,' said Jim.

'Jim, you're not really paying attention to me, are you?'

'Yes I am.'

'No you're not. You've gone all vacant.'

'No I haven't.'

'Then why are you stirring your tea with your toast? And you're glowing, Jim. You have a definite glow on. You're not—'

'I am,' said Jim. 'I'm in love.'

'No, no, no.' John shook his head fiercely. 'You don't want to be in love. You really don't.'

'I do, John. I really do.'

'No, trust me, you don't. Love is . . . well, love is – love is marriage, Jim, marriage and babies and a mortgage and not going out with your mates and having Sunday lunch at home instead of the pub and it's mowing the lawn, Jim, and cleaning the car and having respectable friends round for dinner parties and—'

'Turn it up, mate,' said a married man at the next table. 'We all know what it's like, don't rub it in.'

'Marriage doesn't have to be like that,' said Jim. 'Not if you're married to your best friend.'

'I'm not marrying you, Jim.'

'No,' said Jim. 'You're not.'

'But I'm your best friend.'

'*I* used to have a best friend,' said the married man wistfully. 'My wife soon put a stop to that.'

'Listen to him, Jim. The man knows what he's talking about.'

'John, I'm in love. I can't help it. I don't have any control over it. I've fallen in love.'

'No.' John shook his head once more. 'No, Jim, no, Jim, no.'

'I'm sorry, John, but there it is.'

'Another best friend gone,' said the married man. 'What a tragedy.'

'Quite right,' said John. 'Listen to this poor wretch, Jim. You don't want to end up like him.'

'Steady on,' said the poor wretch.

'Ground down, henpecked, under the thumb.'

'I said steady on!'

'A shadow of his former self, doomed to hoovering and babysitting, while the wife goes out to her story circle and—'

'I said steady on and I meant it.'

'See that? Hair-trigger temper, brought on by too many nights of walking the baby up and down while his wife snores away in her hairnet.'

'Right, that does it.' The married man had possibly been quite an accurate puncher in his youth, before he got all ground down and henpecked and under the thumb. He took a mighty swing at John.

And he hit Jim right on the nose.

Jim went down amidst tumbling crockery, two eggs, bacon, sausage, a fried slice and half a cup of tea with a bit of toast in it.

'Fight!' shouted the lady in the straw hat, who was just coming in.

John brought down the married man, but also two of his colleagues. These were unmarried men and still quite useful with their fists. They set about John with a vim and vigour most unexpected for that time of day.

Jim struggled to his feet and leapt into the fray to aid the man who was still his best friend. Further tables were overturned and others joined in the mêlée.

Lily Marlene, who ran the Plume, issued from the kitchen, her mighty mammaries sailing before her. As a married woman she knew exactly how to deal with men. She laid about her with a wok spoon.

'This is the kind of stuff I like,' said the lady in the straw hat, seating herself at a respectable distance from the fighting. 'I've just come from this PARTY. It was pretty crap until the stove blew up.'

'My stove blew up?' Jim raised his head from the fighting.

'Your mate there did it. Said he knew this trick with an unopened can of beans.'

'What?' But Jim got hit by an unmarried man and went down again.

'What exactly are they fighting about?' the lady asked Lily Marlene.

'Marriage,' said Lily.

'Bastards!' said the lady, taking off her hat and wading in.

The police got there in remarkably good time. They were just passing by, as it happened, on their way to investigate a report of an explosion that had blown a kitchen wall down. They whipped out the electric truncheons and did what had to be done.

'That does it,' said Jim. 'That absolutely and utterly does it.'

'What does it do?' John asked.

Jim made a very bitter face. 'Just tell me where we are,' he said.

'We're in a police cell,' said John. 'But look on the bright side.'

'There isn't any bright side. And look at me. Look at me.'

'You'll heal. It's not too bad.'

'I've got a black eye and a fat lip and—'

'Don't go on about it. I'm hurt too.'

'There's not a mark on you.'

'I'm hurting inside.'

'You lying bastard.'

'Language,' said John.

'Don't you language me. This is all your fault.'

'It's not my fault. You started it with all your talk about falling in love.'

'I never did. You wound up that married bloke.'

'And that's just how you would have ended up. You've learned a summary lesson there, Jim. You should thank me for it.'

'What? *What?*'

'Love and marriage, they're all very well for some people. Ordinary people. But not for the likes of us.'

'But we are ordinary people, John.'

'We are not. We are John and Jim. We are individuals.'

'I've had enough,' said Jim. 'If I hadn't had enough before, then I have certainly had enough now. This is the end, John. Our partnership is dissolved. Our friendship is dissolved. When we get out of here I never, ever, want to see you again.'

'Come off it, Jim. Don't say such things.'

'You blew my kitchen up.'

'I was just trying to make breakfast. You didn't have a tin opener.'

'That is quite absurd.'

'Yes, sorry, I know. It was a bit of a laugh.'

'It's all a bit of a laugh to you, John. Everything. Do it for the crack, eh? Let's go for it, Jim. Well, I've had enough. I quit.'

'You're just a tad overwrought.'

Jim raised his fist and shook it. 'John, I am in love, and I do not need you any more.'

There was a terrible silence.

'You don't mean that,' said John. 'You can't.'

'I do. And I can.'

'She's married,' said John.

'What? Who?'

'Suzy. She's married.'

'She never is. You're lying.'

'I'm not, Jim. That uncle Rob isn't her uncle. He's her husband.'

'But she called him uncle Rob.'

'It's some kind of pet name. Married people do that.'

'People in love do that,' said Jim and he sat down upon the bunk beside John.

'I'm sorry,' said John. 'But there it is.'

'It's *not*.' Jim jumped up. 'You're lying, John. I can hear it in your voice.'

'All right, Jim, yes, I'm lying. But I'm lying to save our friendship.'

'That was a low-down filthy rotten trick.'

'Desperate men do desperate things.'

Jim sat down upon the bed once more. 'I'm desperately in love,' he said.

'I know. And I won't stand in the way. But we will stay friends, won't we? Best friends?'

'Yeah,' said Jim, extending his hand. 'Put it there.'

'Yeah,' said Jim, extending his hand. 'Put it there.'

John put it there.

With his free hand Jim hit him right in the mouth. 'That's for blowing up my kitchen and lying to me,' he said.

23

'One hundred hours of community service!' Jim threw up his arms. '*One hundred hours!* And what is *community service* anyway?'

'Just what it says, serving the community.'

'And how come you only got fifty hours?'

'I plea-bargained.'

'What is *that*?'

'I haven't the faintest idea. But it seemed to work.'

'Work.' Jim made a gloomy face. 'Work.'

'It's not like real work.' John unfolded a piece of paper and spread it over his knees. They were sitting on the concrete bench before the library. It was no more comfortable than before. Autumn now, and cold it was, the nights were drawing in. 'Here's the roster,' said John. 'Ah, there, you see. A little dig and dab.'

'Dig and dab?'

'Yes. You have to dig over Old Pete's allotment then redecorate his house.'

'What?'

'A piece of cake. Good exercise for you, restore you to full vigour.'

'I'm supposed to be convalescing. And what's on the roster for you?'

'Hard graft, I'm afraid.'

'Give me that piece of paper.' Jim snatched it away. 'Dog walking!' he shouted. 'You got *dog walking!*'

'It's Old Pete's dog. A regular hound of the Baskervilles.'

'It's a half-terrier.'

'And half-wolf.'

'It's all too much. It's all too *very* much.'

'I blame you,' said John. 'You took your eye off the ball.'

'Oh yes, and what ball was this?'

'The ball that would have scored the winning goal. The Millennium Fund money, you remember.'

'That's all history. Look around you, John. What do you see?'

'The noble town of Brentford.'

'A sleeping suburb. Do you see any banners and balloons? Any bunting? Any written proclamations announcing the forthcoming festivities nailed to the lamp posts? Does this look to you like a town bursting with excitement at the prospect of celebrating the millennium two years early?'

'No,' said John. 'But then it wouldn't. It was all as the Professor predicted. Fred made great congratulatory displays, then inundated the mayor with so much paperwork that he couldn't get into his own office. The story was quietly gagged in the press, turning up only on the occasional quirky TV show as a comical aside that made us all look like a pack of twats.'

'That's real life for you,' said Jim.

'Listen,' said John. 'I have raised a small amount of capital. I've gone into partnership with Norman and we've rented a building down near the old docks. The Millennial Brewery is still a goer.'

'The *John Omally* Millennial Brewery.'

'Actually it's the *Norman Hartnell* Millennial Brewery. But you can come in on that with us. There's money to be made. There's always big money in beer.'

Jim shrugged. 'I suppose to be a director of a brewery would have a certain cachet.'

'Ah,' said John. 'Well, we don't actually have any vacancies for directors.'

'What then?'

'Porters we need. You could work your way up.'

'I'm going home.' Jim rose to do so. And then he sat down again.

'Are you OK?' John asked.

'I think so. I just got this odd shivery sensation.'

'You probably do need a bit more convalescence.'

'No, it's *them*.' Jim pointed.

Across the road were two boys. They looked to be about ten years of age. One had a golden look to him, the other was all over dark. They stood together silently and stared at John and Jim.

'Oh, them,' said John. 'Damien and the Midwich Cuckoo.'

'Who?'

'Nobody seems to know who they are. They

263

wander about the borough staring at people. It fair puts the wind up you, doesn't it?'

'Don't they go to school?'

'Why don't you go over and ask them?'

'OK.' Jim rose to do so. 'Oh, they've gone. I never saw them go.'

'No one ever does.'

'Well, you can watch me go. Because that is exactly what I'm going to do.'

'How about coming for a beer instead?'

'What, at the Road to Calvary? I don't think so.'

John gave his head a scratch. 'That is something that I'll have to deal with. Neville is not a happy man.'

'I'll bet he's not.'

'He has to wear a costume now, robes and a false beard.'

'That's something I'd like to see.'

'Oh no you wouldn't.'

'Tell you what,' said Jim. 'Let's go round there now. I'm meeting Suzy at eight, we're going for an Indian. But in the meantime why don't you and I apply ourselves to a *really* worthy cause? To restore the Swan to its former glory and re-establish ourselves on the drinking side of the bar.'

'Put it there,' said John, extending his hand.

And Jim put it there.

'So,' said Old Pete. 'There are these two sperms swimming along and one says, "Are we at the fallopian tubes yet?" and the other says, "No, we're hardly past the tonsils." ' Old Pete raised his glass, but no one laughed.

'Fair enough,' said Old Pete. 'So who's going to say it, then?'

'Say what?' asked Celia Penn.

'Say surely that is a somewhat misogynist joke, or something.'

'Not me,' said Celia Penn. 'It's just that I've heard it before.'

'Oh,' said Old Pete.

'A one-legged Lesbian shot-putter told it to me last week.'

'Oh.'

'I heard it from an Irishman,' said Norman.

'An Eskimo told me it,' said a lady in a straw hat.

'A rabbi,' said Paul the medical student.

'I heard it through the grapevine,' said Marvin Gaye.

'God told *me*,' said David Icke.

John and Jim now entered the Road to Calvary.

'Aaaaaagh!' cried the assembled multitude, catching sight of them. 'Out Demons out! Out Demons out!'

Neville rose from behind the bar counter. And yes, he *was* wearing the robes, and yes he *did* have the false beard. And, my oh my, didn't he look like Moses, and, my oh my, didn't he look mad.

'Judas!' cried Neville. 'The Judas twins, no less. Slay the evildoers who have brought woe unto the house of Neville.'

'Hold it, hold it.' John put up his hands. 'We are

265

here to help. Jim and I have come to save the situation. To restore the Swan to—'

'And there shall be a weeping and a wailing and a gnashing of teeth.' Neville reached for his knob-kerrie. 'And fire shall rain down from the heavens and smite the tribes of Pooley and Omally and even their children and their children's children. For they that fuck with the house of Neville, verily they shall all get the red-hot poker up the bum.'

'Now I know you're upset,' said John.

'Spawn of the pit!' Neville raised his knobkerrie. 'Foul issue of the Antichrist!'

'Very upset,' said Jim.

'Burn the heretics,' shouted Old Pete.

'Now you keep out of this,' John warned him.

Neville climbed onto the bar counter. With the robes and the beard and the knobkerrie and every-thing, he looked mightily impressive. 'This day shall be known as the Day of Retribution,' he roared.

'Just calm down.' John made calming gestures. 'Things are never as bad as they seem.'

'*Never as bad?*' Neville flung wide his arms. 'Look at my pub. Just look at my pub.'

John cast a wary eye about the place. The Swan had been converted. Where once had stood the Britannia pub tables and the comfy chairs, now there was a row of pews. The dominoes table too was gone, replaced by a font with a little fountain rising from it. The walls, so long the haunt of mellowed sporting prints, were presently festooned with portraits of saints, garish plastic Virgin Marys that lit up from the inside, fake icons with holographic images, and neon crosses flashing on and off.

And from the ceiling hung plaster cherubim and seraphim, fat-bummed and grinning, holding little bows and arrows, fluttering their tiny wings.

And here and there and all around stood statues, garishly painted theatrical prop statues, of Tobias and the Angel, St Francis of Assisi, Matthew, Mark and Eric Cantona. *Eric Cantona?*

John Omally crossed himself.

'You piss-taking bastard.' Neville made to leap from the counter.

'No,' said John. 'No really, this is dire. We'll get it fixed, we really will.'

'Liar and hypocrite!'

'No, I mean it.'

'Oh yes?' Neville's voice rose by an octave. '*Oh yes?* Don't think I haven't heard about your evil schemes to ruin me further. The John Omally Millennial Brewery and the Jim Pooley.'

'Ah,' said John.

'I think we should be off,' said Jim. 'Before the, you know, flagellating and the nailing up.'

'And the burning at the stake,' said Old Pete.

'Why are you dressed as a Buddhist monk?' Omally asked. 'And wearing a mitre?'

'Just trying to fit in.'

'By Baal!' cried Neville. 'By Belial and—'

'I suppose it must make it worse, him being a pagan and everything,' Jim whispered. But nobody heard him.

'Ye Great Old Ones. Ye Deathless Sleepers.'

Omally pushed his way through the congregation and squared up beneath the ranting Neville.

'Stop it!' he shouted. 'I will fix it for you. I promise. Cross my heart and . . . no, forget that. I give you my word.'

'Oaths are but words, and words but wind,' said the lady in the straw hat. 'Claude Butler said that.'

'*Samuel* Butler,' said Paul. 'He was an English satirist, 1612 to 1680, born in—'

'Stop that!' John Omally raised his fist.

'John,' called Jim from the door. 'John, I'm leaving now. I may not be able to foresee the future, but I know just what's coming next and I have no wish to endure another thrashing.'

'No one is going to get thrashed, Jim.'

'Shame,' said the lady in the straw hat.

Neville opened his mouth to issue curses.

'Stop!' John put up his hands. 'Stop all this *now*. Neville, I promise to sort it out. I promise to have the Swan restored to its former glory. I will swear upon anything you wish. I promise, Neville. I promise.'

'Did you hear that?' asked Neville, gazing around.

'We did. We did.' The patrons' heads bobbed up and down. Old Pete's mitre fell onto the floor and his dog did a whoopsy on it.

'Right,' said Neville. 'I give you until the end of the week, Omally.'

'The end of the week? That's impossible.'

'Bring in the wicker man!'

'No, all right. The end of the week. Whatever you say.'

'Swear it, Omally. Shout it loud for all to hear.'

'I'll get it all sorted by the end of the week,' shouted John. 'I swear upon all that is holy.'

'Fine,' said Neville, climbing down. 'Pint of the usual, is it?'

'You've got a bloody nose,' said Suzy. 'Did someone hit you again?'

'No.' Jim managed half a sniff. 'I was just going up to the bar for a drink when I slipped on this bishop's mitre that was covered in poo.'

Suzy put a finger to his lips. 'You do take a terrible hammering,' she said.

Pooley kissed her fingers. 'I'd like to feel that there's some purpose behind all my suffering, but I'm quite sure there's not.'

They sat in Archie Karachi's Star of Bombay Curry Garden (and Tasty-chip Patio), sipping Kingfisher lager and taking tastes from bowls of Kashmiri rogan josh, Rasedar shaljum, Kutchi bhindi, and French-fried potatoes.

'So, are you going into the brewery trade?' Suzy asked.

'No I am not. I'm going to help Omally sort out the Swan for Neville. Do my community service. Then I'm going to seek proper employment, and then I hope to ask you something.'

'What kind of something?'

'Something I can't ask you now. Not until I've got myself sorted out.'

'Don't sort yourself out for me, Jim. I like you just the way you are.'

'But I'm a loser and I'm fed up with it.'

'You are an individual.'

'That word is beginning to grate on my nerves.'

'Oh, I'm sorry.'

'No, I didn't mean you. Here, have another chip.' Jim fumbled with the bowl. 'I can't even eat properly when I'm with you.'

'Nor me. It's good, isn't it?'

'Yes, it's very good.'

'Bad,' said Dr Steven Malone. 'Very bad boys.'

The two boys looked up at him. One golden, one dark, but otherwise so very much alike. They stood in a downstairs room of that house in Moby Dick Terrace. The house where the old couple had died of natural causes.

'You mustn't keep wandering off,' the bad doctor told them. 'You might get yourselves lost.'

'We cannot get lost, father,' said the golden child, gazing up with his glittering eyes. 'We remember everything, every moment, everything.'

Dr Steven smiled a twisted smile. 'Digital memory,' he said, 'total recall with absolute accuracy. And what about you?' he asked the dark one.

'I forget nothing,' the dark one replied.

'That's good.'

'Father,' said the golden child. 'You said you would choose names for us today.'

'And when did I say that?'

'Precisely one hundred and twenty-three minutes ago.'

'Very good. And so I have. You', he pointed to the golden child, 'will henceforth be known as Cain. And you', he pointed to the other, 'Abel.'

'As in the Bible,' said Cain. 'Genesis chapter four, verse one.'

'Bible?' Dr Steven's face, already ashen, grew more ashen still. 'What do you know about the Bible?'

'All,' said Abel. 'We go to the library and read the books.'

'We are hungry to learn, father. Everything there is to be learned.'

'I will teach you all you need to know. Stay away from the library. Do not go there again, or—'

'You will punish us,' said Cain. 'Lock us away once more in the dark place.'

'I like the dark place,' said Abel.

'Do not defy me.' Dr Steven rocked upon his heels. 'You are too precious to my purpose.'

'And what is your purpose?'

'My purpose, Cain, is my own affair. But by the end of this year all will be made known.'

'Given our unnaturally accelerated growth-rate,' said Abel, 'by the end of this year we will be the equivalent of thirty-three normal years of age.'

'Precisely correct. And then I will do what has to be done. And then I shall know all.'

'No man can know all,' said Cain. 'Only God knows all.'

'Go to your room.' Dr Steven turned in profile, something he hadn't done for a while, and pointed off the page. 'No, wait. You, Abel, go to your room and switch on all the lights. You, Cain, go once more to the dark place.'

Bastard!

24

'Two gentlemen to see you sir,' said Young Master Robert's secretary. 'A Mr Pooley and a Mr Omally.'

Young Master Robert fell back in his highly cushioned chair. 'Not those bastards. Don't let them in here.'

'Morning, Bobby boy,' said John Omally, breezing in.

'Wotcha, mate,' said Jim. 'Nice office.'

John Omally gazed about the place. 'A regular fine art gallery,' he observed.

'Or a shrine,' said Jim. 'It all being dedicated to a single young woman.'

'Get out of my office or I'll call for security.'

'This one's signed,' said Jim, pointing to a poster. '*To my greatest fan, love Pammy.*'

'And look at this bookcase,' said John. 'He's got the complete collection of *Bay Watch* on video.'

'What are all these boxes of Kleenex for?' Jim asked.

'*Get out!*'

'Relax.' John made the gesture that means relax. It's not quite the same as the calming gesture, but there's not much in it. 'Relax and take it easy. We've come here to make you rich.'

'I'm already rich.'

'Richer, then.'

'What's that sticking out from under your desk?' asked Jim. 'It looks like a plastic foot.'

John took a peep over. 'It's an inflatable Pammy,' he said.

'Call security!' cried Young Master Robert. 'Call that new bloke Joe-Bob, tell him to bring the electric truncheon.'

'Calm down,' said John, and he made the calming gesture this time. 'We really have come to make you richer.'

'As if you have.'

'We just want you to sample something.'

'Sample?'

'Jim, the bottle and the glass.'

'Coming right up.' Jim produced a bottle and a glass from his pockets, placed the glass upon the Young Master's desk, uncorked the bottle and poured.

'Sample,' said John.

'Yes I bet it is. Your wee-wee, probably.'

'It is ale. Just take a taste. Spit it out if you want. Over me if you want.'

'Over you?'

'That's how confident I am.'

'No, it's all a trick. Ms Anderson, call security.'

'Ms Anderson?'

'He made me change my name,' said the secretary. 'And I have to wear this padded bra.'

'Suits you,' said Jim. 'But I don't know about the wig.'

'Just taste the ale,' said John. 'Here, I'll have a little taste first, to prove it's not poison.' John took a taste. And then he took another taste and then another taste. 'Magic,' said John.

'You've drunk it all,' said Young Master Robert.

'Jim, the other bottle.'

Jim took out the other bottle, uncorked it and refilled the glass.

'Trick,' said Young Master Robert. 'The second bottle's poisoned.'

'Oh dear me.' John took up the glass once more.

'No, all right, I believe you.' Young Master Robert took the glass, sniffed at it suspiciously, then took a taste. And then he took another taste, and then another taste.

'Yes?' said John.

'Well, it's all right. It's OK, I mean.'

John Omally shook his head. 'It's magic,' he said. 'That's what you mean. It's the finest ale you've ever tasted in your life.'

'It's fair to middling.'

John Omally shrugged. 'Well, Jim,' he said. 'I suppose I lose the bet.'

'What bet?' said Young Master Robert.

'Jim bet me that the master brewer in Chiswick was a better judge of beer than you were. Naturally I defended your honour. It looks like it's cost me a fiver.'

'You took this beer to the rival brewery?'

'Chap called Doveston. He's won several awards. Certainly knows his beverages.'

'The man's a buffoon. Fizzy drinks merchant.' Young Master Robert tasted the last of the ale. 'It's pretty good,' he said.

'Pretty good?' John laughed. 'Mr Doveston was quite ecstatic in his praise of it. Heaping eulogies upon every savoured gobful. What was that song he sang for us, Jim?'

'Wasn't it "Money Makes the World Go Around"?'

'Yes, that was it.'

'It's *very* good,' said Young Master Robert. 'Do you have any more?'

'Crates,' said John.

'And you brewed it?'

'A colleague and I.'

'This bloke?'

'Another colleague,' said John.

'Well, I'll have to get this analysed. Make sure there are no impure chemicals.'

John snatched back the glass and bottle. 'Oh no you don't. The only way you will get it analysed is by pumping it out of your stomach.'

'I wouldn't mind doing that,' said Ms Anderson. 'In an anal-ized fashion.'

'Do you have a sister called Celia?' Jim asked.

'Well, we must be off,' said John. 'I'm sorry we couldn't do business with you.'

'Not so fast,' said Young Master Robert.

★   ★   ★

'You certainly think fast, John,' said Jim, as they sat once more upon the concrete bench before the library. 'A ten-thousand-pound advance. Incredible.'

'Not bad, is it?' John waved the cheque in the air. 'I'll have to open a bank account.'

'And on condition that he restore the Swan to its former glory by the end of the week. Genius.'

'We function best under pressure, Jim. I've always found that.'

'Making him cough up the fiver you supposedly lost to me in the bet was rubbing it in a bit.'

'Yeah, but he didn't complain.'

'So hand it over, then.'

'What?'

'The fiver. I won it fair and square.'

'You never did. We never went to the rival brewer.'

'But *he* doesn't know that.'

John handed over the fiver. 'Petty,' said he.

Jim pocketed the fiver. 'I hope Norman will be happy with the advance. Did you agree the figure with him?'

'Ah,' said John.

'I like not "Ah",' said Jim. 'What does "Ah" mean?'

'It means I haven't actually got round to talking to Norman about this yet.'

'What?'

'There wasn't time. The idea came to me over breakfast. So I just went for it.'

'Same old story.' Jim shook his head. 'Omally rushes in where angels fear to tread.'

'Just leave Norman to me,' said John. 'Norman will be fine.'

Norman didn't look fine. He had a worried expression on his face. As Omally breezed into his shop, he offered him a grunt.

'Thanks,' said Omally. 'I'll smoke it later.'

'Look at my sweeties,' said Norman.

Omally looked. The jars were bright with sweeties. All the Fifties favourites. Humbugs and jujubes. Liquorice pipes and sherbet lemons, Bright Devils and Waverley's Assorteds. Space Rockets and Google's Gob Gums.

Omally tapped the nearest jar. 'They look a bit, well, guggy,' he said.

'Very guggy.' Norman took up the jar and turned it upside down. A kind of blobby mass oozed towards the lid. 'Entropy,' he said.

'What's this?'

'They don't last,' said Norman. 'It's been like this for months. But I didn't like to mention it to you. I thought I could iron out the problem.'

'The sweeties don't last?'

'A couple of weeks,' said Norman. 'Then I have to throw them away, clean out the jars and make another batch.'

'Rotten luck,' said John. 'It's a good job it isn't like this with the ale.'

Norman glanced up from the sweetie jar. 'It's far worse with the ale,' said he.

★   ★   ★

'*What?*' Jim glanced up from his pint of Large. 'He said *what?*'

'Highly volatile,' said John. 'Like nitroglycerine, the slightest tap and it explodes.'

'*What?*' Jim huffed and puffed. 'I had a bottle in each of my trouser pockets. I could have blown my—'

'It was a fresh batch; you weren't in any danger. It has to be two weeks old before it—'

'*Nitro-bloody-glycerine!*'

'Not so loud.' Omally ssshed him into silence. 'We don't want Neville to hear.'

'No we don't,' said Jim. 'But I can't believe it. Everything was sorted. And all so quickly too.'

'Yes, I've been thinking about that. And I've come to the conclusion that every time we sort something quickly, it ends up like Norman's sweeties.'

'It's probably some cosmic law,' said Jim. 'But look on the bright side.'

'What bright side is this?'

'Well, at least you didn't pop in here and tell Neville you'd sorted everything out before you popped into Norman's and discovered that you hadn't.'

A new blonde waitress appeared at the table with a tray. On it were two pints of Large. 'Courtesy of the management,' she said.

John Omally looked at Jim.

And Jim looked back at John.

'You stupid twat,' said Jim.

*   *   *

'There has to be a solution.' John drummed his fingers on the pew end. 'There just has to be.'

They were several pints in credit now and Neville kept on smiling and giving them the old thumbs-up.

'The solution is as plain as a parson's nose,' said Jim. 'You'll have to return the cheque, tell Neville the truth and emigrate to Tierra del Fuego.'

'I don't call that much of a solution.'

'It's the only one I have.'

'Look,' said Omally. 'I have a cheque for ten thousand pounds in my pocket. *Ten thousand*, Jim. We must be able to do something with that.'

'You got it under false pretences. Do you prefer prison to Tierra del Fuego?'

'You would hate Tierra del Fuego, Jim.'

'I'm not coming with you.'

'We're in this together, we shook hands on it.'

'There has to be a solution,' said Jim, drumming his fingers on the other end of the pew.

'Progress report,' said Fred, drumming his fingers on Clive's head. 'What, if any, progress do you have to report?'

'Happily none, sir.' Clive edged out of drumming range. 'We did a pretty thorough job on the media. No one's taking Brentford's claims seriously. You've effectively stymied the mayor with all the paperwork and the louts are just blundering about.'

'Tell me about the lout who found the scrolls.'

'He spent nearly two months in the Cottage Hospital and while he was there we put an implant into his head. Just to keep track of him. He's no

threat, he wants nothing more to do with the celebrations.'

'And the Irish lout?'

'No threat, sir. He's a wanker.'

'And what of the Professor?'

'He's preparing himself for the ceremony. He
has gone on a magical retirement. Put himself
into solitude. But he's wasting his time. Unless
thousands join in the celebrations, he won't be able
to raise sufficient power to succeed in the ceremony.'

'Looks like they're all in the shit then, doesn't it?'

'Seems so, sir.'

Fred leaned back in his chair. His desk had a dust
sheet over it. Scaffolding surrounded the desk, men
upon that scaffolding worked to restore Fred's ceiling. These things take a great deal of time.

'Well, just keep me informed,' said Fred. 'In case
something unexpected occurs.'

'Unexpected?' said Clive. 'Whatever could possibly occur that's unexpected?'

'A gentleman said that I was to give this to you,' said
the blonde barmaid, handing Jim an envelope.

'Gentleman?' said Jim.

'Big fat fellow,' said the waitress. 'Spoke with a
posh voice.'

'Thank you.' Jim took the envelope, opened it and
pulled out a small white piece of card.

On it was written, *Come at midnight to my office. You
may bring your companion. This is* very *important*.

Jim turned the card over. It was a business card. A

name and address were printed in elegant script upon it.

The address Jim recognized.

Also the name.

The name was that of Mr Compton-Cummings.

25

'Well,' said Jim. 'What an unexpected occurrence.'

'My surprise exceeds your own,' said John. 'When it comes to unexpected occurrences, this one is truly in a class by itself.'

'Are you taking the piss?' Jim asked.

'Yes. Weren't you?'

Jim nodded, tore up the business card and dropped the pieces into the ashtray. 'Compton-Cummings indeed!' he said. 'Meet me at midnight indeed!' he continued. 'As if there is any way I'm going to fall for *that*!'

'What time is it?' Jim asked.

Omally turned back his shirt cuff and consulted *his* running gag. 'Midnight,' he said.

Jim looked up at the moonlit building. 'There's a light on in his office. What should we do, just knock at the door?'

'That would be the obvious thing, yes. But are you absolutely certain you wouldn't prefer spinning round in circles, flapping your hands, or simply running away to your cosy bed?'

'Are you implying something, John?'

'Oh no. Absolutely not. But would you just care to tell me exactly what we're doing here?'

'We've come to see Mr Compton-Cummings.'

'But Mr Compton-Cummings is dead, Jim.'

'Yes, I know that. I'm not stupid.'

'You don't feel then that the fact that he's dead might make conversation with him a rather one-sided affair?'

'I'm going to knock at the door,' said Jim. 'And find out just what's going on.'

Omally shook his head. 'I don't believe this,' he said. 'I really don't.'

KNOCK KNOCK KNOCK, went Jim. And it really does go KNOCK at midnight. A light came on in the hall. Bolts were drawn and the door opened a crack. The face of Celia Penn looked out. 'I knew you'd come,' she said.

'There you are.' John grinned at Jim. 'Logical explanation. *She* sent the card.'

'I did,' said Celia, ushering them inside and closing the door.

'So what is it?' John asked. 'What's up?'

'Mr Compton-Cummings wants to speak with you.'

'Ah.'

Through the outer office and into the inner. And there he was. Bulging away behind his desk. Mr Compton-Cummings, large as life. Well, larger really. And Professor Slocombe was with him.

'Ah,' said John once more.

'Stone me,' said Jim.

'Gentlemen,' said the larger than life genealogist. 'Welcome. Pray sit yourselves down.'

Jim nodded towards the Professor. 'Hello,' he said.

'It's good to see you, Jim. All the broken bones thoroughly mended?'

'Temporarily.'

'Sit down then.'

Pooley and Omally took their seats by the door. Well, somehow you just would, wouldn't you?

'You're not dead,' Jim observed. 'How do you account for that?'

Mr Compton-Cummings had a bottle of brandy on his desk. He also had five glasses. These he filled. And these he passed around. 'A ruse,' said he. 'A necessary one.'

'You certainly had me convinced.'

'And others, hopefully.'

John sipped his brandy. 'Magic,' he said.

Jim sipped his. 'I hope it goes down well with that champagne Neville gave you.'

'You didn't drink any of yours, Jim.'

'Curiously I didn't feel I deserved it.'

'Gentlemen,' said the Professor. 'Mr Compton-Cummings has much to say to you. Do you feel that you're up to listening?'

'Absolutely,' said John.

Jim made a sound which might have meant yes.

'Good. Mr Compton-Cummings, if you will.'

'Thank you, Professor.' The fat man put down his glass and interlaced his fingers over his ample belly.

285

'Mr Pooley,' he said. 'As you must now be aware, you play a most important role in matters appertaining to Brentford and indeed the rest of the world.'

'Eh?' said Jim.

'When I traced your lineage and discovered the "great wind from the East" passage, I also discovered what it actually meant: that one of your forefathers had murdered the monk and acquired the Brentford Scrolls.'

'Such is sadly the case,' said Jim.

'And as you also know, Ms Penn here encoded the location of the scrolls into my book. And you were sent the only unpulped copy.'

'Yes, but that wasn't how I found them.'

'No, the Professor has told me about the time travelling.'

'He's very good at it,' said John. 'Well, going backwards, anyway.'

'Quite so. But whatever the case, it had to be *you* who found the scrolls. And you did.'

'Why did it have to be me?' Jim asked.

'You are the last of your line.'

'So why does that matter?'

'These things do,' said Mr Compton-Cummings. 'Trust me, they just do.'

'I thought something really clever was coming then,' said John.

'I expect it's being saved for later,' said Jim.

'Do they always do this?' the genealogist asked the Professor.

'They are individuals,' said the ancient.

'Don't start on that.'

'Sorry, Jim.'

'It was necessary for me to fake my own death.' Mr Compton-Cummings tinkered with a Masonic watch fob which had escaped previous mention. 'Certain dark forces, who do not want the millennium celebrated on the correct date, would have snuffed me out.'

'Fred and his crew.'

'Exactly. I had hoped that between you, you would have been able to get things moving along.'

'I fell down a hole,' said Jim.

'And he fell in love,' said John.

'Well, whatever the case, things have *not* been moving along.'

Jim held out his glass for a top-up. Mr Compton-Cummings topped it up. 'I've had enough,' said Jim. 'I'm sick of getting beaten up and arrested and generally misused. All I want is a normal life. A normal *married* life.'

John groaned. 'We've been through that,' he said.

'Yeah, well. You've been through it. And I got beaten up again.'

'Gentlemen, please.' Professor Slocombe held up his hands. 'This is most important.'

'I was quit when I came in here,' said Jim. 'And I'm twice as quit now.'

'One of my favourite movies,' said John.

'Did you know that Ridley Scott used to do Hovis commercials on television?' asked Professor Slocombe.

'Yes,' said John.

'I didn't,' said Jim. 'But I should have.'

'Nevertheless,' said Mr Compton-Cummings, 'things must be made to move along. And you are the men who should do the moving.'

'We can't,' said Jim. 'This Fred bloke is in control. And he's head of the baddies.'

Mr Compton-Cummings leaned back in his chair, but as he filled it so completely anyway the effect was negligible. 'We can deal with Fred,' he said.

'Oh yes?'

'Certainly. Fred will not hand over any money willingly. So he must be made to do it against his will.'

'And how do you propose to do that?'

'I propose that *you* do that.'

'Do the "I was quit" line again, Jim,' said John. 'I'll join you in the last part.'

'No, no, no.' The fat man waggled his fat fingers. 'I'm not expecting you to meet this man head on in some kind of confrontation. There is more than one way to skin a joint.'

'Shouldn't that be cat?' said Jim.

'I think it's *khat*,' said Professor Slocombe.

'Didn't I just say that?'

'I have *this*.' Mr Compton-Cummings held *this* up for all to see.

'Isn't that one of those new miniature LPs?' Jim asked. 'The ones you can supposedly spread strawberry jam over and they still play?'

'It's a computer disc,' said Mr Compton-Cummings. 'With a virus on it.'

'Don't say it,' said John.

'I wasn't going to,' said Jim. 'He means a *computer* virus, I understand that.'

'Well, it's not so much a virus.' Mr Compton-Cummings twiddled his porky digits and turned the twinkling thing in the air. 'It's more of a program. When put into the computer system at the Millennium Committee's offices, it will siphon off huge amounts of money into bank accounts in Brentford and then erase all record of the transactions.'

'I like the sound of that,' said John. 'Whose accounts did you have in mind?'

'Mine,' said Professor Slocombe.

'And mine,' said Mr Compton-Cummings.

'Ah,' said John.

'But,' said the genealogist, 'this money will be made available to you, to do all the things you were planning to do.'

'Magic,' said John, rubbing his hands together.

'No,' said Jim. 'Not magic. There simply isn't enough time. It's September now. Whatever building projects could even be started would never be completed by December.'

'Sadly,' said John, 'Jim does have a point.'

'I'm sad about it too,' said Jim. 'Don't get me wrong.'

'However,' said Professor Slocombe, 'these large amounts of money could be channelled into Brentford. To raise morale, to enthuse, to engender support, to ensure that when New Year's Eve comes round, everyone in the borough will be celebrating. It is absolutely essential to my ceremony that thousands celebrate. A great rush of positive energy is necessary for it to work.'

'I think we could handle that,' said John.

'The John Omally Millennial Fish and Chip Van fleet,' said Jim.

'The Devo concert,' said John.

'I think I prefer the Hollow Chocolate Bunnies of Death, now.'

'Jim,' said John. 'We could get the Spice Girls.'

There was a silence. It kind of hung in the air. The way they do.

'Surely the Spice Girls are this year's Bros,' said Professor Slocombe.

'Trust me,' said John, 'there are certain important differences.'

'Well, get the Spice Girls,' said Mr Compton-Cummings. 'Get the Hollow Chocolate Bunnies, get the Rolling Stones. The sky's the limit.'

'Let's get them all,' said John.

And there was another silence.

This one was broken by Jim Pooley.

'About putting this program into Fred's computer,' he said. 'Wouldn't that be a somewhat hazardous job? I mean I'm not a coward, or anything. Honestly. But, believe me, there is no way on Earth that I am going to get involved in *that*.'

'So,' said John. 'After I have let off the smoke bomb, you abseil down from the roof, in through the window into the computer room. We've synchronized watches and you have forty-five seconds. I back the van with the mattress on the roof up against the building, you come down on the paraglider and we're away into the night.'

'And no flaw in this plan is immediately apparent to you?'

It was the next day. They were sitting on the concrete bench. The weather was nice, but nippy. The bench was still uncomfortable (although less so for Jim, who had brought a cushion).

'OK, you have fifty seconds,' said John.

'John, if I had an hour, or a day, or a week, I could never, ever, do this. You know how I am with electronic equipment. I would blow the place up. Anyway it's a duff plan. Why don't *I* let off the smoke bomb?'

'Because I thought of it.'

'No.' Jim shook his head. 'This is another of your fast solutions, the ones that end up like Norman's sweeties. All guggy.'

'A minute and a half,' said John. 'Two minutes.'

'No, John. I'm not doing it. It's a ludicrous idea.'

'But it's worth millions. Millions of pounds for three minutes' work.'

'John, I don't know anything about computers. I never have and hopefully I never will. Nobody around here knows anything about computers.'

'Someone must.'

'Who then?'

John scratched at the stubble on his unshaven chin. 'Norman might.'

'Yes well, Norman might. Didn't he build his own once? Out of Meccano?'

'I think it was Lego. But he might. We could ask him.'

'Computers?' said Norman. 'A piece of cake, computers. I built one out of Duplo once.'

'So you do know about computers?' John peered at the guggy contents of a sweetie jar. 'You would know about this?' He held up the glittering computer disc.

'Certainly. Isn't that one of those miniature LPs that you can spread strawberry jam on?'

'Who else do we know?' Jim asked.

'Not too many people,' said John from his side of the concrete bench (and seated now upon Jim's cushion). 'None, in fact.'

'Oh well, throw the thing away.'

'Not a bit of it. This is the big one, Jim. And I'm not going to let you back out again.'

'There's nobody we know, that's it.'

'Nobody you know about what?'

'Who said that?' asked Jim.

'I did.'

Jim turned round on the bench. Behind him stood a child of perhaps ten years of age. He was a golden child. All golden, golden hair. Golden eyes.

'My name is Cain,' said the golden child.

'Jim,' said Jim. 'And this is—'

'John,' said the golden child. 'John Omally.'

'How do you know that?' asked John.

'I don't know. But I do.'

'Do you know about computers?'

'No, stop,' said Jim. 'He's a child.'

'Children are great at this stuff, Jim. Hackers and suchlike.'

'*Hackers?*'

'You really wouldn't want to know.'

'I know about computers,' said Cain. 'I have read all about them.'

'Would you know what to do with this?' John displayed the little disc.

'Of course.'

'How would you like to earn yourself some extra pocket money?'

'No!' Jim snatched away the disc. 'He's a child, John. Get a grip of yourself.'

'Where's your brother?' John asked.

'Abel is in the library. He's reading all about drag.'

'Drag?'

'Cross-dressing. We're up to the Ds now. We're reading the entire contents of the library.'

'Don't you go to school?'

'What is school? We haven't reached the Ss yet.'

'You must have done D for Dictionary,' said Jim.

'What do you want to do with the computer disc?' asked Cain.

'Put it into someone's computer,' said John. 'And turn it on, that's all.'

'No,' said Jim. 'Not a child.'

'You want to put it into Fred's computer,' said the child.

'A mind-reader,' said John. 'You can read people's minds.'

'Some, not all. I cannot read the mind of my father.'

'What number am I thinking of?' asked Jim.

'Twenty-three,' said Cain.

'He's right,' said Jim.

'Incredible,' said John.

'Sixty-nine,' said Cain.

'Pardon me?'

'Sixty-nine's the number *you're* thinking of.'

'What a surprise,' said Jim. 'But you couldn't—'

'Predict the numbers on the National Lottery? No.'

'Shame,' said Jim. 'But incredible, none the less. Can your brother do this?'

'Abel can do other things.'

'And Abel knows all about computers too?'

'Abel might not choose to help you. I will.'

'Why?' asked Jim.

'Because', said Cain, 'something wonderful is about to happen. I can feel it in the air. Can't you?'

Jim stared into the eyes of Cain. The golden eyes blinked, became a pair of amber eyes. The amber eyes of Suzy. Those marvellous, wonderful, beautiful eyes, that made Jim ache inside.

'Give me the disc,' said Cain.

And Jim gave Cain the disc.

26

'Who is he?' Suzy asked, over her bowl of Dilli ka sang ghosht.

'I don't know.' Jim pushed nan bread into his mouth. 'But he can read minds and he said to me exactly what you said to me when we were on the canal bridge.'

'You're going to see this through now, aren't you?'

'Well, I have to, don't I? I'm part of it.'

'You're a very big part of it. But what changed your mind?'

'Just that. That I am a big part of it. That one of my ancestors murdered the monk. That I found the scrolls. All of it. I can't walk away. I have to do it. I know that I do. But when it's done – if it gets done, and I get out of it in one piece – I *am* going to ask you that question.'

'I'll be waiting for you when you do. And the answer will probably be yes.'

'Probably?'

'You have to ask it first. Do you want to come back to my flat after we've finished our meal?'

'For a cup of coffee?'

'Perhaps for more.'

'Perhaps?'

'Probably for more.'

'How could I refuse? But you remember what I told you.'

'That doesn't matter.'

'It does to me.'

'You matter, Jim.'

'I do?'

'You know you do.'

'Suzy.' Jim wiped crumbs from his chin.

'Yes, Jim?'

Jim took a very deep breath. 'I'm in love with you,' he said.

Suzy smiled. That fascinating mouth, those marvellous, wonderful, beautiful eyes. 'I love you too,' she said.

'No,' said John. 'Oh, no Jim, no Jim, no Jim, no.'

They were in the Swan now.

Lunchtime of the next day.

'I couldn't help it,' said Jim. 'The time seemed right and it just came out. And she said she loved me too. She said, "I love you too," just like that. I got all knotted up in my throat then, and I knocked a bowl of Punjabi rajma right into her lap.'

'Very romantic.'

'Do you think so? She didn't seem to think so.'

'And you went back to her flat?'

'We did, yes.'

'And what happened?'

'We had a cup of coffee. Two cups in fact.'

'And?'

'Biscuits,' said Jim.

'And?'

'Just biscuits.'

'Then you didn't, you know . . . ?'

'No, John, we didn't.'

'Jim, you have got to pull yourself together. All this soppy stuff is all right in its place. But if you don't do the business, you'll lose the woman.'

'Do the business?'

'You know exactly what I'm talking about.'

'There's more to a relationship than that.'

'Yes, you're right, there's much more. But, in my opinion, doing the business is the best part.'

Jim sighed. 'I'm gagging to do the business,' he said. 'But the time has to be right. I want everything to be special.'

'Believe me, Jim, whenever you do the business, it's special.'

'Like it was for you at my PARTY, do you mean?'

Omally finished his pint. 'Same again?' he asked.

'So,' said Old Pete, 'there's this, er, this—'

'Irishman?' asked a lady in a straw hat.

'Welshman?' asked Paul the medical student.

'Dwarf?' asked Small Dave.

'Er . . .' said Old Pete.

'Two pints of Large please, Neville,' said John Omally.

'Bloke,' said Old Pete. 'And he goes into this bar, or was it a—'

'Library?' asked the lady.

'Church?' asked Paul.

'Wendy House?' asked Small Dave.

'Some place,' said Old Pete. 'And he's with this other bloke or was it a—'

'Woman?' asked the lady.

'Gorilla?' asked Paul.

'What's going on?' asked John Omally.

Neville did the business. This was the *other* business. The business that most men do much more often than the other other business.

'He's run out,' said Neville.

'Of what?' asked John.

'Jokes,' said Neville. 'He's dried. Look at him.'

'Has this operation,' said Old Pete, 'or did he go into a monastery?'

'Perhaps it was a bank,' said the lady.

'An Irishman went into a bank once,' said Paul. 'He said, "Stick 'em up" and the bloke behind the counter said, "You're Irish, aren't you?" and the bank robber said, "How do you know that?" and the bloke behind the counter said, "You've sawn the wrong end off your shotgun." '

The lady in the straw hat laughed uproariously.

'I don't get it,' said Old Pete.

'Young Master Robert came in here earlier,' said Neville, presenting John with his pints.

'Oh,' said John. 'Did he?'

'He was looking for you. I asked him about the decor.'

'Oh yes?' said John.

'He said they'd be coming in to change it all back tomorrow.'

'Oh good,' said John.

'And I gave him your home address.'

'Oh bliss,' said John. 'Are these on the house, by the way?'

'No,' said Neville. 'They're not.'

'Chimpanzee,' said Old Pete. 'No, nun, no chimney sweep . . .'

'I wonder when we'll hear from the wee boy,' said John, returning to Jim's pew.

'Cain? That was wrong, you know, letting him go off with the disc.'

'He seemed to know what he was up to. He seemed to know every damn' thing.'

'It will all go guggy,' said Jim. 'It was all too fast.'

'No it won't, it will be fine. There was something about him, wasn't there? Something almost inspirational. I don't know how to describe it.'

'Nor me, but I know what you mean. Very strange.'

'Very strange indeed.'

'The Midwich Cuckoo, you called him.'

'He's a pretty weird lad.'

'Not that weird,' said Cain.

'Aaaaagh!' went Jim.

'I'll join you in one of those,' said John. 'Aaaaagh!'

'I'm sorry,' said Cain. 'Did I startle you?'

'You're not supposed to be in here,' whispered Jim. 'You're under age.'

'But this is a church, isn't it?' Cain glanced around.

'No,' said Jim, 'it's not a church. It's a pub.'

299

'Den of Vice,' said Cain. 'D is for Den of Vice. Also depravity, debauchery, dereliction, dipsomania, delirium tremens—'

'Delight and dominoes,' said John.

'Dominoes?' said Jim.

'Discussion,' said John. 'A place of discussion.'

'Drink not only water,' said Cain, 'but take a little wine for thy stomach's sake.'

'My sentiments entirely. How did it go with the disc? Did you—'

'All wrong,' said Jim. 'This is so wrong.'

'I put it into the computer,' said Cain. 'In Penge, which is a very nice place, I might add.'

'You did it?' Jim shook his head. 'And nobody saw you do it?'

'I don't have to be seen if I don't want to be.'

'Buy the child a lemonade,' said Jim. 'And a packet of crisps.'

'I'd prefer a gin and tonic,' said Cain.

'Cup of tea?' asked Clive.

'I'd prefer a gin and tonic,' said Derek.

'That's hardly a macho drink, Derek.'

'James Bond used to drink Martini. And he was pretty macho.'

'Martini is a tart's drink.'

'Babycham is a tart's drink.'

'No, a Bacardi and coke is a tart's drink.'

'Posh tart's drink.'

'I've never met a posh tart.'

'Is a tart the same as a slapper?'

'Aaaaaaaaaaaagh!'

'It wasn't an unreasonable question.'

'It wasn't me going "Aaaaaaaaaaaagh!" '

'Who was it then?'

'Aaaaaaaaaaaaagh!'

'Fred,' said Derek. 'It was Fred.'

Clive and Derek raced along the Corridor of Power. They reached the Chamber of Power. Derek won by a short head. Clive pushed open the mighty door.

'Aaaaaaaaaaaagh!' went Fred again. He was standing behind his desk. The desk was still covered by the dust sheet. Not too much more had been done to the ceiling. Fred held a computer print-out in his hand. It was one of those financial jobbies. A bank statement affair. Fred went 'Aaaaaaaaaaaagh!' once again.

27

Now Small Dave was a postman.

A postman, Small Dave was.

At one time he had the reputation for being a vindictive grudge-bearing wee bastard. But after a very nasty experience involving the ghost of Edgar Allan Poe, a zero-gravity camel named Simon and a mothership from the lost planet Ceres, he had mellowed somewhat and was now, for the most part, quite easy-going.

For the most part.

But not this morning.

This morning Small Dave was all in a lather. All in a lather and a regular foam. He'd arrived at the Brentford Sorting Office with the not-unreasonable expectation of finding the usual two sacks of mail awaiting him.

But not this morning.

This morning there were twenty-three sacks.

'Aaaaaagh!' went Small Dave, all in a lather and a regular foam. 'Twenty-three sacks! Aaaaagh!'

Mrs Elronhubbard the postmistress looked Small

Dave up and down. Though mostly down, due to his lack of inches.

'I'm terribly sorry, Small Dave,' said she. 'But all these printed pamphlets arrived last night and one is to go into every single letterbox in Brentford.'

'Outrage!' Small Dave knotted a dolly-sized fist and shook it. 'Outrage! Outrage! Outrage!'

'I'm sorry, but there it is.'

Small Dave kicked the nearest sack, spilling out its contents. He stooped (though not very far) and plucked up a pamphlet. And at this he glared, fiercely.

FREE MONEY ran the headline, in a manner calculated to gain the reader's attention.

'Eh?' went Small Dave.

THE BRENTFORD MILLENNIUM FUND IS OFFERING YOU A CHANCE TO SHARE IN THE BOROUGH'S GOOD FORTUNE.

'Oh,' went Small Dave.

ALL YOU HAVE TO DO IS COME UP WITH A PROJECT FOR THE NEW YEAR'S CELEBRATIONS AND THE FUND WILL GIVE YOU ALL THE CASH YOU NEED.

'It's a wind-up,' said Small Dave.

THIS IS NOT A WIND-UP.

'Blimey,' said Small Dave.

SO FILL IN THE ATTACHED APPLICATION FORM. STICK IT IN THE ATTACHED PRE-PAID ENVELOPE AND POP THAT INTO AN UNATTACHED POST BOX. AND LOTS OF MONEY WILL BE YOURS!

'Incredible,' said Small Dave.

YES, ISN'T IT!

'Paragliding,' said Mrs Elronhubbard.

'What?' went Small Dave.

'Synchronized paragliding, like synchronized swimming only up in the sky. I'm going to put in for a grant.'

'But you're nearly eighty.'

'You're only as old as the men you feel.'

Small Dave sighed. 'Sometimes I feel like a motherless child,' said he. 'But of course there's a law against that kind of thing.'

'Quite,' said Mrs Elronhubbard. 'And there should be another about recycling old gags. So, Small Dave, up and at it.'

'I am up.'

'Oh, so you are. Well then, get at it.'

Small Dave made grumbling noises. 'It's no bloody use,' he complained. 'It takes me nearly a day to deliver two sacks. It would take me a month to deliver this lot.'

'Then God bless the Brentford Millennium Committee.'

'What?'

'They've supplied you with ten part-time workers, who are out in the car park even now, awaiting your orders.'

'*My* orders?'

'Yours. You have been awarded the title Millennial Postman First Class and your salary's been doubled.'

'Oh.' Small Dave puffed out his pigeon chest. 'Right then, let's get to it.'

★   ★   ★

'Well,' said Professor Slocombe, reading through the pamphlet. 'When you get to it, John, you certainly get to it.'

'Thank you.' John Omally buttered toast and grinned across the ancient's breakfast table. 'I think it should provoke a positive response.'

'Guggy.' Jim dipped a bread soldier into his boiled egg. 'It will all turn guggy, like this yolk.'

'Why so?' asked the Professor.

'Because every conman and nutcase in the borough will apply.'

'That is the general idea.'

'But they'll only be doing it to grab the cash. There won't actually be any projects.'

'He might have a point there, John.'

'No, Professor.' John Omally shook his head. 'I know who's who in Brentford. Trust me to weed out the wide boys and the moondancers.'

'Set a thief to catch a thief,' said Jim.

'I resent that.'

'Yes, I'm sorry. Let's look on the bright side, shall we?'

'Jim, I think at long last we're actually *on* the bright side.'

'Yes, I think you're right. So would now be a good time to raise the matter of our salaries?'

'Now would be a good time to *raise* our salaries.'

'Jolly good.'

Fred's voice rose. It rose and rose. It rattled the crystals of the new chandelier, it made the window panes vibrate, it caused the nose to drop off a toby jug on the mantelpiece, and if chaos theory is to be believed it buggered up the sprout crop in Upper Sumatra.

'Bring me their heads!' screamed Fred. 'Bring me their frigging heads.'

Clive had his hands firmly clasped over his ears. But his nose was beginning to bleed. 'I really don't think that heads are the solution,' he shouted.

'I do,' shouted Derek. 'I think we should cull the entire population of Brentford.'

Fred's hands were all of a quiver. They clutched in their fingers one of Omally's pamphlets. They ripped this pamphlet into tiny little pieces and flung these pieces into the air. 'I want this sabotaged!' screamed Fred in an even higher register. 'And I want my money back.'

But he didn't get it.

Early the next morning John and Jim sat in the Brentford Sorting Office viewing the twenty-three sacks of application forms which had all arrived by return of post.

'I think we can chalk this up as a one hundred per cent positive response,' said John. 'Shall we dig in?'

'Is this what we're being paid for?' Jim asked.

'Of course. Whatever did you think?'

'Well, it was always my opinion that company directors spent their days swanning about in limousines, eating at expensive restaurants, smoking large cigars and taking the afternoons off with their secretaries.'

'Ah.' John made thoughtful noddings. 'I take your point. You feel that a task such as this should be left to underlings.'

'I hope you don't think I'm getting above myself. But I do have pressing business of my own that I should be attending to.'

'Millennial business?'

'Precisely.'

'And what business would this be?'

'The building of the Jim Pooley.'

'Ah. But don't I recall you saying that there isn't enough time left for anything like that?'

'Aha.' Jim tapped his nose.

'You tapped your nose, Jim,' said John. 'This is a new development.'

Jim tapped it again. 'I have decided to enlist the services of our two local builders, Hairy Dave and Jungle John. They are going to construct the Jim Pooley in the traditional style of a rude hut. A couple of weeks and it will be up.'

'One light breeze and it will be down again.'

'I shall oversee the building work myself.'

'Neville isn't going to like it.'

'I don't think I'll mention it to Neville.'

Omally shrugged. 'Well, please yourself, Jim. If you think this bit of self-indulgence is more important than helping the Professor.'

'I didn't say that. It's my personal contribution to the celebrations.'

'You are, as ever, altruism personified. But

regrettably, as I am the managing director of the Brentford Millennium Committee, and so one up the chain of command from your good self, I hereby inform you that you can't have the time off.'

'What?'

'And you'd be wasting it anyway. Hairy Dave and Jungle John are already at work on Omally's. Arse-ends and everything.'

AND EVERYTHING

Now there is much that might have been written of what occurred during the months that led up to December. Of the many and various projects which were put into operation and the many and various plain folk of Brentford who absconded with large quantities of cash and now live on an island in the Caribbean. Of Fred's doomed attempts to recover his money, of more hair-raising life and death struggles, of how the Flying Swan was restored to its former glory, and then converted once more to the Road to Calvary and then restored yet again, converted yet again, restored yet again and so on and so forth.

And some tender passages might have been included regarding Jim's relationship with Suzy and how the old business was finally conducted. And how the old business was not the old business at all when it came to Jim and Suzy. But how it was making love.

And of just how special making love can be.

But time does not allow. And so let us move

forward to Monday, December the twenty-ninth 1997. To early evening, a new moon rising in the sky, a considerable nip in the air and words being spoken in the Flying Swan.

No, excuse me, the Road to Calvary.

28

'And I'm telling you,' said Neville, 'if it wasn't for this,' he held up a bottle of Hartnell's Millennial Ale: the beer that tastes the way beer used to taste, 'you would be roasting in that grate instead of my yule log.'

Omally gave a sickly grin. 'I will get it sorted, I promise. You are serving the ale strictly in rotation, as I told you?'

'Yes, yes, yes. Numbered crates, red bottle top last week, amber bottle top this week, green bottle top next week. I know all that. The beer has to be served fresh, it doesn't keep. You've told me again and again, and so has Norman. I'm a professional, you know.'

'I know, I know. It's just very very important that you use each batch within a week. It will go off otherwise.'

Jim, who had been drinking at the bar, coughed into his ale, sending much of it up his nose. '*Go off*. Oh my God.'

John steered him away to a side table.

'Do try to control yourself, Jim,' he said.

'Control myself? John, what if he overlooks a crate, or something? The whole pub will go up. People will die, John. Supplying him with that beer is such a bad bad idea.'

'I only supply him with just enough. It's the most popular beer in the borough – there's never any left over the following week. And it's the only reason we're allowed to drink here.'

'It's no fun to drink here any more, with it done up like this.' Jim cast an eye over the religious trappings. They were getting pretty knackered from all the constant moving in and out and in again, but actually they didn't look all that bad, what with the Christmas decorations and everything.

'I'll get it sorted.'

'Of course you won't. You won't get it sorted, the same way Norman will never get the beer sorted.'

'And is the free rock concert in the football ground sorted, Jim?'

'Well.' Jim made the now legendary so-so gesture. The one that means, 'No, actually.'

'No,' said John, 'I thought not.'

'I've had a definite yes from the Chocolate Bunnies, and Sonic Energy Authority are coming, and the Lost T-Shirts of Atlantis.'

'I don't wish to be sceptical, and these are very fine bands. But it's not exactly your all-star Wembley line-up, is it?'

'We would have had the Spice Girls.'

'Ah,' said John.

'Yes, "Ah". If you hadn't *had* the Spice Girls, we would have had the Spice Girls.'

'I didn't have all of them, Jim. I only had one.'

'And which one was that?'

'The vacant-looking one.'

'That's not a particularly specific answer, is it?'

'Look, never mind about that. They split up because of artistic differences.'

'You're only making it worse for yourself. And how is Omally's by the way? I've been expecting my invite to the grand opening.'

Omally made the so-so gesture.

Jim shook his head. 'Guggy,' he said.

'But look on the bright side. The entire borough will be celebrating, just as the Professor wanted.'

'The few remaining who aren't already in the Caribbean.'

'We only lost a couple of hundred, don't exaggerate. And if you'd spent a little less time at your girlfriend's experimenting with the contents of her fridge—'

'Stop that!'

'All right. But if you had spent more time concentrating on the job, a lot more would have been done.'

'Shall we consult our list, just to clarify exactly what *has* been done?'

Omally took a very small piece of paper from his pocket. 'There's the concert in the football ground,' said he.

'Which *I* have been organizing.'

'There's the beer festival.'

'Oh yes. One of yours. The one that will probably end in a nuclear holocaust.'

'The beauty pageant. Ah, no, *not* the beauty pageant.'

'Not the beauty pageant?'

'I don't wish to talk about it. There was some unpleasantness regarding my interview techniques . . . husbands, boyfriends . . . let's not discuss the beauty pageant.'

Jim gave his head another shake.

'The street party,' said John.

'Oh yes, the street party named desire. Or should that be the street party named it's-too-bloody-cold-at-this-time-of-year-for-a-street-party?'

'The beer festival.'

'We've done that.'

'The synchronized paragliding.'

'Oh yes, the synchronized paragliding. Half a dozen grannies plummeting to their deaths from the top of the gasometer. That should draw a big crowd.'

'There's the fireworks.'

'Fireworks?'

'Ha, you didn't know about the fireworks, did you?'

'No, I confess that I did not. And who is putting on the display?'

'Mmmmph,' mumbled Omally.

'Sorry? I didn't quite catch that.'

'Norman.'

'Norman. Oh, perfect. Fireworks the way fireworks used to be, I suppose.'

'Something along those lines.'

'So we can expect to see the word GUGGY lighting up the sky.'

'Norman will be fine. He's constructed a mobile de-entropizer that will reconstitute the fireworks again and again. Until the car battery runs down, anyway. It will be a spectacular event. Trust me on this.'

'Well, with that and the paragliding grannies, I think we have the situation firmly under control. What a night to remember, eh? I only hope I can contain myself and not simply die from an overload of sheer enjoyment.'

'You'll be giving your girlfriend's kitchen a miss, then?'

'I'm warning you, John.'

'It's fun though, isn't it?'

'It certainly is. But listen, John, in all truth, we've really fouled this up. All the money that we've given away, we've not got much to show for it, have we?'

'I've personally got nothing to show for it. The Professor's been really stingy regarding my expenses.'

'And making us do our community service, that was rubbing it in a bit.'

'He said it was good for our souls.'

Jim stared into his empty glass. 'What do you think will really happen when he performs his ceremony on New Year's Eve?'

'Search me. But he seems convinced that it will be something wonderful. Dawn of a new age, step closer back to THE BIG IDEA.'

'THE BIG IDEA.' Jim pushed his empty glass aside. 'I think I'll go round to see Suzy,' he said.

'Well, steer clear of the live yoghurt. It gives you thrush.'

'John!'

'Well, it does.'

'I'll steer clear of it then. What are you going to do?'

'Relax.' John drained the last life from his pint. 'Have a few more beers here and relax. Nothing's going to happen tonight, is it? I mean, what could possibly happen tonight?'

Jim looked at John.

And John looked back at Jim.

'Why is it', Jim asked, 'that I really wish you hadn't said that?'

As Jim left the Flying Swan he passed between two men who were entering it. They were tall men and well proportioned. They looked to be in their early thirties and were dressed identically in grey tweed suits. One had long golden hair and a golden beard, the other's hair was dark and so too were his whiskers. As Jim passed between them he experienced a most alarming sensation. It was as if one side of him had turned as cold as ice and the other fiery hot.

Jim gathered his senses together with some difficulty and put what spring he could into his step.

Suzy's flat was in Horseferry Lane, a little up from the Shrunken Head. It was one of those smart newish three-storey affairs, peopled by good-looking arty types with whom Jim had absolutely nothing in common. He spent a great deal of time agonizing over exactly what Suzy saw in him. He was a layabout, there was no getting away from it. A dreamer and a romantic maybe, but a layabout. An individual, she kept on telling him, in a world where few exist. And the two of them did have something. Something wonderful. Something that made differences in their lifestyles totally irrelevant. And when two people know that they're meant for each other, nothing will stand in their way.

Jim had been given a key of his own. Well, it hadn't been a proper key, not in Jim's opinion anyway. It had been a plastic card thing that you pushed into this little black box by the front door. Jim had almost got to grips with it on several occasions. The engineer who had come to fix the little black box said he was totally mystified by the way it kept breaking down. Jim didn't have the plastic card thing any more, Jim had to ring the bell.

Jim rang the bell.

But there wasn't any answer.

Jim inspected the bell push. It was possible, just possible, that the bell push was broken. Stone at the window? No, that wasn't such a good idea, not after what happened last time. Jim shrugged. She was probably out somewhere. Should he hang around, or just go home? Jim leaned back against the front door. The front door swung open and Jim fell backwards into the hall.

'Ouch,' said Jim, struggling to his feet.

The door swung shut, but it didn't lock. The keep was hanging off the wall.

'Well, that wasn't my fault,' said Jim. 'I didn't do that.'

Jim now did those dusting downs that people do after they've fallen over. They do them no matter where they fall, even if there isn't any dust. It's probably some racial memory thing, or a primordial urge, or a basic instinct or a tradition or an old charter, or something.

Jim straightened his shoulders and marched upstairs. Suzy's flat was number three on the second floor. Lovers of illuminati conspiracy theory could get a 23 out of that.

Jim didn't bother with the bell push. He knocked on the door. And as his knuckle struck the black lacquered panel the door swung open to reveal—

A scene of devastation.

Jim stepped inside, in haste and fear. The flat had been ransacked. And viciously so. Curtains torn down, cushions ripped to ribbons, vases broken, books shredded, pictures smashed from their frames.

'Suzy.' Jim plunged amongst the wreckage, righting the sofa, flinging aside the fallen drapes. Into the kitchen, the bathroom.

The bedroom.

The bed was made. The duvet spread. The pale silk curtains hung, untorn. An eye of calm in the centre of the evil hurricane.

Jim felt sick inside. As he stood and stared into that bedroom, the reek came to his nostrils. Jim flung himself across the room, dragged aside the duvet and the bed cover.

To expose a human turd lying in the middle of the bed.

'My dear God, no.' Jim turned away.

The bedside phone began to ring. He snatched it up.

'I'll bet you're really pissed off, aren't you?' said the voice of Derek.

'Who is this?'

'You remember me, or at least my nine-gauge auto-loader.'

Jim's heart sank. His knees buckled. 'Suzy,' he whispered. 'You have Suzy, don't you?'

Jim heard the noise of struggling. And then a slap. And then the awful sound of Suzy weeping.

'I'll kill you.' Jim shook uncontrollably. 'If you harm her I'll kill you.'

'I'm sure you'll try. But it won't be necessary. You can have her back. Possibly even in one piece, if you do what you're told.'

'And what is that?'

Derek spoke and Jim listened. And Jim's face, pale and ghostly as it was, grew even paler and ghostlier still.

29

And the band played 'Believe It If You Like'.

A big brass band it was, of big beer-bellied men. They had such smart uniforms, scarlet with golden sashes, the borough's emblem of the Griffin Rampant resplendent upon them. And big black shiny boots and trumpets and cornets and big bass bassoons.

And they marched through the Butts Estate and they played 'Believe It If You Like'.

And children cheered and waved their Union Jacks.

And old biddies cheered and fluttered their lace handkerchiefs.

And old men nodded their heads to the beat.

And a lady in a straw hat said, 'They're playing in the key of C.'

And a medical student named Paul said, 'Oh no they're not.'

And the weather forecast said 'no rain'. And the winter sun shone brightly and today was a special day indeed.

Today was New Year's Eve.

John Omally glanced at his gold Piaget wristwatch. (Well, he had been able to wangle one or two expenses.) 'Nearly four,' said he. 'Where is Jim?'

Norman Hartnell hurried up.

'Any word of him?' John asked.

'No,' said Norman. 'It's the same all over. You were the last person to see him, John. The night before last.'

'What about his girlfriend? He said he was going there.'

'She's not home. I've rung loads of times, but I don't get any answer. And I don't have the time to keep doing this for you. Do you think the two of them have—'

'What?' Omally stiffened. 'Run off together? Eloped or something?'

'It's more than possible. He's well smitten, that Jim.'

'No.' Omally made fierce head-shakings. 'He wouldn't have done that. Not without telling me.'

'Perhaps he was afraid you might talk him out of it.'

'Oh no.' Omally glanced once more at his wristwatch. If he himself had been able to hive off enough expenses to purchase this, Jim might well have been salting away sufficient cash to do a runner. His need was the greater of the two.

John suddenly felt quite empty inside. Somehow the thought that he and Jim would not remain best friends for ever had never really entered his mind.

They were a team. They were the lads.

They were individuals.

'I have to get back to the brewery,' said Norman. 'I've got crates of ale coming out of the old de-entropizer and I have to get them over to the Swan. I'll see you later at the fireworks, eh?'

But John did not reply.

In that house in Moby Dick Terrace, where the old folk died from most unnatural causes, Dr Steven Malone paced up and down. In the sparsely furnished sitting room, with its curtains drawn and a single low-watt ceiling bulb creating gloom, the floorboards creaked beneath his feet and the two tall men sat in armchairs regarding him in silence.

'Tonight,' said Dr Steven, 'we return to Kether House. I have made all the preparations. Tonight you will learn my purpose and I will learn all—'

Cain opened his mouth to speak.

'No, Cain, only listen. I brought you into being just for this. Do you know who you really are?'

'I am Cain,' said Cain. 'And you are my father.'

'And you, Abel? What of you?'

'I am part of Cain,' said Abel. 'He is part of me. The two of us are one.'

'This is so. And tonight you shall be joined. The two made truly one and at the moment of this joining—'

'We shall die,' said Cain.

'For we belong dead,' Abel said. 'Is that not so, father?'

But Dr Steven did not reply.

Professor Slocombe's study had been cleared of every antique book, every glass-cased creature, every precious artefact, each table, chair and couch. The sconces from the walls had gone, the curtain rails. The carpets, rugs and dhurries. And the walls and the ceiling and the floor and all the woodwork and the very panes of glass in the French windows had been painted black. And on the blackened floor, wrought in white, the sacred circles had been drawn enclosing the hexagram, that six-pointed Star of Solomon, the great seal of the mysteries. And the names of power had been inscribed between the outer circle and the inner. ADONAI and MALKUTH and AUM and TETRAGRAMMATON.

And at the very centre of the hexagram, wrought in red, the sacred symbol Om.

There were no candles in this room, no lamps of any kind, but an astral light illuminated all.

Gammon knelt in silent prayer as Professor Slocombe, in the seamless floor-length robe of white, the robe of the Ipsissimus, intoned the words to cleanse the temple, and begin the operation.

The Lesser Ritual of the Pentagram

And touched his forehead, saying *Ateh* (Unto Thee)
And touched his breast while saying *Malkuth* (The Kingdom)

322

And touched his right shoulder, saying *ve-Gaburah*
  (And the Power)
And touched the left, saying *ve-Gedulah* (And the
  Glory)
And clasping hands upon the breast, he said
  le-Olahm, Amen.

                    (To the Ages, Amen).

Gammon rose and, bowing to the East, the South,
the West and then the North, he said, 'I will leave
you now, sir. Blessed be.'

Professor Slocombe did not reply.

Fred sat in his office with his feet up on the desk.
The dust sheets had gone and the scaffolding was
down. The paintings were up again and so were
Fred's spirits.

Derek and Clive stood to either side of Fred.
Derek had a nice new gun. A small but useful-
looking weapon. An Uzi nine-millimetre. Clive held
a little black bag. Something wriggled uncomfortably
within it.

Before Fred's desk stood Jim Pooley.

And Jim didn't look very well.

'You've got a bloody nose again, Jim,' said
Fred.

Derek giggled. 'He got a bit boisterous. I had to
give him a little slap.'

Jim trembled and knotted his fists. 'Where is she?'
he spat through gritted teeth. 'What have you done
with her?'

'She's safe enough for now,' said Fred. 'Although

I know that Derek is just dying to get to know her a little better.'

'I've filled up my fridge,' said Derek. 'I've got some real prize-winning fruit and veg.'

Jim turned on Derek. Derek just held up his gun.

'You'll do exactly what we want you to do, won't you, Jim?' Fred smiled a smile of such pure wickedness that even Dr Steven Malone would have been hard pressed to match it.

'What *do* you want me to do?'

'A small act of sabotage, nothing more.'

'Where is Suzy?'

'Nearby. Safe for now.'

'I want to see her.'

'Well, you can't. Now what was I saying? Ah yes, a small act of sabotage. Clive here has a little bag. Did you notice Clive's little bag?'

Jim said nothing.

'You wouldn't want to look inside. There's something deeply unpleasant in there. Something unworldly.'

'Go on, show him,' said Derek. 'It frightens the shit out of me.'

'Derek did a shit in the Suzy woman's bed,' said Clive. 'And he didn't wipe his bum afterwards.'

Pooley's knuckles clicked.

'What you are going to do, Jim, is to take Clive's little bag to the house of Professor Slocombe and at the stroke of midnight, as he is bringing his ritual to its climax, you are to open the little bag and release what is inside.'

'Never,' said Jim.

'Jim, you will do this, or the next time you see Suzy there will only be certain pieces you recognize. Now, in case you are thinking of pulling any strokes on us, let me introduce you to this.' Fred opened a drawer and took out a small black electronic item. He extended its aerial and pressed a tiny red button.

Pain exploded in Jim's head. He sank to his knees and screamed.

Fred touched the button again. Pooley looked up, fear and hatred in his eyes.

'Have a little feel of your right temple, Jim.'

Pooley felt with a shaking hand.

'Feel that little lump?'

Pooley nodded.

'An implant, a tracking transmitter. We put it in you during your stay at the Cottage Hospital. We know exactly where you are at any time. And if you're not where you're supposed to be at midnight, we will be terribly upset. Derek and Clive will be waiting outside in the car with your girlfriend. Be a good boy and you can have her back unharmed. Play me false and I'll know.' Fred touched the button and Jim collapsed once more.

Fred touched the button again and Pooley looked up.

'You are going to be a good boy, aren't you, Jim?'

But Pooley did not reply.

Old Pete sat at the bar counter of the Road to Calvary, a most miserable look upon his face.

'What troubles you, Old Pete?' asked Neville the

part-time barman. 'This is a day for celebration, half-priced beer until midnight.'

Old Pete sniffed. 'Take a look at this,' he said, and reaching down he brought up a carrier bag and placed it on the counter.

'What's in there?' asked Neville.

Old Pete rooted in, lifted out what looked to be a toy piano and a toy piano stool. Rooting again he lifted out what appeared to be a tiny man in a dress suit.

Old Pete placed the tiny man upon the bar top. The tiny man bowed, clicked his fingers, sat down upon the stool and rattled out 'Believe It If You Like' on the piano.

Neville stared, his good eye wide.

When the tiny man had finished, Old Pete snatched him up and thrust him, the piano and the stool back into the carrier bag.

'That's the most incredible thing I've ever seen in my life,' said Neville.

'Huh!' said Old Pete, in a depressed tone.

'What do you mean, "Huh"?'

'Well, let me tell you what happened. I was walking down by the canal earlier and I saw this woman drowning. I pulled her out and she said to me, "Thank you, sir, for saving my life." I said, "No problem," and then she said, "I am a witch and to thank you properly I will grant you a single wish."'

'She never did?' said Neville.

'She did,' said Old Pete. 'But she was either a bit deaf or had water in her ears, because I now possess this *ten-inch pianist*.'

'I've heard it before,' said Neville.

'Everyone's heard it before,' said Old Pete. 'But it's a blinder of a joke, isn't it?'

'A classic. Same again?'

'Cheers,' said Old Pete.

'But surely . . .' said Norman. 'I mean, you have . . . I mean . . .'

'What?'

Norman Hartnell shook his head. 'Nothing,' he said. 'I'm sure I'll figure that out, given time.'

'Amber bottle tops,' said Neville.

'Sorry?' said Norman.

'Amber bottle tops this week, red last week, green the week before.'

'Oh yes,' said Norman. 'Amber this week. Don't serve anything else, will you?'

'I am a professional,' said Neville. 'Do I have to keep on telling you? And what would happen if I did make a mistake? It would hardly be the end of the world, would it?'

Norman did not reply.

The big brass band played the theme tune from *Blue Peter*. The world-famous Brentford Girls' School Drum Majorettes high-stepped and baton-twirled; carnival floats manned and womanned by Brentfordians who had actually spent their Millennium grant money on what they said they would followed behind.

These fine-looking floats were constructed to display tableaux from Brentford's glorious past.

Here was a great and garish Julius Caesar,

fashioned from papier mâché, dipping his toe in the Thames, prior to crossing it down by Horseferry Lane. Here were the king's men, ready to hammer the parliamentarians at the historic Battle of Brentford. Here too the Bards of Brentford, the poets and playwrights, the literary greats, born to the borough and now beloved the world over.

And there was, well, there was – er . . .

Moving right along, here come the all-ladies over-eighties synchronized paragliding team.

And the band played 'Believe It If You Like'.

30

Tour trucks rolled into Brentford. Mostly Bedford vans they were, all knocked and knackered about. They had the names of the bands who travelled within them spray-painted on the sides. There were also one or two of those VW campers. You know the ones, the old lads with the two-tone orange and cream colouring. The ones that German terrorists always drive in movies that have German terrorists in them. Have you ever noticed that? It's always two-tone VW campers. And if that's not a tradition or an old charter, or something, then gawd knows what it is.

Hollywood again, probably.

A big bad black Bedford van drew up outside the football ground and a man with considerable hair, considerable piercings, considerable tattoos and a bulge in his leather pants which merited considerable consideration stepped down from it.

He flexed his arms, which did not have particularly considerable muscles on them, and cried out to the groundsman who was lounging outside smoking a cigarette.

'We are the Hollow Chocolate Bunnies of Death,' he cried out. 'And we have come for your daughters. Those we can't screw, we eat.'

'It's a shame Jim couldn't get the Spice Girls,' said the groundsman. 'Park your old van round the back, mate. There's booze laid on in the bar.'

A two-tone VW camper pulled up behind. It was driven by an Aryan type in a roll-neck sweater and denim cap. His name was Axel and he was a member of an organization known as the Black Umbrella Militant Faction Underground Communist Killers. Which was the kind of acronym that didn't bear thinking about.

'You round the back too, mate,' called out the groundsman. 'Park in the bay marked Terrorists.'

The big parade kept on parading by and a carnival atmosphere was beginning to grow. Jim and John had splashed out on vast quantities of bunting and balloons to decorate the streets and the town looked a treat. And what with there being a free rock concert in the evening, and the free beer festival all day and night, and the free fireworks sometime later on, the numbers were swelling, as out-borough types arrived to lend their heartfelt support. There was even a hippie convoy on the way, with a chap called Bollocks driving the lead bus.

It certainly looked like being a night to remember.

At the Hartnell Millennial Brewery (two lock-up garages knocked into one, near the clapped-out trading estate down by the old docks), Norman tinkered happily away at his mobile de-entropizer.

It was constructed mainly from Meccano and mounted upon pram wheels. There was a conveyor belt running through it and the general principle was that you put the item you wanted de-entropized in at one end and it came out of the other – well, de-entropized.

Of course there was no end to the complications of gubbinry crammed inside. Lots of old valve-radio parts, whirring cogs and clicking mechanisms, all beavering away at the ionization of beta particles, thus creating a positronic catalyst, which bombarded an isotope with gamma radiation, giving rise to galvanic variations and the transperambulation of pseudo-cosmic anti-matter.

The way these things do.

Norman twiddled with his screwdriver and whistled an old Cannibal Corpse number. He set the dial to *repeat*, placed a long-defunct penny banger onto the conveyor belt, watched it pass into the de-entropizer and smiled hugely as, one after another, bright new reconstituted clones of the former firework poured out of the other end.

'I must get around to patenting this,' said Norman Hartnell.

By eight o'clock the Road to Calvary was filling nicely. The beer festival proper was in a big marquee in the Memorial Park. On the very spot, in fact, where the John Omally Millennial Bowling Green had been planned. And beneath the very tree where Jim had done his travelling in time. But what the marquee didn't have, but the Swan did, was Hartnell's Millennial Ale.

'Another bottle, Neville, please,' said Old Pete, as he stood at the bar chatting with an Englishman, an Irishman and a Scotsman.

'You were saying', said the Scotsman, 'about your family.'

'Oh yes,' said Old Pete. 'I come from a very musical family. Even the dog hummed in the warm weather.'

'How interesting,' said the Englishman.

'Oh yes, very musical. When I was only three I played on the linoleum. We had a flood and my mum floated out on the table. I accompanied her on the piano. Talking of pianos, the cat sat down at ours once and played a tune, and my mum said, "We must get that orchestrated," and the cat ran out and we never saw it again. Now my father, my father died from music on the brain. A piano fell on his head.'

'Was that the same piano?' asked the Irishman.

'Same one,' said Old Pete. 'I never played it myself. I was going to learn the harp, but I didn't have the pluck.'

'Might I just stop you there?' asked the Scotsman.

'And I was thinking of becoming a homosexual,' said Old Pete. 'But I was only half in earnest.'

'I really must stop you there,' said the Scotsman.

'Oh yes, and why?'

'Because you're telling such shite jokes.'

'Here, look at that,' said Old Pete, pointing to a

nun riding by on a jester's back. 'Is that vergin' on the ridiculous, or what?'

Omally pushed his way up to the bar. 'Has Jim been in, Neville?' he asked.

The part-time barman flipped an amber cap from a bottle of Hartnell's finest and shook his Brylcreemed head. 'Haven't seen him since the night before last,' he said. 'But shouldn't he be at the football ground organizing the free rock concert?'

'I'll go and see.'

Like the Road to Calvary, the football ground was filling nicely. All traffic in the Ealing Road had come to a standstill as crowds milled pavement to pavement. Omally pushed his way into these crowds and into the floodlit stadium.

At the far end, flanked by mammoth speakers, Sonic Energy Authority were already on stage. The lead singer, the now legendary Cardinal Cox himself, was giving a spirited solo yodelling rendition of the *Blue Peter* theme.

'Far out,' said a lady in a straw hat. 'And in C.'

'A minor,' said Paul.

'Have you seen my friend Jim?' John asked the lady.

'My name isn't Jim,' the lady said.

'No, I meant have you seen my friend whose name is Jim?'

'The one whose kitchen you blew up?'

'Yes,' said Omally in a dismal tone. 'That's the one.'

'Actually, yes,' said the lady. 'I saw him down at the Butts Estate about half an hour ago.'

'What was he doing?'

'He was being thrown out of a long black limousine.'

'Ah,' said John Omally.

Jim Pooley sat all alone in a corner of the Shrunken Head. But for Sandy the sandy-haired barman, Jim was the only person in the place. (Well, the Memorial Park was only a beer can's throw away, and the beer there was free.)

Jim stared into his second double vodka. He was trembling from head to toe. Unshaven, pale of face, bruised and bloody about the nose regions, Jim looked the very picture of despair, which indeed he was. After giving Jim a warning kick or two in the ribs, Derek had driven the limousine back to Penge, supposedly to collect Suzy, who would be delivered safely to Jim as soon as he had delivered the unsafe contents of the nasty little bag to Professor Slocombe.

But what was Jim to do?

Could he really bring himself to destroy the Professor's ceremony and probably even the Professor himself, knowing as he did, or at least felt reasonably certain he did, that the ceremony, once successfully performed, would elevate mankind to some almost god-like state?

If it worked.

But then what if it wasn't going to work anyway? Then it really wouldn't matter if he destroyed it.

And ultimately what did matter, other than Suzy? Not much, in Jim's opinion. Not anything at all, in fact. When you love somebody as much as Jim loved Suzy, the rest of the world can go to hell.

Jim downed his second double. His fingers strayed to the little lump on his right temple. Fred's blokes knew exactly where he was at any given moment; he couldn't trick them. He could dump the horrible wriggling bag into the canal, but perhaps that had a transmitter stuck inside it too. He was in really big trouble here, and he was all on his own this time.

Jim looked down at his wrist, to the place where, had he worn a wristwatch, he would have worn it. The one he wasn't wearing now had belonged to John Omally. John had given it to Jim as a present.

'Nine o'clock,' said Jim. 'What am I going to do?'

'I'll tell you what we're going to do,' said Derek.

'What are we going to do?' asked Clive.

Clive was driving, Derek was in the back. Fred was in the back too, and Suzy was sitting between Derek and Fred. They were out of Penge now and heading for Brentford.

'We're going to party big time,' said Derek. 'Roll into Brentford, let some blood and party big time.'

'Shut your mouth,' said Fred.

'Aw, come on, Fred.' Derek waved his Uzi in the air. 'We're mean sons of bitches, ain't we? We're the God-damn horsemen of the Apocalypse.'

Fred made low growling sounds. 'You can let as

much blood as you like, once that Pooley has put paid to the Professor.'

Derek cocked his weapon in the manner that sometimes got a cheap laugh. 'I don't know why you've bothered with all this subtle stuff. You should have arranged a nuclear accident, flattened the whole frigging borough.'

'Dear oh dear.' Fred rolled his eyes. 'You really don't get it, do you? When Pooley introduces our little bagged-up friend into the Professor's magic circle, the entire ceremony will be reversed. Goodness won't come flooding into the world. Its opposite number will. Mr Pooley will turn this entire planet into a seething cesspit of evil. Which is just the way my master wants it to be.'

'You're one bad mother,' said Derek.

'Yeah,' said Fred. 'Ain't I though.'

There really didn't seem any way that Fred's car would actually be able to drive into Brentford. All the roads in were now blocked by other cars, engines off, doors locked, their owners and passengers gone to join the party. And it really was growing into some party. A PARTY! in fact. Folk from all around were descending on the borough, eager to engage in the free festivities. The novelty of this little west London town's genuinely celebrating the millennium two years before the rest of the world had a certain pulling power.

Fred's limo ground to a halt.

'Get a move on,' said Fred.

336

'I can't,' said Clive. 'The traffic's all snarled up.'

'Then put the car into overdrive.'

'Overdrive? What good's that if I can't move?'

'Didn't you ever see that film *The Car*?'

'I did,' said Derek. 'Absolute corker. This big evil black car comes out of the desert and wipes out all these people in a little mid-west American town. And *The Car* is really the Devil.'

'Wasn't Bradford Dillman in that?' asked Clive.

'Nah, Bradford Dillman was in *Bug*.'

'Now *that* was a good movie.'

'*The Swarm* was better.'

'*The Swarm* was crap.'

'Shut it!' shouted Fred. 'What I am trying to say to you, Clive, you little twat, is that you're driving *The Car*. Stick it into overdrive.'

'Overdrive,' said Clive, finding the switch. 'Overdrive, OK.'

Clive flipped the switch and *The Car* rose up and crunched over the roofs and bonnets of the unparked cars.

'Nice,' said Fred.

'Rock'n'roll,' said Derek.

'Let's all Rock'n'roll,' cried the lead singer of the Lost T-Shirts of Atlantis. 'This one's called "Happy in the World".'

The crowd roared approval and the Lost T-shirts launched into a classic.

'Now that one's in C,' said the lady in the straw hat.

'I agree,' said Paul. 'Fancy a bunk-up?'

'Stand up,' said Dr Steven Malone. 'It is time for us to go.'

'Father,' said Cain. 'Are you absolutely certain of what you are doing?'

'Never more so,' said the mad doctor. 'Very soon I will know all there is to know.'

'Abel says that we should kill you, father,' said Cain. 'What is your opinion of this?'

'Now in your opinion,' asked Norman, who was setting up a formidable array of fireworks to the rear of the rock concert stage, 'should I start with the thunder flashes or the really big rockets?'

'Don't ask me now,' said the lady in the straw hat. 'Can't you see I'm being taken from the rear by a medical student?'

As all students of the occult will know, concentration is everything. Unwavering concentration. The mind must be cleared of all extraneous thought. The pathway opens. The magician focuses totally upon the operation in progress. Numerous mental exercises have been formulated to perfect the technique. One is a visualization exercise. Close your eyes and picture an egg with a crown above it. You'll get it for a moment, but then your mind will wander. Try again and again and slowly, slowly you will be able to hold it for two seconds, three, four, five. When you can hold it for five seconds, lie in bed next to your sleeping partner and do it. Your sleeping partner will jerk awake crying something about an egg. Try it, it works.

The Professor could hold the image of an egg with a crown above it for as long as he wished. He was an Ipsissimus, a master of the temple. A magus. He was totally focused.

Within his study the astral light glowed bright. Within the sacred circle the ancient stood reciting the first words of the ceremony.

'Ten o'clock,' said Jim, finishing his sixth double vodka.

'And bloody closing time,' said Sandy. 'I'm off to join the PARTY!'

'We are the Hollow Chocolate Bunnies of Death,' howled the lead singer with all the considerable attributes through the microphone on stage. 'And we have come for your daughters. Those we can't screw, we eat.'

'It's a great line that,' said the groundsman, backstage, to Norman. 'But I suspect probably the only one he's got.'

'This first number's called "I Love You So Fucking Much I Could Eat Your Shit".'

'Or perhaps not,' said the groundsman. 'What exactly are you doing there, Norman?'

'Well,' said the scientific shopkeeper, 'we want to go into the millennium with a big bang, don't we? So I've cranked up the old de-entropizer here, to double the strength of whatever it de-entropizes. So once I've set off a firework, you stick the burnt out remains into the de-entropizer and it will produce a brand new one twice as powerful for the next setting-off.'

'No problems,' said the groundsman. 'But just one question.'

'What's that?'

'Would it be all right with you if I stuck my willy in your machine?'

Time moved forwards, as time generally does, and the countdown to the New Millennium became minutes rather than hours.

31

'No, Cain, no.' Dr Steven Malone stood in his basement laboratory at Kether House. All its horrors had been removed by the police months before, but new horrors now replaced them. 'We have been arguing over this for hours. I should not be the one to die. I cannot be the one to die. For what I shall learn will affect all mankind.'

'What *will* you learn, father?' asked Cain.

'All, Cain, all.'

'No, father, that is the answer you have given before. No man can know all. All can never be known. Only God knows all.'

'I will know more than God,' said Dr Steven Malone. 'For I will learn what makes God God. Of what God is composed.'

'And how could you possibly learn this?'

'From the DNA of God. The DNA which is THE BIG IDEA. The first thought. I will possess this and from it I will clone myself.'

'That's a crock of shit,' said Abel.

'Hold your tongue, boy.'

'Boy? I am now the same age as you.'

'But you can grow no older.'

'This I know. But I do not know how I know this.'

'Because you do not know who you are.'

'Then tell us, father,' said Cain. 'Tell us who we are.'

'You are the clones of Jesus Christ.'

'No.' Cain shook his golden head. 'This cannot be. This is madness.'

'We should put the bastard out of his misery,' said Abel. 'He's clearly a stone bonker.'

'I am telling you the truth.' Dr Malone thrust his pale white hands into the pockets of his grey tweed trousers. 'Cloned from blood taken from the Turin Shroud. I have puzzled long regarding your differences. But then I checked my case notes. You, Abel, the blood from which you were cloned came from scourge marks. While yours, Cain, came from the rib where the spear of Longinus the Centurion pierced you. The Agony of Life and the Ecstasy of Death. But I must take my samples at the next stage. The moment of resurrection.'

Cain stared into the eyes of Dr Steven Malone. 'And you do not think that God will strike you dead for this? For surely you seek to commit the ultimate blasphemy.'

'No, Cain, I do not. For God does know all and God exists outside time. God knew, before the dawn of creation, that his son would die upon the cross. So he also knew of the Turin Shroud and of the blood and of twentieth-century science. All this is for a purpose. Ultimately God's purpose. The difference between myself and others who believe in God is that I deny God's divinity. I do not believe that God is to be worshipped, I believe that God is THE BIG IDEA. What will come when I clone God is of God's purpose. I am following his passive will.'

'The man's a frigging space cadet,' said Abel.

'No,' said Cain, 'I don't think he is.'

Howl, shriek and scream.

Having three lead guitarists who played three different lead guitar solos simultaneously gave the Hollow Chocolate Bunnies a certain edge.

Norman had his earplugs in, so he wasn't too bothered about edges. He was focused on his rather splendid switchboard. This was covered, as switchboards so often are, with switches. Each of these had a little label above it. On one the words *Big Rockets* were pencilled, on another *Catherine Wheels*, on yet another *Starfires*, and on yet another still, *Golden Showers*.

Cables led from the switchboard up the scaffolding at the rear of the stage to a gloriously ramshackle framework to which were attached hundreds of Roman candles arranged to spell out WELCOME TO THE YEAR 2000. All at the flick of a switch, of course. Norman did further screwdriver twiddlings, then looked upon all that he had made and found it good. He turned to the groundsman and grinned. 'We're rocking and rolling here,' he said. 'Now please take your willy out of my machine.'

'A bull's heart?' said Clive. 'He stuck his willy in a *bull's heart*?'

Derek grinned. 'That's what it said in this article I read. He'd wired it up to make it beat. But he'd wired it up to the mains and he was electrocuted to death. When they found him he was fried. Looked like a doner kebab.'

'Or a *beef* burger,' said Clive. 'But I still don't believe it.'

'It's true. I read it in *Fortean Times*.'

'Then it must be true. So where is Mr Pooley?'

'Here it comes,' said Fred.

And here Jim came.

Jim had his head down, a flat cap like Fred's pulled low over his face. He walked in a curious manner as of one tiptoeing along. As of one who is very drunk, doing his best to pretend that he's sober, perhaps? *The Car* was parked across the street from Professor Slocombe's house. Pooley tiptoed up against it and knelt down. The electrically operated window on Fred's side swished down into the door.

'You'd best get a move on,' said Fred.

Pooley leaned into *The Car*. 'Are you all right, Suzy?' he asked. 'Have they done anything to you?'

'I'm fine, Jim. Just get me out of here, please.'

'I love you, Suzy.'

'I love you, Jim.'

Fred pressed the button and the window rose.

'Just do what I told you,' said Fred. 'Take the bag into the Professor's circle. I'll know if you don't.'

Professor Slocombe stood within the sacred circle, performing the Ritual of the Star Sapphire.

Bowing to the East, he said, '*Pater et Mater unus deus Ararita*[1].'

To the South, '*Mater et Filius unus deus Ararita*[2].'

To the West, '*Filius et Filia unus deus Ararita*[3].'

To the North, '*Filia et Pater unus deus Ararita*[4].'

Jim Pooley stumbled across the street towards the Professor's garden door.

'He's going for it,' said Derek.

Fred pulled up the aerial on the little black box device and watched the little red blip that was Pooley move across the screen. 'He'd better,' said Fred. 'Or I'll blow his frigging hat off.'

'This is going to blow their socks off.' Norman flicked the switch labelled *Big Rockets* and the first of the big rockets shot into the sky. Starbursts and great chrysanthemum flares crackled over Brentford.

'Oooooooooo,' went the stadium crowd. Even above the roar of the Hollow Chocolate Bunnies.

'Oooooooooo,' went Clive, peering out through the tinted windscreen. 'Fireworks.'

'There very soon will be,' said Fred.

And not fifty yards away in the basement of Kether House, Dr Steven stood in profile, pointing. 'Go

---

[1] Father and Mother one god Ararita.
[2] Mother and Son one god Ararita.
[3] Son and Daughter one god Ararita.
[4] Daughter and Father one god Ararita.

[NB *Ararita* is Hebrew, meaning *One is His beginning: One is his individuality: His Permutation is One.*]

into the chamber, Cain,' he said.

Cain glanced at the chamber. It had the look of a large glass shower cubicle. There were two chairs in it. These were bolted to the floor. On one wall of the cubicle was a canister with a tiny stopcock. The canister was marked POISON.

'Death chamber,' said Cain. 'You would really kill us, father?'

'I must do what has to be done.'

'I understand. I myself did what had to be done.'

'You? What did you do?'

'I helped a man called Pooley. A man who is in love. I helped him so that something wonderful could happen. Something I could feel in the air.'

'Enough of this nonsense, Cain. Get into the chamber. I order you to do it. Obey my command.'

'You really think we're going in there?' sneered Abel. 'Get real, you twat.'

'You are powerless to resist. I have programmed your minds. Put you into deep trance again and again. I now command you to enter the chamber.'

Cain walked slowly across the basement floor and entered the chamber. Abel twitched and shook, but he too, with faltering steps, followed Cain.

With faltering steps Jim Pooley approached the Professor's French windows. From within came the sound of the magician's voice rising higher, calling out the Latin phrases that would herald the new dawn. Bringing the ceremony to its climax. For the most part, though, these were drowned by the screams and whistles and bangs of Norman's firework display.

Jim reached into his pocket and pulled out the wriggling bag and then he pressed his fingers to the blackly daubed French windows.

'No, Jim.' A hand grasped his wrist.

Jim turned. 'John?'

'Don't do it, Jim. Whatever it is, don't do it.'

'I have to, John. What are you doing here?'

'I heard about you being thrown from the limo. Suzy's gone missing. I put two and two together. They've got her, haven't they? They're blackmailing you to destroy the ceremony.'

'Let me do it my way, John. I have it under control.'

'Oh no you don't, Jim. A man in love is never in control.'

'I know what I'm doing. Leave it, John.'

'No, Jim. I won't let you.'

Jim swung round and hit John in the face with something hard. Omally went down and Jim pushed open the French windows.

'He's going inside,' said Fred, watching Jim's little blip. 'He's going to do it.'

'And now you are inside,' said Dr Steven Malone. 'And now I must do what must be done.'

'Don't do it, father, please.'

'Have no fear, Cain. You return to God. You become God once more.'

'I have no fear for myself, father, or for Abel. My fear is for you.'

'Waste not your fear then. Because I have none at all.' Dr Steven Malone bolted the chamber door and turned the stopcock on the canister of poison gas.

'Yes!' cried Fred. 'He's entering the circle. He's entering the circle.'

John Omally lurched into consciousness, clutched at his jaw and shook his head. The French windows were open, and a bright light shone from within. John dragged himself to his feet and fought to enter the Professor's study, but the light held him back, pushed him away. 'Dear God, no,' cried John. 'No.'

'Yes,' cried Fred. 'Yes, yes, yes.'

Overhead the fireworks exploded, golden showers, starbursts, great flowers of light. Church bells began to ring. Folk prepared for the Auld-Lang-Syning, clutched each other by the hands. Couples in love prepared for the New Year kissing.

'No!' John fought at the light but the light held him back.

'Yes.' Fred's finger hovered over the deadly red button on the nasty little black box. 'And it's good-night to you, Mr Pooley,' said Fred.

'Oh no it's not.' The rear door flew open on Derek's side. Something hard came in very fast and struck Derek a devastating blow to the face. As

Derek fell sideways, Jim leapt in and snatched the Uzi from his hands.

'You?' Fred's face contorted. 'You? How?' He thumbed the button on the box. 'Die, you bastard,' he said.

'No.' Jim ripped the flat cap from his head. A bloody gash yawned in his temple. 'I cut it out,' said Jim. 'No anaesthetic but vodka. I rolled the implant into the Professor's study. Oh yes, and you can have this back.' He pulled the heaving bag from his pocket and flung it onto Fred's lap. 'Give it back to your guvnor.' Jim levelled the Uzi at Fred. 'Get out, Suzy. Hurry now.'

Suzy scrambled over Derek and Jim dragged her from *The Car*. 'Run with me,' he shouted, 'and run fast.'

Omally appeared at the Professor's garden door. 'What the—'

'Duck,' shouted Jim as he and Suzy ran by. 'Duck, John.'

'All right, I'm ducking.'

'After them! Step on the bloody gas, Clive.'

'Yes, Fred, OK. OK.'

Clive stepped on the gas. Wheels burned rubber. *The Car* rushed forward.

The explosion drowned out the noise of the fireworks. The rear of *The Car* lifted into the air. Somersaulted down to the road in flames and sparks and shrapnel. Smoke and debris. Destruction.

And there would have been silence, if it hadn't been for the fireworks and the ringing bells and the Auld-Lang-Syning.

Quite a big silence there would have been.

John Omally's head appeared through the garden doorway. 'What the—' he said once more.

Jim's face appeared from behind one of the mighty oak trees. Suzy's also.

'What did you do, Jim?' asked Omally.

'I stuck a bottle of your two-week-old beer under the back wheel when I knelt down to speak to Fred. I kept one in case of emergencies. Two in fact, just to be on the safe side. I told you I had this under control.'

'Well, hats off to Mr Pooley. You've certainly saved the day.'

'*Aaaararghoooowaaghooow!*'

Now, that's a sound you don't hear every day. Especially on one that's just been saved.

Jim turned, John turned and Suzy turned also.

The Car turned. *The Car* was still intact. And *The Car* turned back onto its wheels.

'Oh shit!' said Jim.

'Did you say run?' asked John.

'No, but I was about to.'

Jim ran and John ran and Suzy ran.

Run, run, run.

And *The Car* rolled after them, keeping just behind, its engine growling and its horn going BAA-BA-BA-BAAAAA, just like in the movie.

32

Glass shattered and stormed and the chamber collapsed.

Abel stepped from the wreckage and stared down at the man now cowering on the floor.

'How?' gasped Dr Steven Malone. 'What?'

'There are many differences between Cain and I,' said Abel. 'And one of these is that I can read your thoughts. I emptied the gas canister last night. And now I must do what must be done. Cain told you that he feared for your life. His fears were not unfounded.'

'No,' screamed Dr Steven Malone. 'Get away from me. No, no, noooooooo.'

'Whoa!' went Derek. 'What happened? Ouch, my bloody head!'

'The bastard played us false!' Fred's face was most unpleasant. It was almost as unpleasant as that of the creature that now sat between him and Derek. This creature had a seriously unpleasant face. All scaly it was, with a lolling black tongue and glaring red eyes.

'Oh, shit a brick,' said Derek, staring into this face.

'You've grown a bit, haven't you? I mean, pleased to meet you again, sir, I mean—'

'Shut up, Derek,' Fred roared. And a roar it was. 'Keep right up behind them, Clive, don't let them out of your sight.'

'They're running into the crowd at the top of the street, sir.'

'Well, there's nowhere else for them to run, is there? Mow the crowd down, Clive, mow the crowd down.'

'Like that sea shanty,' said Derek. 'Mow the crowd down, Clivey, mow the crowd down. Hey, ho, mow the crowd down.'

'Shut it,' said Fred.

'We've got to get out of this crowd,' shouted Jim. 'He'll just drive through it and kill people.'

'Into the football stadium,' shouted John.

'Are you jesting? There's even more people in there.'

'That car will never get through this turnstile, will it?'

'I wouldn't be too sure about that.'

Omally shinned over the turnstile and helped Suzy after him.

Jim glanced back over his shoulder. Screams and shouts and BAA-BA-BA-BAAAAA. Jim leapt over the turnstile.

On stage the Hollow Chocolate Bunnies were giving it the freeform Auld Lang Syne. Behind them the groundsman fed defunct fireworks into the mobile de-entropizer, while Norman prepared to flick the big switch and set off WELCOME TO THE YEAR 2000.

'Any particular place you'd like to go for?' Jim asked John, as they pressed into the assembled throng.

Omally pointed to the stage. 'Make for the high ground,' was his suggestion.

BAA–BA–BA–BAAAAA.

'This was a very bad idea.'

'But we're committed to it now, Jim. Get a move on.'

'I'm with you. Come on, Suzy, come on.'

The Car burst through the turnstile and swept down the walkway into the stadium. The crowd scattered before it. A crowd of laughing, cheering folk, well buoyed up with alcohol and New Year jollity. They skipped aside this way and that, convinced that this must surely be some extra entertainment laid on for their enjoyment.

The crowd swarmed from the pitch up into the stands and then sat down to watch the show.

On stage the Hollow Chocolate Bunnies gaped in awe as *The Car* rushed towards them in pursuit of three racing figures.

'Now that is one tasty automobile,' said the lead singer.

'Split up!' shouted Omally. 'I'll meet you backstage.'

'You have an idea?' Jim huffed and puffed.

'It's a long shot.'

'Oh dear.'

And *The Car* was on them.

Jim dragged Suzy to the right and John dived to the left. *The Car* smashed into the stage, dislodging Chocolate Bunnies, who tumbled down to the football pitch.

Norman's finger hit the switch and the Roman candles flared up the rickety scaffolding, spelling COME TO THE EAR 20, which was a start.

The Car reversed then ploughed once more into the stage, buckling scaffolding. Up in the stands the crowd roared applause. A bit like a bullfight was this.

Norman clung to his de-entropizer. The groundsman clung to Norman.

'Was this supposed to happen?' asked the groundsman.

Back and forwards went *The Car*, growling and smashing and crashing. John Omally was up on the stage now, clawing his way towards Norman. Jim was climbing the scaffolding, pushing Suzy before him.

The stage slewed forwards. Marshall stacks, amps and speakers toppled and fell, mikes and drum kits, all those wonderful guitars that rock musicians rack up to make you jealous, down they came, wires and cables, sparking electrical flares. *The Car* backed away. Its doors opened.

Fred climbed out. And Clive climbed out. And Derek climbed out. And something really vile sort of slurped out.

'Well well well,' shouted Fred. 'It all looks a bit precarious up there. Why don't you come down for a little chat?'

'Boo,' went the crowd. 'Boo and hiss.'

'Stuff you!' shouted Omally.

'Hoorah,' went the crowd, and 'Cheer.'

The Bunnies' lead singer crawled over to Fred. 'How much do you want for this mother-crunching motor?' he asked.

Fred kicked him in the head.

'Ouch!' went the lead singer.

'Boo!' went the crowd.

Fred pointed at Pooley. 'You are a very dead man,' said he. 'You will know such torment as you never knew could be.'

If Jim had had a spare hand free he might have managed a two-fingered salute. But he didn't so he just climbed higher.

'There's nowhere to go.' Fred did a bit of the old manic laughing. 'Bring him to me, Igor.'

'Igor?' said Derek. 'Is its name Igor?'

'Like Dr Frankenstein's assistant,' said Clive. 'And Dr Frankenstein was of course played by Colin *Clive*. How about that?'

'So who played Igor?'

'Bela Lugosi.'

'Oh yeah, old Bela. His real name was Marion, you know.'

'That was John Wayne.'

'The hell it wa—'

'Shut your bloody mouths!' Fred rose quivering on his toes. Higher than his toes, in fact. An inch or two higher. 'Igor, fetch him, bring him to me.'

'Slurp,' went the creature, then 'Aaaararghooo-waaghooow!' like it did the last time. And then it unfolded hideous membraney sort of wings and took flight.

'Oh shit!' went Jim, as you would.

And 'Boo!' went the crowd.

'Get the Irishman,' Fred told Derek and Clive.

'Yes *sir*!' said Derek.

Igor swept up from the pitch, over the sloping stage and flung itself at Jim, talons clawing, jaws going snap, snap, snap. Jim kicked it away, but it lunged at him, again and again, ripping, tearing, and then it fastened hold and clung right on. The scaffolding shivered. Roman candles, fast giving out on their surreal message, dropped from their sockets. Dropped upon John and Norman and the groundsman.

'Ooh! Ouch! Aaagh!' they went, skipping this way and that.

Rip went a sleeve from Jim's jacket and the taloned claws bit into his arm. Suzy clung on to him, but the beast pulled and pulled.

Norman's de-entropizer started to roll down the sloping stage. Omally put his foot against a wheel, and his hand fell upon a very huge firework that was spilling off the conveyor. Above him the beast pried Jim loose from his precarious mooring.

'Fetch him down!' shouted Fred.

'Boo, boo,' went the crowd.

'I wonder where this is leading?' asked the lady in the straw hat.

'There'll be a trick ending in it,' said Paul. 'There always is.'

★   ★   ★

356

'*Omnia in Duos: Duo in Unum; Unus in Nihil,*' Professor Slocombe concluded his rite.

Within the basement at Kether House, Cain and Abel stared down at the broken corpse of Dr Steven Malone.

'All in Two,' said Cain, touching the hands of his brother.

'Two in One,' said Abel, holding tight to his hands.

'One in Nothingness.'

A bright light glowed. Brighter than a summer sun. And All in Two and Two in One, the brothers vanished into nothingness.

A bright light flared on the concert stage, a Zippo lighter it was. As Igor tore Pooley from the scaffolding, John angled up the very huge firework, lit the blue touch paper and did not retire to a safe distance.

'Aaaaararghoooowaaghooow!' went Igor, victorious.

'Whoosh,' went the very large firework.

'Huh?' went Igor, looking down.

'Whoosh,' went the firework, heading up.

Then Huh?

Then Whoosh!

Then, THUNK!

Now what is that sound? THUNK?

That is the sound of a firework entering the anal cavity of a creature named Igor at about one hundred miles an hour. And then,

*All in Two: Two in One: One in Nothingness.

AAAARARGHOOOWAAGHOOOW!

Pooley fell from the creature's grasp. The creature rocketed into the sky (as well one might) and the very huge firework exploded.

CRIMSON SMOKE.

STARBURST FLARE.

GOLDEN SHOWERS.

'Oooooooooooooo,' went the crowd, cheering wildly.

'Told you,' said Paul.

'The show's not over 'til the lady in the straw hat sings,' said the lady in the straw hat.

'That was a good one,' said cowering Norman, and then 'Ooow!' he continued as Pooley fell upon him.

'Take them!' ordered Fred.

Clive and Derek were on stage now. Derek was rolling up his sleeves. Clive had his fists up in a rather foolish fashion.

'Just do what I do,' said Derek. 'Poke 'em in the eyes and kick 'em in the bollocks.'

'Right,' said Clive. 'I'll try to remember that.'

Pooley scrabbled up and Omally scrambled up. The groundsman scrambled up (and ran). Norman just lay there moaning.

'Sorry, Norman,' said Pooley.

'Oh, I'm all right,' said Norman. 'I'm just faking it in the hope I won't get a thrashing.'

'Very wise!'

And Clive took a swipe at Pooley.

The crowd now roared further approval. They'd had the rock concert, the fireworks, an automotive bullfight, the Ray Harryhausen special effects flying creature that got a rocket up its arse, and now they were getting *Rocky 6*, or was it 7? Bloody good value for free of charge.

Pooley ducked and hit Clive in the stomach.

'Ow!' said Clive, stamping on Jim's foot.

Derek took a swing at John, who side-stepped and kicked him in the nuts.

'Bloody unsporting,' howled Derek.

'You fools,' shouted Fred. 'Kill them. Kill them.'

'Boo,' shouted the crowd. 'Boo boo boo.'

Fred turned upon the crowd. 'No more!' he screamed. 'No more. I will destroy you all.'

'Oh no you won't,' the crowd chanted.

'Oh yes I will.'

'Oh no you . . .'

There was a bit of hesitation there, prompted no doubt by the look of Fred. It wasn't so much the look he was giving them. More the look *of* him. The look of what was happening to him.

Fred rose once more upon his toes. Threw wide his arms.

Joints crackled, clothing tore. His flat cap rose as monstrous horns sprouted from his head. With sickening crunches and hideous bone-snapping reports Fred began to swell and distort.

All semblance of human form was gone. The Beast rose grinning. A medieval monster of depravity. The evil one made flesh.

The fighting came to a standstill on the stage. The bell seemingly called for the end of round one.

'Oh shit,' said Jim. 'Are we in trouble now.'

Abaddon, the arch-fiend of the bottomless pit, fallen angel, dweller in Pandemonium, denizen of hell, stood upon the sacred turf of Brentford football ground. Cloven hooves dug into the eighteen-yard line, forked tail curling, brimstone-breathed and hung like a python with the mumps.

'Avert your eyes,' said Paul.

'No way!' said the lady.

'*All of you.*' The Beast's voice echoed, rumbled thunder-like and awesome, quivering the scaffolding to which Suzy clung, rattling ten thousand teeth. '*All of you will die. All of you.*'

And fire belched from the belly of the Beast, and sulphur smoked and people cowered and screamed and made to flee.

And then.

And then.

A golden glow lit up the sky.

A false dawn?

What?

And a sound, far distant, yet close at hand. A sound that filled the air and the substance of the air and all the matter of the planet. The note. The Universal note.

Of Om.

That symbol given with love to be received with love.

An act of love.

And all the people stared. And the Beast turned and glared and breathed his fire and pawed the ground with cloven hooves.

And a man stepped out onto the turf. A golden man shining like the sun. And he walked forward, hands raised.

And the golden light surrounded him and the sound that was Om was everywhere.

'No,' cried the Beast. 'Not you. Not you.'

'This is not your time,' said he that was All in Two and Two in One and One in Nothingness. 'Return at once to whence you came. Get thee behind me, Satan.'

And the Beast screamed and clawed at the sky and squirmed and writhed and shook and moaned and trembled and was gone.

And the golden man held up his hands, and faded, and he too was gone.

And then there was a silence. And some silence it was.

And then the crowd looked up.

For the heavens seemed to part, the moonlight cleft the clouds and down swept beings, beautiful in white on wings of gossamer. Down and down, circling and swaying. Angels of light.

Derek looked up and Clive looked up.

And the beings swept down upon them.

And kicked them clean off the stage.

'Whoops, pardon,' said Mrs Elronhubbard. 'I'm sorry we're a bit late, but it's a right old struggle to the top of the gasometer. I had to help my friend Doris here with her Zimmer frame.'

'Hi,' said Doris, waggling her fingers. 'I hope we haven't missed anything.'

        ★   ★   ★

And then the crowd really cheered. Cheered and cheered. Gave a standing ovation. Clapped their hands and cheered again.

Oh yes indeed.

And the lady in the straw hat began to sing.

'Amazing Grace', I think it was.

33

'I'm sorry I missed all that,' said Neville, flipping the top from a bottle of Hartnell's Millennial Ale. 'It must have been a sight worth seeing.'

'Oh, it was.' Omally raised the bottle in salute.

It was early in the morning now, and but for a few stalwarts the crowds had all gone home to bed, well satisfied with the Brentford millennial celebrations.

In the Road to Calvary stood Professor Slocombe and Mr Compton-Cummings and Celia Penn and Old Pete and Small Dave and the lady in the straw hat and Paul and Suzy and Jim. Minor members of the cast stood about in the background going 'rhubarb, rhubarb, rhubarb' whilst trying to remain on camera.

'Jim did it,' said John. 'He saved the Professor's ceremony, and rescued Suzy. Jim is the hero.'

'You're the hero, John,' said Jim. 'Shooting that rocket up the monster's arse saved my life.'

'I think we have someone else to thank,' said Professor Slocombe, turning his eyes skyward.

'Oh yes,' said Jim. 'Oh yes indeed.'

'Now surely,' said John, 'that was what they call a *Deus ex Machina* ending?'

'How could you have had anything else?'

'Quite so, Professor. And all went well with your ceremony?'

'Oh yes. All went perfectly.'

'I can't actually feel anything,' said Jim. 'Well, I feel something, happy, content, something.'

'I don't think that's the Professor's magic,' said John.

Jim put his arm about Suzy. 'No,' he said. 'I don't think it is.'

'Well, cheers, everybody,' said John, raising his bottle once more.

Jim took Suzy aside. 'I never did get that regular job and get myself all sorted out,' he said. 'But I want to ask you that question anyway.'

'Go on then,' said Suzy. 'Ask it.'

'Will you marry me, Suzy?'

Suzy stared into Jim's eyes. Those beautiful eyes of hers, those wonderful, marvellous, amber eyes made Jim go all weak at the knees.

'No,' said Suzy. 'I won't.'

'You won't?'

Suzy shook her head. 'Marriage is all the things John told you it was, washing the car, mowing the lawn, having dinner parties with terribly nice respectable people. That stuff isn't for me, Jim, and it isn't for you.'

'Oh,' said Jim. 'So what then?'

'Would you like to come and live at my flat?'

Jim chewed upon his lip. 'Well,' said he.

Suzy shook her head once more. 'No, you wouldn't. I know you wouldn't. And I wouldn't want to live at your house either. But what we have is so special, so absolutely special, that one day, one day when everything is right, when everything is resolved, we will be together, won't we?'

'Yes.' Jim smiled. 'I know we will.'

'Good. Then you can kiss me if you want.'

Jim took the beautiful woman in his arms and kissed her. 'All is perfect,' he said. 'All will be perfect. After all this, all we've been through, how could it ever end up anything but perfect?'

'Neville?' John Omally stared at the part-time barman. 'Neville, what colour was the cap you just flipped from my bottle?'

Neville picked the cap up from the counter. 'Green,' he said.

'*Green*?'

'Yeah, well, I thought I'd run out. Luckily I found two bottles left in my fridge. You've got one and Jim there's got the other. It doesn't matter really that they're a couple of weeks out of date, does it?'

Omally held his bottle in a quivering hand. 'No-body move,' he said.

But it really would be mean to leave it there like that, wouldn't it? And so, of course, the beer did not explode. The sun rose over Brentford and a new dawn began. Though subtle at first, the spirit moved across the face of the Earth, across its people, touching them as gently, gently, the wheel began to turn, the holy mandala, returning mankind to THE BIG IDEA.

And Jim and Suzy stood upon the canal bridge watching the new sun rise above the windscreen wiper works and Jim took Suzy once more in his arms.

'I love you, Suzy,' said Jim.

'I love you too, Jim,' she replied.

THE END

SPROUT☖LŌRE

The Now Official
RŌBERT
RANKIN
Fan Club

Members Will Receive:

Four Fabulous Issues of the *Brentford Mercury*, featuring previously unpublished stories by Robert Rankin. Also containing News, Reviews, Fiction and Fun.

A coveted Sproutlore Badge.

Special rates on exclusive T-shirts and merchandise.

'Amazing Stuff!' – Robert Rankin.

Annual Membership Costs £5 (Ireland), £7 (UK) or £11 (Rest of the World). Send a Cheque/PO to: **Sproutlore, 211 Blackhorse Avenue, Dublin 7, Ireland.**
Email: sproutlore@lostcarpark.com WWW: http://www.lostcarpark.com/sproutlore

Sproutlore exists thanks to the permission of Robert Rankin and his publishers.

A SELECTED LIST OF FANTASY TITLES AVAILABLE FROM CORGI AND BLACK SWAN

13017 6	**MALLOREON 1: GUARDIANS OF THE WEST**	*David Eddings*	£6.99
12284 X	**BELGARIAD 1: PAWN OF PROPHECY**	*David Eddings*	£6.99
14254 9	**WINTER WARRIORS**	*David Gemmell*	£6.99
14255 7	**ECHOES OF THE GREAT SONG**	*David Gemmell*	£6.99
14256 5	**SWORD IN THE STORM**	*David Gemmell*	£6.99
14627 7	**FREEDOM'S CHALLENGE**	*Anne McCaffrey*	£6.99
14621 8	**ACORNA**	*Anne McCaffrey and Margaret Ball*	£6.99
14274 3	**THE MASTERHARPER OF PERN**	*Anne McCaffrey*	£6.99
14598 X	**JINGO**	*Terry Pratchett*	£6.99
14614 5	**THE LAST CONTINENT**	*Terry Pratchett*	£6.99
13703 0	**GOOD OMENS**	*Terry Pratchett & Neil Gaiman*	£6.99
13681 6	**ARMAGEDDON THE MUSICAL**	*Robert Rankin*	£5.99
13832 0	**THEY CAME AND ATE US, ARMAGEDDON II: THE B-MOVIE**	*Robert Rankin*	£5.99
13923 8	**THE SUBURBAN BOOK OF THE DEAD, ARMAGEDDON III: THE REMAKE**	*Robert Rankin*	£6.99
13841 X	**THE ANTIPOPE**	*Robert Rankin*	£5.99
13842 8	**THE BRENTFORD TRIANGLE**	*Robert Rankin*	£5.99
13843 6	**EAST OF EALING**	*Robert Rankin*	£6.99
13844 4	**THE SPROUTS OF WRATH**	*Robert Rankin*	£5.99
14211 5	**THE MOST AMAZING MAN WHO EVER LIVED**	*Robert Rankin*	£6.99
13922 X	**THE BOOK OF ULTIMATE TRUTHS**	*Robert Rankin*	£6.99
13833 9	**RAIDERS OF THE LOST CAR PARK**	*Robert Rankin*	£5.99
14212 3	**THE GARDEN OF UNEARTHLY DELIGHTS**	*Robert Rankin*	£6.99
14213 1	**A DOG CALLED DEMOLITION**	*Robert Rankin*	£5.99
14355 3	**NOSTRADAMUS ATE MY HAMSTER**	*Robert Rankin*	£5.99
14356 1	**SPROUT MASK REPLICA**	*Robert Rankin*	£5.99
14580 7	**THE DANCE OF THE VOODOO HANDBAG**	*Robert Rankin*	£5.99
14589 0	**APOCALYPSO**	*Robert Rankin*	£5.99
14590 4	**SNUFF FICTION**	*Robert Rankin*	£5.99
14741 9	**SEX AND DRUGS AND SAUSAGE ROLLS**	*Robert Rankin*	£5.99
14742 7	**WAITING FOR GODALMING**	*Robert Rankin*	£5.99
14743 5	**WEB SITE STORY**	*Robert Rankin*	£5.99
14897 0	**THE FANDOM OF THE OPERATOR**	*Robert Rankin*	£5.99
99777 3	**THE SPARROW**	*Mary Doria Russell*	£7.99
99811 7	**CHILDREN OF GOD**	*Mary Doria Russell*	£6.99